THE FAKE HUSBAND DEAL

SPECIAL ILLUSTRATED EDITION

SPENCER BROTHERS
BOOK 2

ANA ASHLEY

Illustrated by
CARAVAGGIA

The Fake Husband Deal- Spencer Brothers, book 2
© 2025 by Ana Ashley
Special Illustrated Edition

ALL RIGHTS RESERVED
No part of this publication may be reproduced, distributed, or transmitted
in any form or by any means, including photocopy, recording, or other
electronic or mechanical methods, without the prior written permission of
the author, except in the case of brief quotations embodied in critical reviews
and certain noncommercial uses permitted by copyright law.

The Fake Husband Deal is a work of fiction. Names, characters, businesses,
places events and incidents are either products of the author's imagination or
used in a fictitious manner. Any resemblance to actual persons, living or
dead, or actual events is purely coincidental.

Cover design: Ana Ashley

Illustration by Caravaggia

Editor: Abbie Nicole

Join Ana's Facebook Group Café RoMMance
(facebook.com/groups/CafeRoMMance) for exclusive content, and to learn
more about the latest books at anawritesmm.com!

To all the characters whose personalities who jump off the page so vividly we wish they were real.

ABOUT THIS BOOK

Love, as it turns out, is the most complicated deal of all.

I'm the one-and-done, allergic-to-feelings, marriage-is-for-suckers guy.

That night with him? Unforgettable.
Learning he's my new client? Unexpected.
Pretending the spark between us isn't a forever flame?
Impossible.

My life is a string of bad decisions.
Proposing a fake marriage to the sexy silver fox may be the worst one yet, but he needs me, and I might need him more. Besides, why would I kick him out of my life when he looks so good in it?

What starts as a business arrangement quickly becomes something I can't categorize. Falling in love is definitely not part of our deal.

The Fake Husband Deal *is book two in Ana Ashley's new series featuring the charming and far-too-handsome-for-their-own-good Spencer Brothers.*
Expect romance, heat, fun, and plenty of laughs from a loving but slightly too meddlesome family unit.

LAS
7

AS
7

1

NOAH

SWEAT AND DAY-OLD cologne was not the scent combination I wanted to wear to my family's Sunday lunch.

I knew I could count on either of my brothers to open my old bedroom window to let me climb into our parents' house incognito. I'd grab a shower, get in and out again, all fresh and ready for what I affectionately called the Spencer Weekly.

I loved every single bit of it. The food, the desserts—which had their own category in my mind—chewing the fat with my brothers outside of work and spending time with my parents and Avó.

The problem today was that it was not Sunday, which meant I'd been caught with my proverbial pants down when the message notification had come through from one of my brothers.

I parked in my usual spot a few houses down from my parents' and walked up to the door. Before I got my old key out, the door opened. "Thank fuck you're here. Everyone's acting really—" Lex, the younger of my twin brothers, pulled a face. "You stink."

"And you're ugly, but you don't hear me complaining."

"Pfft, everyone knows I'm the prettiest of the Spencer brothers."

I pretend-punched his gut. "What would Adam say about that?"

"That we're so perfect Mom and Dad had to make two of us."

I snorted. "Can you help me sneak upstairs? I need a shower."

"No complaints there from me. Why are you all sweaty? Did you run here or something?"

I ran my hand over my now less-damp hair. "Yeah, something like that."

He gave me a funny look that I ignored. "Are you going to help me or what?"

"Who's that? Is that Noah?"

My shoulders sagged as our mom came out from the living room.

"Honey, you're la— What happened to you?" she asked, inspecting me from head to toe as if to double-check I hadn't been robbed or something.

Jeez, I didn't think I stank that bad.

"Walk of shame, I see," Adam said, joining the party.

"Is that the sound of jealousy?" I cupped the back of my ear.

"You couldn't be further from the truth, as you'll find out soon enough, but please, dude, go grab a shower because you stink."

"Thanks. I love you all too." I took the stairs two at a time to the second floor and went straight to my old room.

After the shower, my muscles felt that kind of good tired you got from a solid workout, and, boy, had I gotten one this morning. I put on some old jeans and a T-shirt I kept here and made my way downstairs.

My parents' kitchen was the heart of the house, so it wasn't surprising to hear all the activity coming from there.

"Oh Adam! This is such great news, honey. I'm beyond happy…with happiness."

I chuckled from the door. "Nice and eloquent, huh, Mamã?"

She gave me a you're-in-trouble look, and I replied with a what-did-I-do-this-time shrug.

I went straight to my grandma, wrapping my arms around her. "Avó, how come you get younger every week?"

"Not to mention more beautiful, but it's my ability to see through your crap that really gives me that edge."

I laughed and gave her a kiss.

"What are we celebrating today that we moved the Spencer Weekly a day early?"

Mom put the casserole dish in the middle of the table, but there were many more pans on the stove, not to mention the smell of homemade bread. "Let's all sit down first."

We all took our usual places, which was when I noticed Adam's girlfriend, Victoria, was in the room.

"Hey, Vicky, I didn't see you there. Been ninja training in your spare time?" I waved at her, ignoring her annoyed expression as she sat next to Adam.

Lex bumped his knee against mine. It was his way of telling me to shut up.

"Why the expensive china?" I whispered to Lex.

"No clue. Big wedding booking at the restaurant?"

I doubted it was that. Since Adam's best friend, River, had taken over managing the restaurant for Dad, they'd had a few large weddings, and it wasn't a big deal.

"Maybe Adam knocked Vicky up."

"You have to stop calling her that. She doesn't like it."

I rolled my eyes. Victoria wasn't my favorite of all the

girlfriends Adam had brought home. She seemed cold and distant, a trait that wouldn't work well in our family.

Everyone was up in everyone's business all the time. My parents had run a restaurant together all their adult lives. My grandma lived with them, and my brothers and I ran a PR and advertising agency together.

Victoria didn't fit in, but it seemed she was here to stay from the way Adam put a protective arm over the back of her chair.

The doorbell rang, so as the ever-dutiful older son, I stood to get it.

River stood on the other side with a couple of champagne bottles.

"Tell me why I had to raid the restaurant's stock supply and rush here, leaving my assistant manager on her own on a busy Saturday."

"Beats me, but if you're here, it has to be important. Like *family* important." Because River wasn't just Adam's best friend and Dad's restaurant manager. He was family.

Lunch was delicious, as it always was. My mom learned how to cook from Avó, who learned from her mom when she still lived in Portugal as a young woman.

Throughout the meal, several knowing looks and smiles were exchanged between my parents, but nothing about what had brought us together.

I was about to demand it when my dad stood, grabbing one of the champagne bottles from the fridge.

Adam cleared his throat. "Mom, thank you for the amazing food. You might all be wondering why we're here today." He looked at Victoria, who beamed.

The rest of us shared confused looks, apart from my mom, who fidgeted in her seat, wearing a beaming smile.

"As you know, Victoria and I have been together for almost a year. It may seem too soon, but when you've met the person you're meant to be with for the rest of your life, you want that life to start immediately." He looked around the table at all of us.

Lex narrowed his eyes, and River stiffened on my other side.

"This morning, I asked Victoria to marry me, and she said yes."

"Isn't this the most excellent news?" Mom stood to hug Adam and Victoria.

While Dad and Avó followed with their questions about the big day, the tension radiating from Lex and River was so palpable I felt like a squished pancake.

Lex stood and hugged Adam. "I'm so happy for you, Adam. I really am."

Adam searched Lex's face for answers but seemed happy with what he saw.

"I'm so sorry, but I have to go back to the restaurant," River said, standing. "I've just gotten a message that we're at capacity, and they need all hands on deck."

Adam deflated while Victoria's smile couldn't have gotten any wider.

I'd always gotten the impression Victoria didn't like River. Why? I didn't know.

"Congrats, dude. You make a great couple," River said before thanking my mom for the food and leaving.

In the scramble for hugs, I followed Lex, who tried to sneak away unnoticed.

I gave his old bedroom door a knock before walking in. He stood by the window looking out.

"Hey, you okay?" I asked.

"Sure, why wouldn't I be?"

"It's okay if you're not, you know? Feeling happy for Adam doesn't mean you can't also feel sad for yourself."

A year ago, Lex's boyfriend ghosted him just after he

proposed. Lex had been a shadow of his old self since. He'd lost his lightheartedness, and some days, he seemed so sad and lonely that I worried he'd never recover from the heartache.

"Adam deserves to be happy. I don't want to cloud his celebration."

"Hey, how about we go out tonight? I'm sure I saw something at Tanner's about a long happy hour today."

"Nah. I'm heading home after this. There's some work I want to catch up on."

I squeezed his shoulder and left him. On my way downstairs, I met Adam coming up, so I pulled him into my old room.

"Dude, congrats. I'm happy for you and Victoria, but couldn't you have given Lex a heads-up?"

To his credit, he looked genuinely regretful. "It all happened so quickly. I proposed this morning, and Victoria said we should tell my family first. When I called Lex earlier, he didn't pick up, and I didn't want to do it over voicemail. Is he…really upset?"

"He's happy for you, but it's not easy for him, you know? You're having what he thought he would have a year ago, and you two are so close."

He dropped on my bed. "I know. I'll talk to him. And how about you? You haven't said much."

And there was the dreaded question.

"Honestly, dude? I think it's too early. You barely know her."

"How can you say that when only a week ago you were moaning that I've missed the last two Friday drinks at Tanner's because I went out with her?"

He got me there. "There's spending time with someone and knowing them. How many family meals has she been to? And when she has been to them, she…hasn't belonged."

"How do you know what it's like when someone belongs? When was the last time you brought someone home to meet the family? Oh wait, that's never. The next time you turn up to the family dinner not stinking like a cheap hookup, I'll take your concerns a little more seriously. Until then…" He stood, but I grabbed his arm and hugged him, brushing off his hurtful words like I was coated in Teflon.

"I love you, little brother, and I'm really proud and happy that you and Victoria are ready for the big M, even if I don't understand it. Just name it, and I'll be there for you every step of the way. Maybe don't get me to organize your bachelor party."

I relaxed when he hugged me tight. "Thank you, Noah. And don't worry, that's a River job, and he's not getting out of it."

Judging by the look on River's face after the announcement, I wasn't sure about that, but it wasn't my business.

Maybe River liked Victoria even less than I did, but I would be a good, supportive brother.

First, I just needed to make my excuses to leave so I could go to Tanner's for one—or ten—stiff drinks.

2

LIOR

"I'm so sorry for your loss."

In the four weeks since my father passed, I'd heard those words more times than I could count. Only a handful of them had been said with genuine care.

"Thank you." I wondered if words could wear out from overuse.

"He was a great man, made from the same cloth as your grandfather. He'll be missed."

I shook the man's hand, placing my other hand on his shoulder, squeezing a little.

Since when had it become the job of the bereaved to console everyone else at a funeral?

A hand landed on my shoulder. "Lior, we must schedule a meeting soon. Your father was overseeing an expansion into the European market, but they have stricter regulations there. Don't worry. I'm happy to teach you the ropes on that front."

I was sure he was, especially since any delays on the expansion would hit his pocket directly. Not that Warren Livingston needed the money. This was just another invest-ment to add to his ever-growing fortune. Or so my father told me when he'd attempted to get me up to date with the business in his final weeks before cancer really took over and made it impossible for him to work.

"Of course, Mr. Livingston. Get your secretary to book something with my father's secretary. She's overseeing my fath—um, my appointments."

He tapped my back. "Sorry for your loss. Your father will be missed."

"Thank you."

I eyed up the bar and wondered if I could get to it without being stopped to console someone or having yet another meeting added to my schedule.

"How are you holding up, sir?" And there they were. The only words that were meant with true sincerity.

"Starting to wonder why I'm the one holding the Kleenex box, Charlie."

"He was a well-liked man."

I snorted, gaining a disapproving look from someone whose name I vaguely remembered. "Funny how everyone seems to think they knew him."

"That's always the way, sir." He turned to face me, whispering imperceptibly. "One nod, and I'll put the exit plan in motion."

"Thank you."

I needed a drink to get through this, and since my mother was clearly hiding somewhere, I couldn't exactly leave.

"Lior."

I froze on my way to the bar. If I'd thought I needed a drink a moment ago, now I needed the whole bottle.

"Pierce. What are you doing here?" My attempt at a detached voice and cold expression had been achieved, judging by the look on his face. I'd take it as my first win of the day.

"I figured you might need a friendly face today."

"What makes you think that?" I wouldn't go so far as saying my ex's face was friendly or the one I wanted to see on the day of my father's funeral.

"Can we put our stuff behind us for a moment? I liked your dad, and I'm here to support you."

"Out of respect for my dad, you can stay, but lose the pretense. We're too old for that shit." I smiled at a woman passing who'd overheard me swear. "It's such a sad day. My mouth is running away from me."

"Understandable, dear," the woman said. "Funerals are fucking depressing. More so when you're at the age when people look at you, wondering if you're going to be next."

My kind of girl. How could I resist?

I took her hand and wrapped it around my arm. "Can I buy you a drink?"

"It's a free bar. Let *me* show a young man a good time."

Pierce called my name as we walked away, but I ignored him.

The bartender came over as soon as we approached.

"Two scotches. Top shelf. Light on the ice," the lady said.

"I love a woman who knows what she likes and likes what she knows."

She winked. "It comes with experience, my dear."

The bartender placed the drinks in front of us. I wasn't sure what the etiquette was with bartenders at a funeral. Although I didn't doubt he was being paid handsomely, I was too well-trained to not give him a tip.

"Thank you, sir." I nodded as he walked away.

"How a person treats those beneath them says a lot more about the person they are than the zeros in their bank account," she said.

The scotch was so smooth that I only choked because hearing the words my dad had said so many times repeated back to me on a day like today hit me where it hurt the most.

"There's no one beneath me in this room," I said. "How did you know my dad?"

"I didn't, actually. My late husband did. He met your father at college, way before I met him. They had a mutual respect for each other. I wouldn't say they were close friends, but they kept in touch."

"It's kind of you to be here." One tumbler of scotch down, and I already felt my tongue loosen. "You may be the only person I've spoken to today that is…a person."

She put her hand on top of mine, and I noticed the soft, wrinkly skin and clear nail polish.

"How about that young man I stole you away from?"

I scoffed. "He's…something else."

"They all are, dear. They all are." She looked at her watch. "I'm afraid I must go. I just wanted to speak to you and give you my deepest condolences. Can I leave you with some parting wisdom?"

"Of course."

"When life drops you in certain positions, you have no choice but to occupy the box you were given. You fight a little when you're young and full of dreams, but eventually, you learn to love the box until it becomes your safe space. Men like your dad and my husband are mostly known for how they ruthlessly built their empires. That generation didn't know how to be anything else. Remember that. They didn't know."

I held her hand up to my lips and kissed the back. "I hear you." And I did. After all, I'd avoided the box all my life.

My dad had loved it. He'd embraced corporate life.

Unlike my grandfather, my dad's creative genius shone through in the way he saw the opportunities for expansion into new markets beyond stained-glass windows.

I was much like my dad in the way the creative gene had skipped my generation, but I loved and appreciated my grandfather's work, maybe more so than my dad ever had.

My grandfather's parting gift to me twenty years ago was the stained-glass museum that had once been the home he'd built for my grandmother with his own sweat, blood, tears, love, and determination.

The museum and my grandfather's workshop I'd renovated and made my home were my safe space. I loved it with all my heart. I felt close to my grandfather there and, to a degree, my father.

Maybe that was why, over the last four weeks, I'd felt like I was getting pushed further and further away from my dream and closer to the box my father had occupied.

It was only as the lady walked away from me that I realized I hadn't gotten her name.

I eyed Pierce in the corner, talking to a couple of my dad's investors. He looked like he belonged there much more than I ever had or wanted to.

"When you marry Pierce, you can share running the company with him and dedicate the rest of your time to the museum. Pierce has a sharp mind, and he's from a good family."

My dad's words echoed in my mind. I was glad he hadn't noticed Pierce's absence from my life. My dad had liked Pierce because he'd never known what kind of man Pierce really was. I hadn't wanted to take something else away from him, but equally, I didn't have to accept it in my future.

"Mr. Van Stern, may I grab you for a moment?"

I took a deep breath and wondered about the merits of asking for a top-up of my scotch or staying sober enough to get out of there.

"How can I help, Mr.…"

"Hoffman." He held out his hand. "I'm your father's attorney."

I tried to hide my irritation. "I know all of my father's attorneys, Mr. Hoffman, and I'm afraid I haven't had the pleasure of hearing your name before."

The man was short, skinny, and had bright-blue eyes that seemed incapable of looking at anyone the wrong way, let alone doing what my father had his long string of attorneys and counselors do.

He didn't seem phased by my rudeness. Maybe I wasn't giving him enough credit.

"There's a reason you haven't heard of me, Mr. Van Stern. Your father wanted it that way."

"Why's that?"

"I'm the executor of your father's last will and testament."

I frowned. "No, you're—"

"The *real* last will and testament."

All day, I'd pushed aside my feelings and the impact of my father's death to give my father's business partners and acquaintances the impression that I was in control.

What forty-seven-year-old man has to prove himself to a bunch of strangers?

I did. Because regardless of my age, I was a Van Stern. My name meant money, status, birthright, and looking like I'd stuffed a big old stick up my ass.

"Why doesn't it surprise me that my father made two wills," I said, not expecting an actual reply from the man. "Does my mother know about this?"

His ears went a deep shade of pink. "She found out within the last thirty minutes."

Well, that explained her absence.

"What do you need from me, Mr. Hoffman?"

He held out an envelope.

"You might want to stay in the city tonight."

I took the envelope and looked inside.

My face must have said it all because, within seconds, Charlie was by my side.

"Charlie, can you drop me off at the hotel? I won't need you again until tomorrow."

"Are you sure, sir?"

"I am."

I'd fulfilled my obligation for today. My dad's investors, money friends, and Pierce could all get stuffed. It was time for some alone time with a bottle of scotch—anywhere else but here.

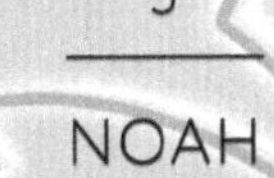

3

———

NOAH

My brother's words followed me home like a bad smell, so I hit the shower as soon as I got back to my apartment.

It wasn't like me to dwell in the past or on what could have been, and Adam didn't know how much those words got to me.

To my family, I was the ever-single, relationship-allergic Noah. My life was all about my family, the PR and marketing agency I ran with my brothers, and hooking up.

They were right on all accounts, but they didn't know why I was like this. And since nothing was going to change, I did the only thing I knew how to do.

I picked up my phone and called my old friend Jax, who'd conveniently just moved into my apartment building.

"Dude. I'm broken. You broke me."

I laughed at his words as he picked up my call.

"No one told you to accept my invitation."

"It was that or going to a practically empty apartment and sleeping off the jetlag. You know I get all weird with time zones."

"I hope you've had some sleep since this morning's workout because we're going out."

He sighed. "We are?"

"Meet me downstairs in ten."

He groaned. "I'm going to regret moving into the only vacant apartment in your building, aren't I?"

"It's the best decision you've made in your life. I promise."

I heard a string of "Yeah, yeah" as he disconnected the call. I finished getting ready, and ten minutes later, I stepped out of the elevator into the lobby of my building.

Jax was already there.

"Damn, man. You look like you'll have no trouble scoring tonight."

"Is that what we're doing?" His eyebrows raised like he wanted no part in whatever I was up to.

"That's what *I'm* doing." Even though I hadn't brought any condoms or lube, I could bullshit like the best of them.

"Crazy me thought you actually wanted to spend time with your best buddy. Where are we going anyway?"

"Best bar in town."

What I loved the most about the location of my apartment was that it was equidistant from both the office and Tanner's. Whether I was grabbing a quick drink after work or hoping to score some fun, it was all within the same square mile.

Tanner's was already showing signs of a busy Saturday night, but we managed to score a couple of stools at the bar and ordered a beer each.

"Happy to be back on US soil?" I asked Jax. When he'd gotten in touch with me a month ago to help him find a place to live, all he'd told me was that he was retiring from the military.

"Ask me when I've had more than three hours of sleep in

a row." He clinked his bottle against mine and drank almost half of it.

"I thought you army guys were all tough and shit. Don't you sleep standing up?"

"Man. It gets old, and so am I. I'm looking forward to starting over."

"Well, I'm glad you came this way. It'll be nice having you around again."

He turned on his stool and leaned his elbow against the bar. "What's the score around here?"

I mimicked his position and scanned the bar. There were a few familiar faces. People who worked or lived nearby.

"I don't mess with the regulars. Things can get awkward, and I like this bar too much."

"That includes the bar staff?"

"Absolutely. Don't fuck where you drink. Or who serves you drinks. There are a few good bars in town, but this one is the best. Also, openly LGBTQ+ friendly."

Jax nodded and grabbed his drink.

It was fun catching up with someone else's life. So much of mine in the last year had been about being there for my younger brother, watching as he hid away more and more, keeping him from slipping all the way down.

Not that I'd neglected my own social life. I still hooked up regularly, but sometimes it wasn't as much fun as it used to be. I shook the thoughts away.

"Dude, you okay? You look like you're having a seizure and I didn't bring my medical bag."

"Haha. I was shaking a funk that slipped through uninvited."

I ordered another couple of drinks. Jax didn't seem too interested in checking out any potential hookups, probably because he was barely alive right now. I shouldn't have brought him out, but I was selfish.

"How did you get started with the kids? This morning was fun. I wouldn't mind doing it on the regular," Jax asked.

Yes! "I was on a morning run one time and noticed the group on the basketball court. They saw me watching and invited me to play. I registered with the Star Finders Youth Network straight after and have been doing it for a few years. The kids are amazing."

Volunteering at Star Finders was my thing. As the oldest of three brothers, I didn't exactly feel excluded. Even with the younger two being twins, we were all super close. But I'd always felt like I needed a thing that was mine and no one else's.

Volunteering my time was that thing for me.

The kids who came to Star Finders were all teenagers in foster care or from low-income families and had various backgrounds. They just needed a little guidance, mentoring, and a sense of belonging. And I wouldn't deny that the weekly basketball game was a good workout.

"Can you give me the details to sign up?"

"Sure." I took a swig of my beer. "Can you keep it between us? You'll meet my brothers at some point, and this is something I…"

Jax raised his beer. "I get it. This is your thing. Your secret is safe with me. Oh, look, I found the person just for you."

My gaze followed his nod.

"Fills out a suit. Broody. Fucking silver fox." I groaned. "I think I just got pregnant."

The man was sex on legs. His silver hair was just long enough to grab hold of while he pounded my ass, which wasn't something I let just anyone do, but this guy? Damn. My dick thickened as the silver fox downed two fingers of scotch in one go.

"You're going to have to get him before the drink does," Jax said.

"You're right there. Let me buy you one last drink."

He laughed. "You're confident."

I gestured to my carefully picked outfit.

"Well, if it isn't my favorite Spencer."

I turned around to greet Tanner. The man had the face of an all-American boy with the body of a Greek god, and best of all, he'd made it clear he was willing to break all his rules for a night with me. Sadly for him, I had my rules, and I wasn't willing to break them.

Tanner gasped as Jax turned around in his seat.

"Jax Fucking Mitchell. What the fuck are you doing here?"

Tanner practically jumped over the bar to hug Jax, who was stunned into silence.

"Hi, Tan...Tanner. Sorry, force of habit."

Tanner smiled wider. "Hey, you know I'll always be Tan to you."

"How do you guys know each other?" I asked.

Tan jumped in straight away. "I dated Jax's little sister in high school before I realized boys were my thing."

"What?" Jax straightened.

"Oh yeah, I guess you'd left for the military by the time I came out."

Jax finished his beer. "So you're...?"

"As gay as a summer's day parade."

"Right."

Someone called Tanner's name from behind the bar, so he had to go back to work.

"If you're going to hit up Mr. Silver Fox over there, I'm going to head out. It's time to catch up on sleep."

"So, you and Tan..." I teased, drawing out the nickname he'd called Tanner.

He snorted. "Dude, I found out he was gay a minute ago. Haven't seen him since he was eighteen."

"Aww, you left for the military because you were in love with your sister's boyfriend. How cute. You know this is the stuff romance novels are made of, right?"

Jax punched me in the gut. "You're a dick, and I'm out."

I watched him walk through the ever-expanding crowds around the tables for a second before setting my eyes on tonight's prize. Sure enough, the sexy silver fox was still on the hard stuff.

"Tough day?" I asked, sitting on the stool next to him.

"You could say that."

He rotated the glass between his fingers, determined to ignore me, but I wasn't going down without a fight.

"Top-shelf scotch shouldn't be enjoyed on your own."

"That so?"

"That is so. But I'm a giving kind of guy, so I'll let you let me buy you the next one."

The guy pinned me with his eyes, and fuck me, I had to suck in a breath. He was…intense…and now I needed to know just *how* intense.

"I'll pass."

"Are you always this hard to charm?" I squirmed in my seat, my belly pooling with need as his lips curled up just a tad.

"Not always. Sometimes, I lower my standards."

"Ouch. My heart breaks."

"How come I get the feeling your heart is the least of your concerns right now?"

4

LIOR

I HAD to admit the guy's confidence was sexy as fuck. I'd take much pleasure in bringing him down a notch or two.

"You're right. My heart is dead, but the whole rest of me is very much alive and at your disposal."

Fuck, he looked like he'd put up with just the right amount of fight to make it fun.

The bartender appeared in my periphery, ready to refill my glass. Without breaking eye contact, I covered my glass with my hand to indicate I was done.

How did I go from a night of destructive thoughts and numbness through alcohol to scoring a hookup?

"You cut right to the chase, don't you?" I drawled, lowering the pitch of my voice.

He turned on his stool to face me. "I know what I like, and I like what I know."

I narrowed my eyes as I heard my own words repeated back to me. "You don't know me."

"I know you'll make it worth my while, and it's been a long time since someone has."

The idea of burying myself in a stranger, without the

expectation for more, was appealing. It was certainly a good way to pass the remaining hours until I had to sit in a room with twelve business partners while I found out what my dad wished for the company and me now that he was gone.

I was going to regret this, but the guy was hot. Young—probably fifteen years too young—but hot and willing, and he didn't seem to have issues hooking up, which meant no attachments, no clingy exes, no awkward morning-after conversations.

I dropped a few bills on the bar. More than enough to cover my drinks and a generous tip.

He was so cocksure in the way he jumped from his stool that, for a moment, I wanted to mess with him.

"Ground rules," I said, loving how I towered over him at six foot two. He'd have to raise his heels a little to kiss me.

The way his gaze scanned me, he'd agree to anything.

"Ground rules," he mimicked, licking his lips.

"I'm in charge."

"That's it?"

I nodded.

"One rule. I can remember that."

Cocky little shit. "I'm on PrEP and recently tested negative. Haven't been with anyone since. Don't have condoms on me since I didn't come out expecting…you."

He bit his lip and swallowed. "Same."

"Say the words."

He huffed. "On PrEP. Negative. Tested recently. No one since. Can we go now?"

I liked his impatience. It matched mine, but I could exercise self-control. Case in point, we were discussing the particulars of a hookup in a bar filled with people because I knew the moment I had him to myself, I couldn't trust myself to remain level-headed.

"We can go."

He grabbed my hand and pulled me toward the exit. I stopped him when we turned into the hallway leading to the restrooms.

"What's wrong?"

"I'm not doing this here."

"This place is very clean."

I pushed him against the wall, placing one hand on his hip and the other on the wall above his head. He went lax under my touch, but his bulge pressing against mine was anything but.

"My restroom hookup days are over," I said into his ear, my lips just on the cusp of touching him.

"You're in charge," he breathed out.

"Damn right, I am."

This time, I took his hand and guided him out of the bar, ignoring how good his slightly smaller hand felt in mine.

My hotel was one block away, but the way my mind raced and my body coiled with anticipation, it may as well have been ten.

The guy walked beside me with the kind of spring in his step that someone without a care in the world had.

I wondered how often he picked up men in that same bar. Something told me his scoring rate was pretty high. Who wouldn't go for someone like him? A little shorter than me, filled out a shirt nicely, short, trimmed beard, and bright blue eyes that oozed confidence.

Suddenly, my carefully put-together facade felt as fragile as a sugar-glass bottle.

"I was thinking…" he said. "Are we exchanging names or…?"

"No names. I think it's better if we keep our information sharing to a minimum."

He leaned into me as we walked and whispered in a

sultry voice that went straight to my dick. "What name will I shout when you make me come?"

I coughed.

"You can call me whatever you want."

He tapped his finger over his pretty mouth, making me reconsider my decision.

How would my name sound coming from those lips?

"We're here," I said.

"You're staying here?"

"Is that a problem?"

He smiled. "None at all. Just funny because I don't live that far. I can see this building from my place."

I sighed but couldn't help warming up to him. He was terrible at keeping personal information to himself.

The ride to the top floor was filled with dirty, promising looks and barely there touches we couldn't take further because we never had the elevator to ourselves.

When we finally got to my room, I took the key card out but paused before tapping it on the pad.

"Cold feet?" he teased.

I leaned against the door, facing him. "Why me? You could have picked anyone in that bar tonight."

He narrowed the gap between us until he was pressed against me.

"Have you looked in a mirror recently?"

"Yes."

"Then you know how hot you are."

I moved my hand behind my back until I heard the click of the door unlocking.

No sooner had the door closed behind us than I found myself pressed against it. I smiled. It was cute that he thought he was in charge.

"I need to kiss you," he said, raising his heels to reach my height.

All I needed was to lean down a couple of inches. "Patience," I whispered against his lips.

"You're a fucking tease."

I wasn't, but the tip of my lower lip was on fire, and it had only barely touched his. How would I survive a whole kiss?

If I blamed his hastiness, I could pretend I wasn't the one on the verge of giving him everything and more.

I couldn't blame him though. Younger guys were always keen to get the first orgasm out of the way. Once upon a time, I could also go on all night, but at forty-seven, I was lucky to have one good one in me. I had to make it count.

"I'm not teasing. I'm drawing it out."

"We're still dressed, and your hands are nowhere near my body. Draw this out any longer and I'll have to put in for retirement."

The soft light from the streets below illuminated the room just enough that I could see his face without turning on any lights.

I shrugged my coat off and threw it at a nearby chair. "Take your coat off," I said, rolling my shirt sleeves to my elbows.

His gaze narrowed on my arms and he sucked in a breath, following my instructions.

"Now, your shirt."

I walked to the floor-to-ceiling glass window, doing my best to ignore the way his muscles rippled as he undressed.

"Next?" he asked from behind me.

Turning around to find him completely naked was the straw that broke my resolve. I swept him into a hard kiss. Somehow today, of all days, the universe had given me the gift of this man. The gift of letting go for a moment, and he didn't even know it.

He moaned as I stroked his tongue with mine. His hands fisted my shirt so hard that one of the buttons popped.

The glass door behind me shook when he pushed me against it.

Hot damn, the guy could kiss. It was almost easy to forget I was supposed to be in charge.

"I need you to wreck me. Make me feel you for the rest of the week," he said before dragging his teeth over my lower lip.

His raspy voice was so full of need.

"You don't know what you're asking."

I wound my hand in his hair, the other firmly placed on his hip. He was going to get a bruise from how hard I gripped. My self-control hung by a thread. One slight pull, and I'd take him into the bed and fuck him into the next life.

He pulled away and flipped us so he faced the street. With his hands on the glass, legs set wide, he all but offered himself to me.

"Jesus, fuck," I growled.

My dick was like steel in my pants. I undid the button and lowered the zipper just enough to take myself out. There was something about remaining clothed while he was fully naked that did it for me.

I didn't know where these feelings of claiming and possession were coming from, but I wanted to own this guy's body. If he wanted to feel me beyond tonight, I was happy to oblige.

"Don't move," I demanded, kissing his neck while my hands explored his body.

"Hmm…more…"

I chuckled.

His nipples morphed into tiny peaks under my touch. I wanted to lick them, to get my hands on his gorgeous cock, to kiss every inch of his body.

I lowered to my knees, spread his ass cheeks, and threw myself in face-first. The longer I fucked his hole with my tongue, the more he pushed back, so needy. His head hit the glass with a thud as I pushed a finger inside him.

"Are you ready for my cock?" I stroked my length. I was so ready to fill him.

"Fuck, yes. Yesterday."

He hissed as I added a second finger. I pushed myself up and covered his body with mine. "How often do you bottom?"

His silence screamed at me to be careful.

"Rarely."

"Why now?"

"I don't know. I just know I need it from you." He tilted his head sideways to look at me with heavy lids. "You're still dressed. Fuck, that's so hot."

He relaxed under my touch and the third finger got him begging.

"You're going to take my cock so well, aren't you?"

He nodded.

I patted my pockets, which was when I realized I didn't have any lube on me because my intention when I'd gone to the bar was to get drunk, not to find the most perfect ass I'd ever seen. "Fuck. I don't have lube."

"I don't need it." He got on his knees and swallowed my cock to the back of his throat. It was slurpy and messy, and fuck, he looked so good down there.

He suddenly stood, leaving me off balance.

"There. You're all good."

I fucking was.

He resumed his position, and I lined up my cock and pushed in.

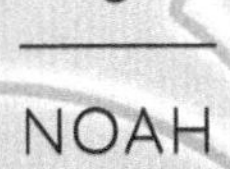

5

NOAH

I GRITTED my teeth as he filled me. It was painful. Also, painfully slow.

What had come over me when I asked him to wreck me? I couldn't remember the last time I'd bottomed, so why had I so eagerly volunteered my ass for this man?

My therapist would have a field day if I had one.

Inch by aching inch, he bottomed out.

"Are you okay?" he whispered in my ear.

His concern was sweet, even as his big body pinned me against the cold glass. The balcony gave us an extra layer of safety from prying eyes, and with the lights off in the room, I knew there was little chance of us being seen.

Well, me, because while I was buck naked and cock-stuffed, my silver fox stranger was still fully dressed. That difference alone brought out something I didn't want to consider in depth. Not when my cock was leaking all over the floor-to-ceiling glass window.

"Just fuck me already."

"You're topping from the bottom, my dear."

I gasped as he pulled almost all the way out before

pushing back in again. In this position, his cock wasn't hitting my spot in the way I needed to come.

"Do that again," I begged.

"Is this what you were looking for when you went to the bar tonight?"

"Yes." No. Maybe?

He held my hands above my head, lacing his fingers through mine. We were a mix of grunts and skin slapping against skin. The smell of sex was intoxicating.

"You're so fucking tight. Your ass is a work of art," he said between gritted teeth as he fucked me senseless against the glass door.

"In the bar," I swallowed a gasp. "You had this big-dick energy."

"Big-dick energy?" He laughed.

I met his thrusts, trying to get him to hit my prostate. "Yeah. The way you held that scotch glass. Your long, sexy fingers. I just knew you'd be so good. I wasn't wrong."

"How close are you?"

"So fucking close."

Without skipping a beat, he pushed my legs open a little wider. His hands went to my hips, and he pulled my ass back. In that position, every thrust got me closer and closer to ecstasy.

Sweat ran down my back. My forehead slipped all over the cool glass, leaving a mark.

He pulled my head back against his shoulder and wrapped his big hand around my throat, squeezing enough that every breath I took was punctuated.

My pulse pounded in my ears and my body ached for release.

"Next time you look up at this hotel from your apartment, I want you to think about this moment. How you were completely owned by a stranger without a name. I want you to wonder if I'll have cleaned your cum from the glass or left it for the maids to find in the morning."

My orgasm built with each thrust into my ass and each word rasped in my ear. His breath smelled of expensive scotch, and I wanted his cologne imprinted on my skin.

"Come for me."

As he said the words, ropes of my cum painted the glass, running down and marking it. Evidence of how I'd been truly wrecked by this man.

I kept my hands on the glass to hold steady as his thrusts lost their finesse, chasing his own orgasm.

He grunted he was coming, and then I felt it inside me. He stilled, breathing heavily against my neck.

Was it sick that I wanted him to stay inside me a little longer? Or that I wanted to keep his cum inside me, at least until I got back to my apartment and showered away the evidence of what had just happened.

He pulled out slowly, kissing my shoulder as he did. Something in my belly felt weird. Probably because I'd never had sex like this in my life. It had been raw, claiming, desperate.

I picked up my clothes, avoiding eye contact, and got dressed, hoping for an easy exit.

When I put my jacket on, he straightened the collar for me.

"Are you okay? Do you want to stay?"

Fuck, he was too sweet, and I couldn't deal with sweet right now when I felt so raw inside.

"I have an early morning tomorrow."

He nodded, his hand came up to my cheek, and he kissed me.

"Thank you. You were an unexpected stop in what would have been an otherwise bad night filled with poor choices."

I smiled. "Glad to know I wasn't one of them."

His fingers ran through my hair, straightening it. "I want to ask your name. Ask if I can see you again or if you'd be up for a repeat."

"Y—" He covered my mouth with his hand.

"Don't tempt me. You're far too perfect for me, which means you'd also be far too bad. I don't have…the capacity to start anything. Even casual."

I took in his dark eyes, salt-and-pepper beard, and the muscles peeking out from under his shirt. Was I responsible for the missing buttons?

"I can't say I'm not sad I didn't get to explore this sexy body. I'll just have to spend the rest of my days by the window, looking up at this place and jacking off to memories of you filling me up and making me come all over the glass."

He groaned. "See? You're far too tempting."

I chuckled. "I'll get out of your sight then." I stood on my toes and kissed him. "Goodnight, sexy silver fox stranger with the big dick."

I walked out and away from the hotel without a single look behind me to see if I could find the window from the outside.

All the way home, my brain was a messy mix of feelings, thoughts, and confusion.

I knew my behavior had much to do with how I dealt with the hurt I was still carrying in my heart.

The way to get over someone is to get under a lot of someones.

That had been my MO for years. Tonight was no different, but it had felt different.

When I got to my building, I debated knocking on Jax's door, but it was late and he was jet-lagged, so he was probably asleep already.

I needed to apologize for ditching him for dick. I also needed a distraction but tonight he wasn't going to be it.

My apartment felt cold and empty. I walked to the window I could see the hotel from and stared out.

I found his window straight away, thanks to the balcony in the room. The hotel was one of those old buildings with a marble front and a distinct old-world look. There was a single balcony that I now knew belonged to the suite I'd just been fucked in.

Fuck, his cum was still inside me.

My dick stirred, which was an indication I needed to push the stranger aside, grab a shower, and go to bed.

Tonight would have to be enough to keep me going for a while. My brothers needed me.

Lex was on the verge of a breakdown or severe depression, and Adam, while he put on a brave face for Lex, felt a lot of what Lex felt.

Now, he was engaged, and while I didn't necessarily agree with it or think he'd done it for the right reasons, I wanted to be supportive.

My phone dinged with a message as I came out of the shower.

LEX

Are you awake?

NOAH

I am. Wanna talk?

The phone rang with a video call. I answered as I pulled a pair of sweatpants from a drawer.

"Hey, Lexy-Loo," I said, calling him by the stupid nickname I picked for him as a kid.

"Hey. I just wanted to talk about…you know, earlier. I'm fine. I know I don't always look like I'm fine, but—"

"Yeah, you're fine." I sighed. "Lex, I love you, bro. Just know that I'm here for you anytime, okay?" Because it took a bullshitter to know a bullshitter, and Lex was bullshitting, though he'd never admit it.

In that respect, it was something all the Spencer brothers had in common. We were fucking stubborn. We got it from our mom's Portuguese blood.

"Thanks, Noah. I just wanted to say that."

"I hear you. See you in the office tomorrow?"

"As always."

I didn't like dwelling on the past because it brought too much pain. I wished I could help Lex get through his, but he wasn't like me. He was better. He loved with his whole heart, like I did once upon a time, but I knew better now.

6

—

LIOR

Silence followed me as I walked into the conference room at the main offices of Van Stern Enterprises.

Thirteen faces stared at me. Twelve business partners, plus my mother.

"I'd love to say good morning, but that remains to be ascertained."

"Lior," my mom said in the same tone reserved for when I was ten and had skipped homework to go visit my grandfather in his workshop.

Stained glass had been his life and his passion. Yes, it had paved the way to a Fortune 500 enterprise, but at heart, he'd been first and foremost a craftsman.

I'd heard the story so many times.

"Don't forget where we come from, Lior. Your Dutch grandfather taught me everything he knew about stained glass so his legacy could be preserved for the new generations after the war ended."

"He let you marry grandma and bring her to America. She was very pretty."

"The most beautiful person I've ever met."

"When you and grandma moved here you opened your work-shop and put to practice everything that great-grandpa taught you. And that's why we have grandma's name."

"Correct."

"Can you help me make a window for Mom's office? It needs more color and her birthday is coming up."

"Absolutely, Lior."

I pushed thoughts of grandfather away. Today was about the other man that had shaped my life and was about to shape my future.

"Hi, Mom." I kissed her cheek and took my chair next to hers at the top of the large conference table.

"You left early yesterday."

I bit my tongue to stop myself from acknowledging the elephant in the room or saying something I'd regret.

Sorry, Mother, I stayed long enough to fill my schedule for the next decade, so I figured grabbing a drink and burying myself in a stranger was my reward for having to do business during my father's funeral. Oh, and forgive me for not wanting to be around people after discovering my dad has a secret will.

Yes, that was going to go down well.

Around the room, everyone talked in whispers, but they may as well be fucking shouting.

Why did Lior Van Stern Sr. have a secret will?

What was in it? A secret child?

Was he going to make his own family destitute?

What's in it for me?

I scrolled through emails on my phone to drown them all out until Mr. Hoffman came in. The attorney my dad had hired without telling his wife and only son.

Thoughts of last night filtered through, and I felt guilty for indulging in the memory.

I couldn't remember when I'd ever had such a quick connection with another man. The way he'd given himself so freely, like it was something he'd needed more than wanted. It called out to a side of me that didn't come out very often.

"Good morning, Mrs. Van Stern, Mr. Van Stern, gentlemen." Mr. Hoffman entered the conference room holding his briefcase to his chest like he was afraid someone would tackle it out of him.

He placed the briefcase on the table. The click of the clasps sounded loudly in the room where silence now reigned.

Did everyone really think my dad was keeping some dark secret that would destroy the company?

"Since I've already introduced myself to each of you prior to this meeting, we'll get straight to it, shall we?" Mr. Hoffman looked at me and my mom.

"Please," I said.

"Mr. Van Stern contacted my law firm shortly after he was diagnosed. He wanted to ensure his wishes were seen to by a third party with no connection to Van Stern Enterprises." He turned to my mother. "Mr. Van Stern was a strong-willed man but just a man, and it was a pleasure working with him. Over the past year, I had access to a side of Mr. Van Stern he perhaps reserved for a select few. We did not always agree, but like I said, he was a determined man."

I held my mom's shaking hand under the table. Unlike many of my parents' friends and close acquaintances, they'd married for love.

Hearing about my dad from someone she'd only just met had to be hard, especially while under close scrutiny from the business partners.

"Before I read Mr. Van Stern's last will and testament, I want to remind you all that he was of sound mind when he wrote his final wishes. This has been co-signed by his doctor as well as my legal team."

I kept my eyes on the table, focusing on a tiny surface imperfection.

With no objections from anyone, Mr. Hoffman pulled out an envelope from his briefcase and started reading.

"Dear Mathilda, Lior, and all you bloodsuckers who are here just for the paycheck."

I snorted as the room remained silent. Dad had always been a candid man, but I'd never heard him call his business partners bloodsuckers to their faces. From the shocked expressions around the table, this was a first for them too.

Mr. Hoffman cleared his throat to continue.

"First and foremost, I have to apologize to my dear Mathilda, the love of my life and the only person strong-willed enough to put up with my cantankerous ass."

I held my mom's hand and squeezed it tight. Her chin trembled a little, and I hated my father for making her go through this in a room full of business partners instead of just close family.

"Van Stern Enterprises started as a work of love. My father took my mother's surname to honor her father, from whom he learned his trade. The story is well documented in our historical archives. Most of them are held in the Cliffborough Stained Glass Museum, which was once the Van Stern family home outside the city.
"When I think of it, my father held beliefs that were modern for the standards of America in the 1940s. This likely has to do with seeing so much death, destruction, and loss when he was stationed in Europe during the Second World War.

"Like many men of his time, he rarely talked of those days unless it was to recount how he met my mother and her family. How he managed to bring them to the United States after the war, and how proud he was to continue the legacy of his father-in-law, my grandfather, whose work had mostly been destroyed when churches all over Europe were bombed.

"From stained-glass windows in public buildings to private commissions to the enterprise we have today, nothing would be possible if a young man hadn't fallen in love with the right person and found passion in the art of stained glass and the possibilities that working with glass offered.

"But enough of the history lesson. Many of you might wonder what will happen to my place in the company now that I'm gone.

"My son, Lior, whom I love more than he probably knows, took over the Stained Glass Museum after my father passed away. It's been his literal home and his passion.

"Since Lior was a young child, I dreamed of passing the family legacy to him. Maybe I failed to bring him into the business as much as I could when I saw he shared more of his grandfather's passion for stained glass than mine for business. Maybe what I did was the right thing.

"Regardless, Van Stern Enterprises needs a new CEO. Unfairly as it may seem, I am leaving that legacy to Lior with one condition."

Mr. Hoffman put the letter down, much to the collective gasp in the room.

He took a pile of files from his briefcase and handed one to each person in the room.

"I beg that you let me finish reading the letter before you open the file," he said.

My stomach churned. I always knew my father would leave me the majority share of the company. The conditions it apparently came with made me sweat under my suit jacket.

When I'd inherited the museum from my grandfather, I'd thought my role within the family and the business had been established. But my father had made it clear he wanted me to take over when he retired.

That was supposed to be a long time from now. I'd started to enjoy my involvement in the company as much as I loved working in the museum, but I'd thought I'd have longer to get used to the idea that I needed to pull away from my hands-on approach to the museum.

Was I ready to run a company that had expanded into a multinational business manufacturing everything made of glass, from housewares to decorations and gifts? Not to mention, we were still the leaders in anything stained glass.

The file burned in my hands. I wanted to open it now and know the stipulation my father had set before I could take on the role he'd left vacant.

Mr. Hoffman returned to his place at the table and continued reading the letter.

"Lior will not take on my role as CEO of Van Stern Enterprises unless he gets married within six months from now. Only then will my sixty percent shares of the company be passed to him."

"I'm sorry, what?" I asked, coughing. I looked at my mom, who looked equally surprised.

"Please, Mr. Van Stern, let me finish the letter, and then I can answer all your questions."

"I'm sorry. I thought I just heard in a room full of business partners that my father wants me, a forty-seven-year-old man, to marry within the next six months in order to take over the role that is my birthright. Forgive me for being a little shocked."

Mr. Hoffman raised the letter and resumed once again.

"I have written a separate letter to my son to explain the reasons behind this decision. This will come as a shock to many, not least to Lior and my dear Mathilda, but I truly believe this stipulation is the right thing to do. While my body is slowly giving in to this awful illness, my mind is sound. Mr. Hoffman will be able to answer all your questions and how this transition might affect each of you."

Mr. Hoffman put the letter down and opened the file in front of him.

I stood. "Is this a joke?"

"I assure you it's not, Mr.—"

"Call me Lior." I paced the room. "What happens if I don't do it?"

"If you aren't married six months from today, your father's shares will go on the market, and you will receive the dividend."

"What about the museum?"

"The museum is tied to the company."

He didn't have to say anything else. I'd lose my home.

7

———

NOAH

I'D BEEN STARING at the same page on my computer browser for at least ten minutes. When I saw the photo, I immediately looked up to ensure no one had seen it. Stupid, since I was in my office, so only I could see my screen.

Also, because, one, no one knew what had happened that day at the hotel, and two, there was nothing wrong about checking a prospective client's website.

It'd been three whole weeks since I'd stared at those dark eyes, and not a day had gone by without me thinking about his dick filling me up. His hand on my throat. His raspy voice in my ear, commanding me to come.

It could be because we'd kept things anonymous. The secrecy was hot as hell. Or that I knew it would never happen again. But that night was imprinted in my brain and refused to let go.

All I could do was jack off daily in front of my window while staring out at the hotel room balcony like a pervert. And while it didn't hold a candle to the real thing, it was the best I could do. The only thing I could do. Until now. Until his face had appeared on my computer.

Lior Van Stern.

The man had a sexy name to go with his broody face, hot body, and big dick.

I was so fucked.

The Cliffborough Stained Glass Museum was looking for a PR and marketing agency to help them with the launch of the new range of summer workshops they were offering to the public.

The museum had been on my hit list for a while. As the account director at the agency, my job was to look after our existing clients and scout for business.

These days, I spent more time looking after our current clients than looking for new ones, thanks to our reputation for delivering creative and successful campaigns that yielded results. But I was always looking to expand our client base.

Van Stern Enterprises was very much a goal in that respect.

What the fuck was I going to do?

There was no way we could afford to ignore an inquiry from the museum. VSE was a huge company, and this could be the break we needed to hit it big.

Working with them would give us our pick of high-profile projects in the future.

Since our company's inception, my brothers and I had always wanted to offer pro bono services to small businesses. Help them get off the ground and get visibility with a good campaign. We could only do this if we had enough income from other projects.

I needed to think about this, but first, I needed some distance, so I closed the browser and shut down my computer. "On your way out?"

I jumped when I saw Adam leaning against my office door. "Jesus fuck, Adam."

He scratched his clean-shaven chin. "I knocked, but you seemed really engrossed. New client?"

"Yeah, potential big new client. Van Stern Enterprises."

He gasped. "You're shitting me."

"Shit you not."

"Whatever they want, we'll do it. Can you imagine the business we could do with them on our books? Not to mention how it would help with our mission statement."

"I know. Leave it with me. Did you want something?"

He looked around and came inside, closing the door. "About Lex—"

"Is he okay?" I stood, ready to run over to his office.

Adam raised his hand for me to sit back down as he took the seat across from my desk. "He's fine. That's the problem. How can he be fine? At my engagement party, he was crumbling, and then—"

"Adam, you held your engagement party in the same place he proposed to his boyfriend, who then disappeared without a trace. How did you expect him to be?"

To give Adam credit, he sank a little in his chair.

"I know. I should have pressed Victoria harder to have the party somewhere else."

I'd already shared my thoughts with Adam at length so there was no point going over it again. "It's in the past now, and Emery is back."

"That's the thing. Lex is determined to get to know Emery again, find out what happened, and how he lost his memory. What if this all ends wrong? We need to help him before he gets hurt again."

I rubbed my temples with both hands. A week ago, Lex had called a Code Red—our brotherly bat signal. When we'd arrived at his place, he'd been on the verge of a panic attack because he'd bumped into his ex-boyfriend at the farmers' market.

Emery, whom I'd always loved like a brother and had thought was the best thing to happen to Lex, told him he'd had a car accident and lost his memory. Their meeting at the market had been purely by chance, and Lex was convinced Emery was being genuine. That was all we knew.

I'd admit my suggestions to get the truth out of Emery weren't the most helpful because while most people think I'm great under pressure, I'm really not. My default is slutty assassin. Kill 'em or fuck 'em. And if you can't decide, then fuck them to death.

"He said he was going to take it slowly," I said.

"I know, but I'm not sure he can. He never stopped loving Emery. How would you be if the lost love of your life appeared in front of you?"

I'd kill her. See? Default.

"I don't know, Adam, but it's up to Lex to figure out if Emery is telling the truth and if there's still anything between them."

He sighed.

"I know this is hard for you with your weird twin connection, but…I don't know. Maybe show your support so he knows he has somewhere to land if it all falls apart."

He stood and held out his hand in a fist. I bumped it.

"And that's why you're the older one," he said. "Maybe not the prettiest, but you're wise."

"Fuck you, I'm gorgeous."

I liked the sound of his laughter as he left the office.

On my way out, I called Jax to meet me at Tanner's. I needed someone to talk to, and for this, it couldn't be my brothers.

"Hot damn, Doctor. Can I tell you where it hurts?" Jax was one good-looking motherfucker. He was smart as fuck, having completed his medical degree while in the military, which required a level of fitness I could never aspire to have. The guy was ripped.

"You're not good-looking enough for me to get my stethoscope out."

"Ouch. Hit me where it hurts, will you?"

He called the bartender and ordered us two beers.

"Tell me why I'm in a bar rather than at home in bed after a thirty-six-hour shift at the hospital."

"Fuck, this is what you look like after a long shift? I look like I've been robbed and beaten up after a single workout."

He looked at me like he doubted that was true, even though he'd witnessed it over the last couple of weekends that we'd played basketball with the Star Finders kids.

"Don't deflect. What's up?"

"Do you remember that guy from three weeks ago?"

His forehead wrinkled. "The silver fox dude?"

"Yeah."

"Well, he was hands down the best sex I've ever had. I can't even begin to tell you how he——"

"Please don't."

I chuckled. "It was good, really good, okay? We didn't exchange names or any personal details. I confess he's been hard to shake off, but he said he couldn't start anything. Even casual."

"Please don't tell me you're going to hire a private investigator to find the guy."

"The thought never crossed my mind. Contrary to public opinion, I do have boundaries." Maybe just not when it came to Lior Van Stern. Fuck, that name sounded so sexy, even in my head.

"So what's wrong?"

"He came to me."

Jax swallowed his beer and put the bottle down. I could be wrong, but I'd swear he was only half-listening to me because his eyes kept going to the area behind the bar that connected to the kitchen.

"He found you, and he wants to hook up?"

"No, he found the agency, and he wants to hire us. He doesn't know I'm…me."

"Would it really be a problem to tell him who you are? I mean, it's not like you knew each other before."

"No, we didn't, but his business would mean big money for us. What if he finds out I run the agency with my brothers and decides he doesn't want to use us?"

Jax glanced behind the bar again before he leaned toward me. "How much involvement do you have with clients?"

"I manage the accounts, but all the creative stuff is with Adam and Lex. Beyond the initial meeting and keeping in touch once the project is delivered, I don't have much contact. The problem is that if we work with his company, I'll want to keep them on board."

"Why don't you send one of your brothers for the initial meeting, then you do the work that doesn't require face-to-face contact? By the time you've delivered the project, it won't matter who you are because he'll be sold on your work."

That was a great idea. I could send Lex to meet with Lior and maybe I would never have to meet him.

Did I want to interact face-to-face with Lior?

Yes. And dick to face. Face to ass. Ass to dick. All the ways under the sun. Nothing had changed in that respect.

If we worked together, we couldn't hook up, which meant I wasn't breaking any rules.

"You're a genius."

"Not to mention good-looking."

"You're right about that," Tanner said, dropping a basket with steaming clean glasses on the counter behind the bar and aiming his usual teasing smile at Jax.

Jax was stunned into silence. A blush crept up from under his shirt collar.

I stood and tapped his back. "Sorry to leave you, bud. I just remembered I have somewhere to be." *In my living room, in front of the window with my dick out while I exorcise Lior Van Stern out of my system before dumping him on my brother.*

Jax gave me a pleading look, but judging by Tanner's expression, I'd made the right decision.

8

LIOR

"LIOR, where are you? I just stopped by the museum, and Charlie said you were out of town."

"Hi, Mom. I'm in Atlanta for a business conference. I just landed and have a bunch of work to do. Can I call you when I'm back?"

"No, you cannot. Lior Van Stern, you've been avoiding me for the best part of a month, and enough is enough."

I sighed. The driver looked in the rearview mirror but quickly looked away when our eyes met.

"I've been working. Believe it or not, stepping into Dad's shoes at the company isn't easily done. Not to mention, I still have my work at the museum."

Charlie had fulfilled more than his personal assistant role since my dad had gotten ill, but I couldn't just dump everything on him and expect him to take it. There were only so many hours in the day.

"I know it's not easy, honey, but we have to talk about our plan to keep the company from being sold off to the highest bidder. I don't know what was going through your father's head when he wrote that goddam will."

That made two of us. I thought I'd get more clarity after reading the letter he'd addressed to me, but that hadn't helped. Well, other than him mentioning how a partnership with Pierce would benefit the business as well as gain the respect of the more conservative partners.

"I'm not marrying Pierce, no matter what Dad may have thought about him. I wish I'd told him Pierce and I had broken things off because maybe he wouldn't have put this ridiculous plan in motion. Do you know how old I am?"

She laughed on the other side of the line. "I believe I was there the day you were born, so yes, Lior, I know how old you are. I also know that however ridiculous this stipulation from your father is, we can't just let the company go. You know what that means."

"I know, Mom."

"You've lost one month already. Don't waste more time. Maybe you could reconnect with Pierce? Were things that bad?"

No, he only cheated on me with one guy that I know of, but don't worry, it was all my fault because I neglected our relationship by working too much.

"I'll see."

It would never happen, but I'd say anything to get her off the call. I loved her for having my back, and I knew that if my dad had run this idea by her, it would never have made it into his will. Maybe that's why he kept it a secret.

Like my grandparents', my parents' love story was beautiful. As they had so often recounted, it had been love at first sight. They met when walking into a restaurant for dates with other people.

Neither date was successful, but my father persuaded the maître d' to give him my mother's name. In the days of phone books, it had taken him a while to find Mathilda Branson, who still lived with her parents at the time.

I could only imagine how many angry dads he must have called to find the right house.

His determination had paid off, even if Granddad Branson hadn't been impressed with his daughter's wannabe stalker.

"We'll be at your destination in ten minutes, sir."

"Thank you."

I scrolled through some emails and replied to a couple of messages from Charlie. He was definitely in line for a bonus this year for all his support. There was no way I'd be standing on my own two feet right now if it hadn't been for him.

The man should have retired already, but I didn't want to think about it too much. I'd already lost one father. Losing Charlie, now the closest thing I had to a father figure, was incomprehensible.

I closed my eyes and leaned my head against the car's headrest. The face I'd been unsuccessfully trying to forget for the last month filled my mind.

The man had given me exactly what I'd needed on one of the worst days of my life. He deserved flowers, an award, or at least more orgasms.

Instead, I'd played it safe and let him go.

He was too young anyway.

What would I have done if I'd met him just a day later? I didn't want to think about that. It was a ridiculous thought, but marrying a stranger like him right now seemed like a good-enough option.

Marry for love, son, not because there's a timeline attached. I know I'm not making this easy on you, but I know you. Stop playing it safe. Life is an adventure, but it's not half as fun if you don't have someone beside you to share it.

My father, ever the romantic, had made legally binding stipulations that made it virtually impossible to fulfill his wishes.

I pushed those thoughts aside as we reached the conference hotel. It was time to put on my professional mask and make connections.

The last time I'd attended the Atlanta Business Symposium, Pierce had come along and worked his charm on everyone. This time, I was on my own.

I'd checked in before arriving at the hotel, so grabbing the room key was a painless process.

"Can my bags be taken up to my room, please?" I asked.

"Of course, Mr. Van Stern."

The conference didn't start until tomorrow morning, so I planned to grab a drink and then figure out where to have dinner before spending the evening working in my room.

The glamorous life of a CEO, I thought.

The bar was busy. Hoping I wouldn't be recognized and pulled into a business conversation, I took the only seat at the bar that wasn't next to someone in a suit.

The bartender put a coaster in front of me. "What can I get you, sir?"

"Scotch, please. Neat. Thank you."

While he poured the drink, I looked at the mirror behind him to take in the room.

"We must stop meeting like this, Mr. Van Stern."

I turned toward the voice and met those blue eyes I'd regretted not looking into long enough the first time. The soft lips. The neatly trimmed distinct jawline.

He was even more beautiful than I remembered.

"I'm afraid you have me at a disadvantage, Mr...."

"Spencer, Noah Spencer."

He held out his hand, and I took it. His fingers wrapped

slowly but intently around my hand. A sign of familiarity no one but us would ever see.

"Spencer, as in…"

"The PR and marketing agency you're working with."

I let out a breath. How fucked up was my life right now?

There was apprehension in the way he stared at me. He looked around before he lowered his voice.

"Disclaimer. I didn't know who you were when we…"

I nodded, praying he wouldn't finish the sentence. As it was, my dick was paying far too much attention to the way he dressed casually but still looked professional and how he smelled. Sandalwood and citrus.

"How did you find out?" I asked.

"Honestly? I should have recognized you then. After all, your company has been on my dream list since we started. But it wasn't until I researched the museum that I found out. That's why…I sent my brother to meet you. I didn't want what happened between us to cloud your judgment about working with us."

To give him credit, he looked embarrassed.

"He did a good job of selling you to me." I groaned. "I mean, your agency."

He bit his lip to hide a smile.

"Gotcha."

"Are you here for the conference?"

"Yeah. It's my first time. You?"

"Second."

"It sounds like we're about to spend some time together, Mr. Van Stern."

I moved my gaze away from him and drank my two fingers of scotch in one go.

"It seems that way."

He chuckled. "Just so you know, I don't sleep with clients."

"It's not the sleeping I'm worried about." *Way to show your hand, Van Stern. Why don't you just tell him to go up to your room, get naked, and be on his knees by the time you get up there?*

My eyes met his in the mirror. He took a sip of his beer. My cock filled as I stared at his mouth around the rim of the bottle. He licked his lips.

I remembered that sinful tongue too well.

Since that night, I'd jerked off more than a few times to thoughts of him. It had been the only thing I'd indulged in because unlike most of my day-to-day life, my thoughts were my own.

"What are you doing for dinner?" he asked.

"Not you."

"Ouch. My heart bleeds."

"Funny. I didn't think you had one." I winked.

"And look at that, it's like you know me inside out." His smirk made me want to break the rules.

You can look but not touch.

I repeated it. *You can look but not touch.*

This was going to be a nightmare weekend.

"Come on, Lior," he said, drawing out my name. "Let's have some food and talk business. My brothers will love me forever if I get more intel to help them put together the concept for your summer courses promotion."

9

___

NOAH

"Not here. I'm not in the mood to get sucked into a business conversation," Lior said.

I stood from the stool a little too eagerly, placing me directly face-to-face with Lior. The top buttons on his white shirt were undone, showing some of that sexy salt-and-pepper chest hair I hadn't gotten a chance to appreciate properly that night.

I lowered my voice so only he could hear. "Want me all to yourself, Mr. Van Stern?"

He placed a couple of bills on the bar and gave me a look that sent a thrill through my spine. "You can't help yourself, can you?"

I shook my head.

"Maybe I should teach you a lesson."

Please. That's what I wanted to say, but I was already skirting too close to the border between flirting territory and full-on propositioning.

I couldn't have sex with him again. There was no way I would jeopardize our working relationship, but I couldn't deny he was an intriguing man.

He was intrinsically linked to the museum, so there was no harm in getting to know him on a professional level. Anything I could get from him would surely help Lex and Adam with the creative process.

Sure. It's all about the job.

"There's a nice steakhouse at the Centennial Olympic Park if you don't mind a short walk," Lior suggested.

"I think we've proven I'll follow you anywhere that seems like a good time."

He moved his hand as if he was going for mine but stopped it just before they touched. I pretended not to notice and followed him out of the hotel into the humid Atlanta evening. Instead of taking the path to the front of the hotel, he took a left. We didn't stop until we'd almost reached the staff entrance.

I thought he was going inside from the way he looked around, but instead, he pinned me to the wall.

"Honest to god, Noah. You need to quit it if you want to keep things professional. I'm one flirty comment away from putting you over my knee and spanking your perfect little ass until all you can think about every time you sit down this weekend is me."

"If this is you trying to get me to stop, I'll let you in on a secret." I looked down to where my dick imprint was very visible in my jeans.

He closed his eyes and let out an exasperated breath.

"I'm teasing you. I wasn't joking when I said I don't mess with clients. Even if you're the only one who's ever made me rethink my policy."

"Good to know. Now, let's go get some steak. While I'm avoiding talking business with other people, I don't mind doing it with you."

He pulled away, and I smiled. "It's because I'm special, right?"

"You're special, all right. Come on."

The restaurant had a premium view of the park. I saw why he'd picked it, but it was also inside a different hotel, which gave us a layer of privacy.

"I bring you to a steakhouse and you order seafood," he said, staring at my barbecued shrimp like it was a personal offense.

I leaned on the table. "Here's a little restaurateur inside scoop for you. The way the chef treats the starter tells you how good the main dish will be, especially in a steakhouse."

He took his red wine glass to his lips. "And you know this how?"

"My parents own a restaurant in Cliffborough. Most kids spend their summer vacation outside playing, we spent it visiting restaurants out of state."

"I spent my summers with my granddad in his workshop, much to my father's annoyance."

"Why's that?"

He moved his ravioli around the plate. "My father thought my granddad should spend more time in the office with him, building the company. Selfishly, I wanted the opposite."

"Your grandfather started the stained-glass business."

Lior nodded. "Yes. He was a true craftsman. Even when he had to be in the office he always stole some time away to work on his pieces. He even built a small workshop there."

"Lex was very impressed with your museum. He wouldn't shut up about how beautiful it was. He wouldn't shut up about you either, but for a different reason." I laughed.

He raised a brow. "How so?"

"He found you intimidating, which I can understand."

"You find me intimidating?"

I smiled, trying to find the right words. "I find you intriguing, captivating, tempting…"

The server took our empty plates and replaced them with our main dishes.

Lior waited until he was out of earshot. "I think you're the one who's tempting."

"And look who's flirting now?"

"It's not flirting if it's a fact."

"Tell me more about your strained-glass workshops," I said, diverting the conversation to a safer topic.

He smirked but took another sip of wine and leaned back in his chair. "Stained glass is a dying art. These days, you can get beautiful glass panels for a fraction of the price. Hell, you can even get them from my own company. My goal isn't to make handcrafted stained glass mainstream. It's to make it special. Timeless. Something you can pass on to future generations. I'll never forget the time I spent with my grandfather learning how to make small decorations. My parents still have Christmas tree ornaments they bring out every year. I made those."

His smile turned into a frown. I'd read his father passed away recently, just before we met. It had to be hard talking about good family memories when he'd just lost someone.

"Who's your target audience?"

"Anyone. We have couples' workshops, family parties, children-only workshops, and we can also deliver team-building exercises."

"I have an idea."

"Shoot."

"I'd like you to run a workshop for me, my brothers, and their partners. I want to see you in your element."

His eyes shot up to his forehead. "You're...no, that's not happening."

"You barely know me," I managed to say with a straight face, "but hear me out. Remember, I'm the marketing dude."

"Hmm."

"This is what I've learned from my research into your company. Your grandfather was the heart of the company, your grandmother the soul, and your father the mechanism that made it a financial success beyond the small business it started out as. But I didn't see you. You are the future of VSE. Anything you do from now on needs to be impactful and with purpose. Your purpose. Even if you don't teach the workshops yourself, your customers want to know you're connected to your family history."

Shit. He didn't look happy. I hoped I hadn't put my foot in my mouth and lost his business because I'd been too honest.

His eyes moved from the wine bottle between us to mine.

"I'm not sure I understand. Can you elaborate?"

Deep breath. I could do this.

"Lior, the way you talk about your grandfather and your business is purely from the heart. I can see it in your eyes. If you want a place where memories are created, you have to share your memories."

"I'm not sure I'm comfortable being a marketing tool."

"You wouldn't be. This is about showing your audience that VSE is a family business. That you've grown in it, and everyone else should experience it. Lex and Adam are the creative heads in our business. If anyone out there knows family business, it's us. I'm confident we'll develop an excellent campaign that not only promotes the workshops but also showcases your values and the values of your family."

"I'll sleep on it."

"I can help you workshop it this weekend."

"That means more alone time, which, as I'm finding out, is a very dangerous activity with you."

"Don't dangle the carrot."

He raised a brow. "No carrots are being dangled."

"You're right. It's more a huge eggplant or a prize-winning zucchini."

"You're incorrigible."

"I'm sure you'd know exactly how to discipline me."

He let out a throaty growl. "Noah."

I leaned over the table, pushing my finished dinner aside. "Just so you know, every time you say my name, I think about your hand around my throat, telling me what to do." I ran my hands over my face. "I'm sorry. I don't know what's wrong with me. I just can't switch off around you. I promise for the hundredth time that I'll keep things professional."

He smiled. "I know you will because I won't let you fail."

"Ugh, don't be nice to me."

"Would you rather I wasn't?"

I sighed. "No. That would turn me on too."

"If it makes you feel better, I also wish we could revisit that night, but apart from wanting to keep things professional, I didn't lie. I really don't have time to start anything."

I rested my chin over my crossed hands, with my elbows on the table. "When we met, I thought you couldn't be more different from me, not just because of the age difference. Now I think we have a lot more in common than we think."

"I am inclined to agree."

"Shall we order dessert?"

He laughed. "How can you still eat more?"

"Several reasons. Dessert stomach is a thing. They have chocolate mousse on the menu, and Mom would disown me for not completing a meal."

"Tell me about your family," he said.

Talking about his family was work. Talking about mine was…getting personal. But just like I knew I wouldn't deny him another go with my body if he really wanted it, I opened up and told him all about my crazy Portuguese family.

10

LIOR

Noah's absence from the breakfast buffet before the start of the conference was explained when he walked on stage for the first session of the day.

I'd sat at the back of the room, hoping to see him as he came in. I regretted that decision now because I wanted to be closer to the stage and ensure I didn't miss a word.

Last night, he'd proven that he was a great businessman. His default seemed to be boosting his brothers' creative skills, but I'd argue his ideas had merit. Even if they'd left me a little uncomfortable at first.

His session was titled *The Friends and Family Plan*. I'd picked the session because, as someone who managed a business passed down the generations, I wanted to see what fresh ideas or perspectives I could take back.

Had I done my research, I'd have seen Noah's photo on the conference website as one of the speakers.

He hadn't even mentioned it last night. I just hoped I hadn't taken up the time he'd planned to use to prepare for his session.

My heart beat faster as he approached the lectern and pulled the microphone closer to his mouth.

"Good morning, everyone. I'm Noah Spencer, co-founder and director of Spencer Brothers Marketing & PR, and your speaker for this session. Usually, you can trust a PR agency to come in with all the bells and whistles, props, dancers, and smart media. After the dancers threw a tantrum over the lack of cupcakes in the green room and left, we now have a tiny issue with our IT system." He winked at the crowd. "It shouldn't take long to fix if you can bear with us for a few minutes."

I watched as Noah worked with the conference team. The room was full, and all eyes were on the stage. He was the definition of cool under pressure.

Someone took the seat next to mine. My face fell when I turned to greet them. "Pierce. What are you doing here?"

"The way you greet me these days, one might think you're not happy to see me."

"I wonder what gave you that idea," I said sarcastically.

"Why don't I take you out to dinner tonight? We can talk properly."

"I already have plans." I didn't, but I wouldn't be opposed to having dinner with Noah again.

"With who?"

I gave him my best are-you-fucking-serious face.

He raised his hands. "None of my business, I get it."

"Okay, folks, we're all set. Thank you for your patience," Noah announced from the stage.

The big screen behind him filled with a photo of his family. I recognized Noah and Lex, although I didn't know which one Lex was. I hadn't realized his brothers were twins.

"Not another millennial. These conferences are becoming really predictable and boring," Pierce complained. He must have taken my silence as agreement with his opinion because he continued, "PR people never know how to wear a suit. Creative types with mumbo-jumbo ideas that will never work in the real world. Try pitching this to a boardroom filled with aging businessmen. What do these kids have to teach us?"

"Manners for a start. If this session isn't for you, the door is only a few feet away."

"Don't be like that, baby. You know what I mean."

"No, I don't know what you mean, and you've lost the privilege of calling me baby. My name is Lior. Now, either leave or let me listen to the speaker."

He harumphed but stayed mercifully silent throughout the session.

Noah was astonishing. He spoke with clarity about his parents' restaurant and how they'd found a way to make sure it would carry over to another generation, even though none of the children wanted to follow in their footsteps.

He talked about change and moving forward. Accepting who you are, your strengths, and how you can make it work even when working with family means you can't fire them or kill them.

That got the audience laughing.

Pierce mumbled a few times, but I didn't pay attention because I felt that Noah was speaking directly to me as a person and a business owner. He was good.

The audience stood in applause at the end. I joined them, ignoring Pierce, who remained seated.

Noah thanked the audience, his eyes scanning it until he found me. His smile widened.

I walked up to the side of the stage to wait for him. I wasn't the only one. Many of the people in the audience wanted to ask him questions.

He gave out his business card and told everyone politely that his inbox was open.

"Congratulations. You were amazing up there," I said at my earliest opportunity.

He walked toward the door with me. "Was it good? God, I was so nervous I thought I was going to shit my pants. And when the server went down." He gasped. "The crew here is amazing. I'd have crumpled under the pressure."

"Are you serious?"

He looked at me. "Yeah, why?"

"Noah, you were fucking brilliant. You're a natural speaker, charismatic, funny, and you know what you're talking about."

His cheeks flushed a little.

"I could murder a coffee. Want to join me?" he asked.

"Do I get to pick your brains about your presentation?"

He laughed. "Sure."

"Then let's go."

After letting me ask all the questions, Noah, amazingly, still stuck with me for the rest of the day. I was pretty sure he'd get tired and would want to network with other people.

"I've been to a few business conferences, but this has been the most eventful." He was doubled up in laughter after the hotel security had to escort out one of the speakers who had drunk a whole bottle of wine at lunch to calm his nerves and who, after a short, slurred speech, fell asleep leaning against the lectern.

I looked at my watch. There was a mixer in the hotel bar now, but dinner was up to us.

"Would you like to grab dinner somewhere?" I asked Noah.

"I thought you already had plans," Pierce said, appearing out of thin air.

"I had hope," I said, keeping my eyes on Noah.

"Aren't you going to introduce me to your *friend*?" Pierce asked, highlighting the word friend.

Noah held out his hand. "Noah Spencer. Nice to meet you. But you already know who I am since I saw you at my session this morning."

I bit my lip, suddenly feeling aroused while watching Noah stand up for himself.

"Pierce Dellcourt, of Dellcourt Industries."

"Oh yeah, I've heard about your company. Weren't you in trouble recently for some kind of tax dodge? Or am I thinking of a different company? You know, us millennials can't hold our attention for longer than a minute."

I laughed. I shouldn't have, but Noah was spot on.

Pierce looked dumbfounded for a second before he turned to me, likely looking for someone to blame. He wouldn't find it in me, and he knew that.

When he recovered, he put his hand on my elbow. I looked at it pointedly, and he put his hand down. "I had an interesting conversation with one of your father's business partners the other day. I'll leave you to your boy-toy because you and I both know the right thing to do. I'll see you around." And he walked off.

"What is he talking about?" Noah asked.

"Nothing important. I've got to know how you know what he said."

Noah smiled. "I'm a little rusty, but I can read lips."

"Really?"

He laughed. "No. I was talking to someone earlier who told me about a guy making rude comments at the start of my talk. The description fit. Doesn't he look like he's picked the biggest fork in the hotel and stuffed it up his ass?"

"He sure does. More than you know."

"It would have been embarrassing if he'd said something else. I also have no idea who he or his company is."

God, I wanted to put my arms around this man and hold

him tight. His snark, when aimed at someone else, was hot as fuck.

"May I take you out to dinner?" I asked again.

"Two days in a row? Well, Mr. Van Stern, I'm going to start thinking you're coming on to me."

There was no one else in the hallway since most people had moved to the bar, so I pulled him close and whispered in his ear. "You'll know when I'm coming on to you."

"Fuck, Lior. Don't threaten me with a good time if you're not going to follow through."

I laughed, and he narrowed his eyes.

"This is the worst weekend ever."

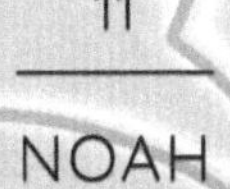

11

NOAH

"The guy is clearly a douche who needs his attitude adjusted, but who is he? I mean, to you."

Lior kept his gaze on the sidewalk in front of us.

"He's just someone. Trust me, he doesn't matter."

I wrapped my arm around his to get closer, happy when he didn't shrug me off. "He's an ex, isn't he?" I gasped. "He still wants you, but you don't want him. Oh man, we could make him so jealous. There's still one day left in the conference."

He snorted. "Jealousy is beneath him. I'm not even sure he's competitive. He's just…never mind. I don't like talking about people behind their backs."

"Not even about how uptight he is? He oozes uptight asshole energy, one hundred percent.."

He laughed. "Not even to talk about how uptight he is."

I knew it.

Okay, so Pierce was an ex. If I was to put my money on it, I'd say he cheated. He seemed the type of arrogant who'd cheat even when he had someone like Lior in his bed.

Why were people never happy with what they got?

"We should go there." I pointed excitedly at the bar with the big Karaoke sign above the front door.

"No."

"Oh, come on, Lioreo. I promise I won't make you sing. Look, they have wings."

He gave me an exasperated but amused look as he reluctantly followed me to the bar. I could work with that.

"For the record, that nickname is ridiculous."

"I think it's perfect because they're my favorite cookies, and just like with them, I could lick your cream all night long."

"Noah. For the love of—" He shook his head.

"I think I figured out why I have this tiny filter problem around you."

"This should be good." He gestured for me to continue as we found a free table in the packed bar. It was a Saturday night, after all.

"I have blue balls."

He coughed. "Thanks for the information."

"And it's your fault. You left me wanting more, and no one else will do it for me now."

He raised a brow. I called the server and ordered two portions of wings and a pitcher of beer.

"You can be very bossy considering..." he said, his dark eyes spelling out exactly what he wasn't saying. *Considering how easily I'd submitted to him.*

"I know what I like, and I like what I know. Back to my balls. They're blue." I pouted.

"We had a deal."

"We still do, but we faced Pickle Pierce together. We're best buddies now, which means you get the honor of knowing these things."

"My dreams have finally come true," he deadpanned.

We practically inhaled the wings and destroyed a couple of beers in no time.

"These were amazing," I said, wiping the sauce from my hands.

"As good as the food at the hotel is, nothing beats dive bar food."

"I never pegged you for a beer and wings guy. You're always so composed, stiff."

"Noah…"

"No." I laughed. "What I mean is that you come across as this corporate type, which doesn't match my image of someone who runs a museum."

"Should I be wearing tweed jackets with elbow patches?"

I scratched my chin. "Hmm, you'd still look sexy as fuck."

We took our time with the third beer, switching to water afterward.

"You're very close to your brothers. What's it like?" he asked out of the blue.

"Only child?"

"Yup."

"Having brothers is great. I love working with them."

His eyes bore into mine. "How about the rest?"

"What do you mean?"

"Are you close, close? I always wanted to have a sibling, but my parents said it just never happened. I always wondered what it would be like to have someone to share secrets with. Like a partner in crime."

I laughed. "I wouldn't say we're partners in crime. Lex and Adam were always closer to each other, which is natural. They even share that weird twin ESP connection where they can sense the other's emotions. It's creepy. We have fun together. We go out most Fridays to Tanner's with Adam's best friend, River. He's my dad's restaurant manager. He grew up with us, and he's practically Adam and Lex's triplet."

Lior finished his beer. "Why do I get the feeling they don't know everything about you?"

I laughed. "Because they'd enroll in a convent and take a vow of silence or send me away to a remote location away from humans."

"You're really good at deflecting attention away from you, and when you seek it, it's not you. It's a mask."

His words hit me right in the feels. No one in my life had ever called me out like this, and he didn't mean it in a bad way. It was like he'd just figured me out, and I didn't know if I liked that.

"Not always." That night, he'd stripped me bare in more ways than I could imagine. Underneath the sex, there had been more. Acknowledging that was terrifying. So I didn't.

I looked at my watch. "It's still early. What do you— Oh, look who it isn't."

Lior turned around to follow my line of sight and groaned.

"I wish I'd known he'd be in Atlanta."

Pierce walked into the bar with the swag of someone who owned it but looking so out of place he may as well be on a different planet. Did the guy have any self-awareness?

Hanging from his arm was a twink who had to be ten years younger than me. I didn't even want to guess the math with Pierce.

"Do you want to go?" I asked Lior.

"No. I'm having a good time. He doesn't get to have a say in this."

I didn't know what "this" meant, but I followed Lior to the bar.

He ordered a couple of shots.

"This looks like a bad idea," I said, laughing.

"All good ideas start off that way."

We downed the shots, and Lior ordered two more. I also asked for another glass of water because if Lior kept drinking like this, one of us needed to keep their head straight.

Whatever happened between him and Pierce clearly still affected him, even when he tried to hide it under his cool and controlled demeanor.

Thankfully Pierce kept his distance, but the way he was exploring the other guy's throat like he was digging for gold with his tongue? He wanted Lior to see.

"Do you think I'm too stiff?" he asked.

"Probably not after four shots."

He laughed and put his hand on my chest. "I think around you, I'll always be stiff. Oops, did I say that too loud?"

His salt-and-pepper hair still looked great even after he'd run his hands through it all day. He'd ditched his jacket and now wore jeans that hugged his thighs and his butt perfectly. The man was aging better than a fine wine.

"I think it might be time to head back to the hotel and have an early night," I said, taking his beer bottle from his hand and placing it on the bar.

I settled the bill and pocketed my card.

"Hmm, the things I could do to you in my bed."

"And I'm sure I'd love them all. Let's make sure we get there first, okay?" I wrapped my arm around his waist, letting him lean on me a little.

He was at that drunken stage when bad decisions were made. Our relationship was complicated. We had work, reputations, and responsibilities. But we also craved each other. The longer I spent with Lior, the more I felt it definitely wasn't one-sided.

The least I could do for him tonight was ensure he didn't

make any bad decisions. I'd leave those to Pierce, who seemed to be eyeing a new man at the bar while the twink still hung on him.

I debated calling a taxi, but the night had cooled a little, which would help Lior sober up.

Once we were inside Lior's room, he started taking his clothes off. I paused for a moment, watching as he unveiled miles of tan skin, salt-and-pepper hair, a chest to die for, and the thick outline of his dick under his boxer briefs. My mouth watered even as my brain told me to do the right thing.

"I should marry you, you know. You'd make it fun, not like Pish, Piss…Pierce, the uptight asshole.

"Come on, let's get you to bed."

"Oh, now you're talking."

We landed on the bed together after he pulled me by the waist and I lost my footing, ending up practically on top of him.

He closed his eyes, and for a moment, I thought he'd fallen asleep, but then he opened them wide, staring into mine. "Marry me, Noah. Help me save my company and my home. I'll even make you happy. I promise." His hand snaked around my neck, pulling me close until our mouths were centimeters apart. He looked so vulnerable. It broke my heart.

Resisting a good thing had never been my strong point, so when he placed his lips on mine, I gave in. It was a sloppy, dirty kiss, and it took me back to that night at his hotel.

I broke the kiss off and sighed. Well, being proposed to by a sexy, drunken man was a first.

"Turn over, Lior. Let me hold you while you sleep."

"No funny business," he drawled as he fell asleep.

"No funny business," I repeated more to myself than

him. As uncomfortable as it would be to sleep in my clothes, I didn't trust either of us to keep our promise to stick to a professional relationship if I undressed.

As it was, there was an excellent case against us in that respect. Professional colleagues didn't sleep together.

12

———

LIOR

My head throbbed like someone was using a jackhammer to pierce through my skull.

"Ugh, you're too fucking old for this, Lior," I muttered to myself, even though it hurt to talk. I deserved it.

I was forty-fucking-seven years old. A fact I'd been repeating over and over again to my mother due to the unfairness of my father's will stipulation. But here I was, acting like a fucking teenager on his first trip away from home.

"Here, have this."

I opened my eyes slowly to find a shirtless Noah sitting on my bed, propped against the headboard, holding a glass of water and two small pills.

"They're for your head. I ordered breakfast to the room so you don't have to face the conference until you're ready."

"Thank you." I took the water to help swallow the pills and get rid of the awful taste in my mouth.

"If you're okay I'm going to head to my room for a quick shower. I'll be back in ten, okay?"

79

"Yeah."

I got up from the bed slowly, looking around for any signs that we'd done more than...well, anything. My memory was fuzzy at best, and the last thing I remembered was the two shots I'd ordered when I'd seen Pierce come into our bar.

The room was as tidy as I'd left it. My jeans were folded and on top of a chair with my shirt hanging from its back.

Did I undress myself? Or did Noah help?

It was hard feeling mortified without knowing how mortified to be.

I'd ask Noah when he got back, but I needed a shower first.

I tried to be quick, but it was as if my body was on vacation from functioning, so by the time I walked out with a towel around my waist, I was met by Noah and a tray of breakfast food.

He looked as fresh as a daisy on a spring morning.

His appreciative gaze over my body made me feel only marginally better. At least I didn't look half as bad as I felt.

I reached for my suitcase to get a clean pair of underwear and jeans.

"You've seen it all before and my head's too heavy for modesty." I turned around and dropped the towel before stepping into my underwear, jeans, and T-shirt.

"You're forgetting that the last time you kept your clothes on. I'm not sure looking but not touching counts as us getting even now, but thank you for the pleasant reminder."

I joined him at the small table, eyeing the fresh fruit, pancakes, and bacon, wondering which option I could stomach.

"Can I ask you a question?"

"We didn't have sex, if you're wondering. You passed out as soon as we got here."

Okay, that was a good thing. We'd acknowledged our chemistry but had held firm on keeping a professional relationship.

"Did I do anything embarrassing last night?"

Noah tilted his head as his lips curled into a teasing smile. "It depends. On the scale from slightly embarrassed to mortified, where would you place proposing to me?"

I massaged my temples. No way I proposed to him. It had to be a joke.

"Hey," he said gently. "It's okay. You were a little drunk, and I'm pretty irresistible. The alcohol talked louder last night. It's normal."

I groaned. "I'm so sorry."

"I'm still here, and we're still good, right? What happens in Atlanta stays in Atlanta. Do you agree?"

"I agree. I'm still mortified. This whole marriage and will thing is on my mind. I shouldn't have gotten drunk in the first place."

His eyes perked up. "What do you mean?"

I filled a cup with coffee from the pot and drank almost half of it in one go.

"My father stipulated in his will that I have to get married in six months or lose the company and the museum. A month has passed already."

"Wow, and I thought my family was crazy. At least all my mom does when she's upset is mix up ingredients and over-bake everything."

I met Noah's eyes, and he paused midway through putting a piece of fruit in his mouth. "You're not joking."

"I wish I was."

"I'm so sorry. How could your dad do that? What happens if you can't or don't want to get married within that time? Or at all?"

I shook my head. "Shares will go on sale. Business partners get first refusal, and I don't have enough personal money to buy them."

"There has to be a way out of it. Shit, Lior, we're not in eighteenth-century Britain."

Yeah, I knew that. My father, apparently, didn't agree. "Trust me, I've been looking at all legal avenues, but everything's a dead end."

"Why would your father do that to you?"

I sighed. "He had an amazing, happy life with my mom, and when he wrote the will, he was pushing me to get married because, at the time, I was—"

"With Pierce."

"Yeah." I couldn't sound more like a deflated balloon.

"Shit."

I didn't want to sit in my room indulging in a woe-is-me pity party. "Are you done with breakfast?"

"Yeah."

"Let's catch some more sessions. The conference isn't over yet."

I couldn't decipher the way he looked at me, so I ignored it. Pity was the last thing I wanted Noah to feel for me.

With my hair still wet from the shower, we walked through the hotel to the attached conference center.

Pierce didn't show his face all day, so I assumed he'd either gone back home early or decided to stay away from the conference.

As the hours ticked by, my time with Noah was coming to an end. Soon, we wouldn't have any reason to be in touch.

I had my plate brimming to the top with work, finding a husband, avoiding finding a husband, and trying to keep my family's business in the family. There was no time to even grab a meal with a business friend. So why was my brain trying to come up with reasons to see Noah again?

"Hey, you okay?" he asked.

We were in the front row for the closing keynote speech. Noah had been invited to be part of a final panel so he had front row seats for him and a companion.

"Yeah, I'm good. Why?"

"Don't know. Seemed like a dark cloud just came over you. Your eyebrows did that thing like when you saw Pierce yesterday at the bar."

"Nah. Just tired. We're not all twenty-something-year-olds who can survive on energy drinks and sunshine."

"First of all, I'm thirty. And second, energy drinks and sunshine are overrated. Give me a greasy breakfast and two Advil any day."

His unbreakable spirit was infectious. Boundless energy, an incorrigible flirt, sweet and caring. Why couldn't I have met him ten years ago?

I cringed. That would have made him twenty.

Business connection or not, he was still too young.

My phone buzzed in my pocket, so when the keynote ended and Noah joined the other speakers on stage, I pulled it out.

MOM

Hey, honey. Don't be mad, but I bumped into a friend, and she told me her son has recently broken up with his boyfriend. I suggested you two could meet up and passed on your number.

LIOR

Mom, you can't just give my number to strangers. Also, it's weird that you're setting me up. I'm not five and don't need playdates to be arranged for me.

MOM

I don't want to know what you do during
your dates.

LIOR

Then stop trying to fix me up. I've got this.

I didn't have anything, and if I was honest with myself, maybe meeting this guy wouldn't be so bad. Mom's friendship circle was tight, and I'd met most of her friends. They all came to the museum at least once a month for tea and cake and usually tried to get me to join them.

They were also charitable women. Surely, the son of someone like that had to be a good person, right?

I put the phone away to pay attention to the speakers on stage, to one speaker in particular.

He smiled at everyone and knew his stuff. I had a fucking competency kink, and Noah ticked all my boxes.

Why did we have to meet at the wrong time in my life?

What would it be like to have him and his free spirit in my life all the time?

I pushed the thought away because it couldn't happen.

We discovered we were on the same flight, so we traveled to the airport together. After a brief call to Charlie, Noah's ticket had been upgraded to business class.

Five more hours with Noah was totally worth the money.

"So..." he said as we waited for our luggage to come through on the belt.

"So..." I smiled.

"This is it."

"Yeah."

"I had a great time this weekend," he said.

"Me too. Noah—"

He put a hand on my chest. "Don't say it. The world has

already put us together in the same place and time twice. Let me hope for a third."

It still won't be enough, I thought, but all I could do was kiss his cheek and make my way out of the airport, where Charlie was waiting to take me home.

13

NOAH

My walk to work in the morning wasn't filled with the same excitement it usually held.

As much as I tried to avoid it, my eyes were suddenly attracted to any gap in the buildings that showed me a view of Lior's hotel. Our hotel.

Every thought in my mind was of Lior.

Was he really going to marry someone he didn't love just to save his company? Would he marry a stranger? Or worse…Pierce?

I stopped by my usual coffee shop to grab coffee for the weekly Monday meeting with my brothers. I didn't know when we'd fallen into this routine, but the bastards hadn't bought a coffee in months.

Maybe I'd ask the barista to make theirs extra weak, or worse, swap it for tea.

As I walked in, I saw West, one of the founders of the Star Finders Youth Network. He smiled as I joined the line with him.

"Hey, Noah. So great to see you. The kids missed you on Saturday."

"Hey, West. Sorry, I was at a conference in Atlanta this weekend, but I'll be there on Saturday."

West held his to-go coffee in both hands. "Sorry to bother you, but since I caught you, do you have a few minutes?"

I checked my watch. "Sure. What's up?"

"It's about Star Finders."

We left the line and took up a table. At this time in the morning, most orders were to go, so there were a lot of empty tables.

West looked a little dejected. I didn't know him well, only through Star Finders, which he'd started with his foster brother, Drew.

"You work in PR, right?"

"Right."

"Um, I'm not sure how much it would cost to hire you, but we need help. Drew and I have been waiting months for the mayor to release the lease on the old hospital building."

"Yeah, Drew mentioned you're planning to open a shelter slash welcome center for foster kids and kids from low-income backgrounds. That building would be amazing."

"It's big enough to add rooms for anyone needing shelter, it has a cafeteria, we could host events, and there's a huge parking lot we could partly use for sports."

"I bet it would save you a lot of money from renting the basketball courts at the park."

West nodded. "You can see why we want it."

"Absolutely. What's the problem?"

"The mayor stipulated that the new leaseholders also need to make a donation to the local community to improve their public spaces. They want fifty grand, which is a lot of money for us but peanuts to the large corporations that have already placed bids on the space."

"Shit, man. I'm so sorry." I stood and paced the space

between our table and the window. "Okay, let's think about this…we can run a campaign in the local community. Tell them your plans and how they can be included. After all, you're welcoming kids from the area who might not have anywhere else to hang out, especially low-income families."

"Absolutely. That area has a lot of low-income families. We want to prevent kids from going into the system by supporting the families and the community."

My phone buzzed with a message, making me jump.

ADAM

You're late. There better be muffins.

"Shit. West, I gotta go, but let me think it through."

He nodded. "Thank you. Um…I hate to ask, but how much do you think this will cost us?"

"Fucking nothing, West. I can't take money from you."

He looked so relieved his eyes went all red. "You're unbelievable, Noah. Thank you so much. And now you made me cry."

West had a heart of gold and wore it on his sleeve. It was such a shame Drew was completely blind to it.

I grabbed the coffee and three muffins and practically ran to the office. Okay, so I wouldn't mess with my brothers today because I *was* late.

When I got to our meeting room, Adam was working away on his laptop while Lex looked at his phone with a smooshy expression.

My brain was running on adrenaline after the chat with West, so I wanted to get our stuff out of the way so I could get to work.

I started with an update on our current clients, a couple of whom had made inquiries for follow-up campaigns, which was always a good sign.

"We get that you probably got laid a lot this weekend,

but we have work to do," I said, leaning over the table toward Lex.

"Yeah, I know," he replied defensively. "What's the issue?"

"The issue, little brother, is that you can't repeat anything said in this meeting so far because you're too busy looking out the window and spacing out. I don't have your twin telepathy, and even I feel slightly horny this morning."

Lex stared at me. "When do you not feel horny?"

"Good point, but we need to wrap this up because I have places to be."

They questioned me about my plans, with reason. We usually caught up with work on Monday and set up the week. I'd barely set foot in the office and was already planning on leaving.

"Hey, speaking of clients, how's the Van Stern account?" Lex asked just as I sipped my hot coffee, causing me to cough and almost spill it all over me.

"What?"

Lex's eyebrows narrowed. "How is it going with the stained-glass museum? Lior seemed very interested in working with us."

I couldn't tell them everything, but I shared what I'd learned about Lior and his business.

"This is all good stuff, Noah," Lex said. "I can already think of some imagery to go with a campaign. Send him the contracts. I'm excited to work on this."

Adam had remained mostly quiet. He usually took notes for the meeting and only spoke when his input was required or had something to update us on.

He closed his laptop and looked at me. "Please tell me you haven't slept with a client."

"I resent that you think I would."

I could see this meeting going rapidly downhill, and I wasn't in the mood to be accused of fucking every person I met. Especially when, one, I hadn't done that in months, apart from the one time with Lior, and two, I hadn't slept with him since discovering he was a client.

My family wasn't openly judgmental of me, but I wasn't blind. My parents wanted me to settle down with someone nice. My brothers lived with a permanent fear that my hooking up with people would be bad for business.

When they stopped asking about Lior, they asked if I was sleeping with Tanner.

It was getting old. Or maybe I was getting old.

"Let's move to the Lusitana anniversary celebration. Lex, what are the options for the visuals?"

Our parents' restaurant was turning thirty, so they wanted to celebrate in style. Naturally, they "hired" us to take care of it, which was an additional project to handle on top of everything else.

With Lex distracted with Emery and Adam with the wedding planning, I had to step up and fill the gaps.

Once the meeting ended, I locked myself in my office and brainstormed ideas to help West for a few hours.

A week later, I had a plan, but I needed to do two things. To tell my brothers about my involvement with the charity and to figure out how to get an invite to the mayor's yearly ball, where I planned on schmoozing the right people to raise money and support for the Star Finders Youth Network Shelter project.

Ever the wingman and soundboard, Jax agreed to meet me at Tanner's before his night shift.

He had a table, a plate of wings, and a beer for me by the time I arrived.

"Man, you're the coolest," I said, bumping his fist.

"I know. What's the emergency?"

I picked up a wing but stopped it on the way to my mouth when I saw Lior across the bar. He was with someone.

"What's wrong?" Jax said.

"Um…nothing."

He didn't buy it because he looked behind him, and judging by his expression, he remembered exactly who Lior was.

"That's your silver Daddy."

"Please don't say that. It's just wrong."

"The silver or the Daddy?"

I snorted. "I refuse to say the word."

I glanced again. They were eating and Lior had a beer, so this wasn't a late business meeting.

Fuck, was he on a date?

My stomach soured at the thought, even though I had no right to stake a claim. I just happened to find that we made a lot more sense together than whoever the guy with the bow tie and glasses was.

"You look a little green, and I don't mean the sick kind of green," Jax said. "Why don't you go and talk to him? You clearly want to."

"I came to talk to you."

"Then talk to me."

The guy Lior was with got up and went toward the restroom. My gaze followed him until Jax got my attention.

"Just go. We can talk tomorrow. But I'm taking the wings for my break later."

"Sorry. It's becoming a habit abandoning you in a bar."

"You'll make it up to me one day. Go get your man."

He wasn't mine. He couldn't be. So why was my stomach turning?

I tried to find the courage to speak to Lior. Why was I even nervous? Just because fate had put us in the same place at the same time again?

He was looking at his phone, so he didn't see me until I approached his table.

"Noah, what are you— Oh, of course, you live nearby."

"Question is, what are you doing here? On a date?"

His cheeks flushed.

"How can I help you?"

He looked tense, but his eyes burned with the heat that always flamed between us, like embers that refused to be snuffed out.

His date could return any moment now, and I still didn't know what I wanted to say.

Why had I come all the way here to interrupt his date? Did I want to interrupt it or disrupt it?

He needed this date to go well because he was on a deadline to find his husband.

As his eyes remained locked with mine, suddenly, everything became clear. I'd found the solution.

I went down on one knee and held his hands in mine. His eyes opened wide and he tried to speak, but no sound came out.

Even if he was unsure about what I was doing, maybe on some level, he wanted it too. Or maybe it was just wishful thinking.

"Lior Van Stern, will you marry me?"

14

———

LIOR

BERNARD APPEARED in my periphery as Noah popped the question and then stared at me impatiently.

"Are you expecting me to say yes?" I whispered, leaning forward.

"That's why I asked the question. Do you need me to come up with a speech? I'm not sure I can come up with one on the fly, considering I didn't know I was going to do this until ten seconds ago."

I shook my head. "Oh, Noah."

He shrugged.

"What's happening, Lior?" Bernard asked.

"I'm so sorry, Bernard. Can you give us a moment?"

He frowned but started walking toward the bar.

"We're going to need a little longer than that," Noah said, looking as smug as ever. Boy, I could spank his perfect ass right now.

I sighed. "Stay here."

"On my knees?" He wiggled his eyebrows.

"Don't make me break the rules, Noah."

"We're making brand-new ones."

I walked to the bar where Bernard stood awkwardly fiddling with his bow tie. I used to think they were cute and matched him perfectly. Now, I wasn't so sure he or his bow ties were for me.

"I'm so sorry, Bernard. I have to…" I pointed to our table, where Noah picked on the wings and drank my beer.

"Okay. Do you want a raincheck?" he asked hopefully, but his face fell when mine gave my real feelings away.

"But your mom—"

I placed my hand on his arm. "Bernard, nothing in this situation should ever start with those words. If you were here because of my mom or yours, then surely you must know that leaving now is the right thing to do."

"I'm sorry. You're right. It's just that before we…you know, it was good."

"It was, but that was twenty-five years ago. We were young, not ready for more, and it barely lasted a few months. We're older now and too set in our ways. Maybe it was never meant to be more than it was."

"Do you really believe that?"

I shrugged. "I don't know, but I can't tell you that I think this could be more when I don't feel that way. It would be deceiving and unfair. I'm sorry I reached out to you. I know our moms are friends. Maybe we can be too."

He sighed. "Thank you for being honest. I think you're right. What are you going to do about…him?"

"He deserves a fucking good spanking."

"You were always good at those." He blushed.

"Find someone who makes you blush like that, Bernard. You're a good man, and contrary to popular belief, it's not yet too late. Our bones might remind us of our age in the morning, but the night is ours."

He laughed and gave me a kiss on the cheek before leaving.

Mr. Spencer's eyebrows were doing a circus number. I stayed put for a moment, trying to figure out what to do with him.

He'd actually proposed to me. Was he insane?

I settled my bill and walked up to the table.

"Come on. We're going to your place to talk."

He shot up to his feet. "My place has a bed."

"Noah Spencer, you just proposed in a public place. I'm sure someone took a photo, although I hope it's for personal curiosity rather than anything else. The last thing on my mind right now is getting you naked."

I made my way out of the bar with him on my heels.

"You don't even know where to go. Come on." He pulled me in the right direction after I went the wrong way.

I lied. The only thing on my mind was getting him naked. In all my adult years, no one had gotten as deep under my skin as Noah.

Going to his place was dangerous. Being alone with him was dangerous, but there was no other way.

As much as this would be an exercise in self-control, I couldn't have this conversation in public.

His apartment was open-plan, the front door leading straight to the kitchen and living area. The large windows with views of the surrounding buildings provided enough light. Before he turned the lights on, it took me back to that night at the hotel when nothing but the light from the street-lamps below had illuminated his beautiful body.

The layout of the apartment and the kitchen were the only modern things about it. Everywhere else, there were rugs, photos, paintings, an old couch. Noah's apartment was a home.

"Okay, hear me out," he said, going to the fridge and taking out two bottles of beer.

"Water for me, please. I'm driving home."

He didn't argue, though I could see he wanted to.

"So…"

"Why do I get the feeling I'm not going to like this?" I sat on the couch, surprised at how comfortable it was.

"You didn't answer my question," he said.

"Hmm, let me think. We have a working relationship, and the last time we saw each other, we agreed to get some distance. Correct me if I'm wrong, but getting married isn't exactly putting distance between us."

"It is if it's fake."

"I'm sorry, what?"

He stood and paced between his coffee table and the large TV.

"Here's the deal. You can help me with something really important to me, and I can help you with something really important to you."

"Such as?"

"You need a husband to keep your company. I need your connections and influence."

"You're forgetting one thing. I need to marry for love."

He gave me a pointed look. "Was that love I saw in your eyes when you were talking to Bernard?"

"Bernard and I have history."

Noah bridged the gap between us until he was in front of me. His gaze burned into my skin, and I wanted to reach out and pull him into my lap.

Why was I so attracted to this guy?

He put a knee on either side of me, his eyes never leaving mine.

I leaned back on the couch.

"We have a history," he said, placing his hands on the back of the sofa. Not a single inch of him was touching me, but I felt his electric pull like a strong current.

"You're too young."

"Bullshit."

"You don't love me."

"This isn't about love. Bernard doesn't love you. He might want to be spanked by you, which I can empathize with, but he doesn't love you."

I grabbed him by the waist and flipped him over on the couch so I was on top of him.

"Now we're talking." He raised his hips up to meet mine, but I kept space between us.

He was rock-hard under his jeans. My own erection was borderline painful. I hadn't had sex with anything but my hand since our last time.

"What do you want from me, Noah?"

He swallowed and his face went serious. "I need your help. The safety of hundreds of vulnerable kids is at risk. I don't know how to help my friends on my own. I need you."

"And it would be fake?"

"The marriage would be real to fulfill the requirement of your dad's will. Everything else would be fake. Once you have the company, we can wait some time and then get a divorce. This is a business transaction. We don't need to complicate it."

I couldn't believe I was actually considering this.

"Why would you do this for me?"

"I told you. To help you. And because you can help me."

"You don't need to marry me to access my connections or influence. You just need to ask."

He closed his eyes, some of his fight leaving him.

"I want to go to the mayor's ball. All the people with

money and influence are going to be there. I need them on board. If I don't get this, my friends won't be able to raise enough money to take over the lease for the old hospital. They want to turn it into a shelter for vulnerable young people, an activity center, and a safe place for kids in low-income families. They don't have anyone to fight for them. Everyone else looks at that building and all they see are dollar signs."

I stroked his cheek. "This isn't a decision to make lightly, Noah. Marrying me will come with attachments."

"Like what?" he asked, leaning into my touch.

"My mother. She's going to want to be your best friend."

"Can't we tell her it's fake?"

"No. It would break her heart to know I was deceiving everyone when, in her eyes, my father's intention was that I was finally happy and settled."

"My family is a little crazy."

I smiled. "I wouldn't expect any less from the people who raised you."

"Hey." He hit my arm.

"How about sex?"

"Yes, please." His voice was deep and husky.

I pulled back and took him with me so we sat facing each other.

"We can't have sex."

"What?" His eyebrows flew to his hairline.

"Noah, don't get me wrong. If there were no consequences, I would take you somewhere and not let you get out of bed for a week straight. But if we're faking a marriage, adding sex will make it messy. We're already too familiar with each other."

"It's like a real marriage then. No sex." He pouted.

"Tell me more about the kids and your friend's project."

"You're saying yes?"

"Ask me the question again."

He smiled and took my hand. "Lior Van Stern, will you agree to be my husband in sickness and health, blue balls and heated gazes, charitable events and business needs, until divorce do us part?"

I laughed. "Yes, Noah. I'll marry you."

15

NOAH

"You're getting worse, Grandpa," West shouted from the other side of the court.

I passed the ball to my nearest teammate, Joel, who then cut to the opposite block to clear out the ball side.

"Have you seen the white hair?" Avi yelled.

I flipped him the bird.

"Are you allowed to do that?"

I smirked. I probably wasn't. As a volunteer mentor, I was supposed to be supportive and help these cocky teenagers navigate the challenges of life. But this was the Star Finders youth on the basketball court. It was an all-out war.

Joel lost the ball to the defense, but I saw an opportunity for a backdoor play and went for it. My sneakers scuffed on the concrete. I loved that sound. It meant I was moving, doing something. A rush of adrenaline coursed through me, making me feel alive.

"He's definitely slowing down. Must be arthritis," Avi yelled back at his teammate.

Fucking kids with their young energy and unfiltered confidence.

West, who was usually on my team, had deflected to the enemy team because Drew had to go in to work, so the kids were already one teammate down.

Not only had he deflected, but he was joining in with their jabs.

"There's no white hair," I said between my teeth, stealing the ball from the point guard and dribbling through the offense into the paint. "Or arthritis."

The defense guys tried and failed to block my play. Grandpa, my ass. I took a step back and shot. Well, overshot by about a quarter of an inch, but it was enough that we wouldn't have scored if Joel hadn't saved it at the last minute with a dunk.

Game over.

The kids all groaned, throwing themselves dramatically onto the floor.

I laughed, high-fiving the other mentors. "And I believe that's a winning game for the geriatric team."

Applause sounded from the side of the court. I turned to find Lior walking toward us. In jeans and a polo shirt, he had no right to look this good when I was hot, sweaty, and probably looked like I'd been run over.

"Who's that?" one of the kids asked.

"He's a friend."

"Hmm," they said with an attitude and suspicious smile.

Everyone sat on the floor in a circle with their water bottles and towels. Lior sat next to me, whispering "You stink" in my ear.

"What have you learned today?" Joel asked.

The kids avoided answering the question by sipping water and wiping the sweat off their foreheads.

Alma, another mentor, sat next to us. "No one learned anything? For real?"

"Um..." Remi said, "We shouldn't underestimate our opponent, even if they're from the Cretaceous period?"

"Why is that?" I asked, throwing him a sweaty towel, which landed right on his face.

They all shrugged. "Because you won even though you're old?"

I chuckled. "Yes, we won and we're old. Why do you think that is?"

Ted, who was splayed on the floor, raised his hand with a thumbs-up. He was by far the oldest of us at forty-five. With three young kids at home, he always moaned about being too old for this, but he still turned up every week without fail.

I'd always thought of him as being part of a different generation from the rest of us in the mentor group, but he was younger than Lior by two years. I definitely didn't see Lior as old or like I didn't have much in common. Quite the opposite.

"No," I said. "Forget the court for a moment. How many of you have part-time jobs?"

They all raised their hands.

"So you've already met someone with more experience, who's been there longer, right?"

"Yeah, one of the servers at the diner is almost seventy," Lucas said.

"I bet they're a lot slower doing certain tasks, right?" I waited for their nods of agreement.

"Okay, I have a challenge for you this week."

They all groaned. "We already get homework from school."

"This isn't homework. I want you to find someone at work who's older than you, and I want you to strike up a conversation and learn something about them."

"Like what?"

I shrugged. "Anything you want. When we meet next week, I want you to introduce them to us as if they were here. Without telling us their name, age, or what they do, I want you to tell us what you've learned."

More groans. I threw Joel's sweaty towel in their direction and sent them all home.

We usually hung around until everyone was gone and then loaded the balls into West's car.

Some of the kids didn't have great conditions at home, so if anyone needed something from us—a chat, some food, or a lift—we'd be here for them.

Lior hung back while I caught up with the mentor crew.

"That was a good game," Joel said, holding his fist up for a bump.

"Cheaper than a gym membership, that's for sure," Ted added.

"Hey, guys," Alma said. "There's this girl in my sister's class. She just moved into the city. Looks like her foster parents are cool people, but she's struggling to adjust. You think the guys would mind having a girl around?"

Somehow, through kids moving in and out of the system, getting adopted, or moving away with their real or foster families, we ended up with an all-boys group.

"They've had girls in the group before. Besides, it's a good learning opportunity," I said.

West added. "It'll be good to introduce someone new to the group. I'll give Drew the heads-up."

Alma nodded. "Thank you. I'll get word back to my sister and her new friend. Anyway, what are you guys doing now? Anyone up for a drink?"

Everyone gave their excuses. Joel had work to do, Ted's wife was out tonight with her friends so he needed to take care of their children. In the past, I'd have made an excuse because I'd have gone home, showered, moped around the house, and then went out to hopefully find someone to hook up with.

"I'd love to, but we have plans." I pointed at Lior.

"The kids are right. You're all geriatric." She shook her head and started walking to her car with a trail of boos behind her.

I turned to my fiancé. Weirdly, thinking of Lior as my fiancé didn't make my skin break out in hives.

"Walk home with me?"

"You're certainly not getting in my car smelling like gym socks," he said.

I lifted my tank to show my abs. "It's all worth it to get these, don't you think?"

He groaned and looked away.

The advantage of living in Cliffborough was that the downtown was self-contained within the boundaries of the surrounding river. And while the city had definitely expanded beyond the river, it still had a small-town feel.

It didn't take long to get to my place from the park.

My phone screen was filled with notifications when I got home. I'd started leaving it behind on the days I volunteered because it was hard sometimes to switch off from work, especially when you worked with your brothers.

A short glance showed there was nothing from the family, so I left the phone where it was and hit the shower while Lior hung out in the living area.

When I came out, there was a message from Jax.

JAX

WTF, dude. Tanner sent me a message saying you're engaged. He saw it happen at the bar the other night.

NOAH

Oh, you have Tan's number? When did you two go steady?

JAX

Ignore my concern. It's your funeral, but I expect to be the best man.

NOAH

You've been back five minutes. Surely, my brothers are first in line.

JAX

Nah. Brothers don't make good best men. They'll be too afraid of your mom to let you do something really stupid.

NOAH

What? Like get married?

My phone rang, so I put it on speakerphone while I got dressed.

"You're serious?" Jax asked.

"I am. Want to be my best man?"

"Dude. Backtrack. Wait…Mr. Sexy Silver Fox?"

I laughed when Lior walked into the room, having heard Jax.

"Yes, Mr. Sexy Silver Fox. Are you on shift tonight?"

"No, I'm off."

"Come over for dinner."

"Okay. See you later."

I ended the call. "Sounds like I got us a best man. What are you bringing to this wedding?"

He gave me one of his looks that told me I was in trouble. If only he'd follow through. I wondered what would make him snap and make good on his spanking promises.

"Mr. Sexy Silver Fox is going to raid your fridge and find something to cook for dinner since we have guests."

We. Fuck. I liked the sound of that.

A new notification came up on my phone. A reminder to fill out the marriage license application.

Shit. This was really going to happen.

16

LIOR

As it turned out, planning a small Vegas wedding when money was no object was surprisingly easy, especially when the grooms wanted a low-key affair.

The only problem we'd encountered so far was timing. Since we hadn't told anyone in my or Noah's family about the wedding, there was always a chance of something we didn't plan coming up.

That's what happened when, a week ago, Adam announced that he and his fiancée were having a family gathering to try the wedding caterer. *Today.*

I looked at my watch. We needed to board the private jet I'd chartered in forty-five minutes, and there was no sign of Noah. I just hoped he'd made it out of the event with plenty of time to get to the airport.

Flying from the small airport outside of town instead of going to the bigger airport in New Haven made it all a little faster and more flexible, but I knew we could lose our departing slot if we were too late.

I scanned the small terminal lounge again, and this time, I saw Jax and Tanner walking toward me with another guy.

"Hey, Lior," he said, dropping his bag on the ground. "Hope we're not too late."

"Hi. Thank you for coming. You're on time. Noah, on the other hand…"

I glanced at my watch again until Jax said, "Here comes the groom."

Noah rushed through the small crowd, almost tripping over someone's bag before he crashed into me with a thud.

"Fiancé!" he grinned. "See? You said I'd never fall for you, and here's me *literally* falling."

I laughed. "I never said that. That's what you promised."

"Oh yeah. Bad Noah. I shall not fall for my big, sexy silver fox future husband."

Jax coughed a "too late," which Noah missed, thankfully. I didn't, but I ignored it.

I was already too nervous about the fact I was going to be legally married. I didn't need to panic over feelings I may or may not have toward Noah and that more than once in the last couple of weeks, I'd wondered if I could keep him for real.

Like he said, this was a business transaction. Okay, we had insane chemistry, but we'd agreed we wouldn't act on it so things didn't get complicated. I needed to remember that before my own emotions got in the way. I had a company to take over and run so I could live up to my name.

"Tanner, what are you doing here?" Noah asked when he decided to untangle himself from me and look around. He gave me a panicked look.

"Your best man needs his own best man," Jax said. "Plus, you also need two witnesses, and for credibility, you may not want one of them to be Elvis."

"Besides, I have to make sure this guy isn't going to come back married to some stranger," Tanner added.

Noah turned to me, running his hand over my chest, resting on my peck. "We're going to have the best time, right, babe?" That was way over the top, even for him.

I shot him a pointed look. "Tanner knows. When Jax suggested bringing Tanner, he told him. I thought you'd like having another friend around."

He looked a little disappointed. "Shame. I was so ready to practice my I'm-so-in-love-I-had-to-marry-this-guy-yesterday face."

Tanner shook his head. "You guys are insane, but your secret is safe with me. For what it's worth, I think it's a good idea if it helps you both. And those kids deserve the best. Jax told me about volunteering with Star Finders. I'm not sure I can be alive on Saturday mornings after a busy night at the bar, but maybe I can support in other ways."

Noah pulled Tanner into a tight hug. "Thank you."

"Damn. All this time working on my flirting game and all I had to do to get some action was be nice to kids."

The flight attendant approached us. "Mr. Van Stern, if you're ready to board, we're scheduled to depart in fifteen minutes."

"Thank you. Shall we?"

Jax and Tanner followed the flight attendant. Noah hung back a little. He took my hand and laced our fingers together.

"Are you sure about this?" he asked.

"Are you having cold feet, fiancé?"

"Nope. Feet are toasty warm."

When we boarded the plane, Jax and Tanner had already claimed their seats facing each other toward the front.

"I'm going to take my fiancé to the back so we can make out during take-off. We'll be back in a bit."

Both guys rolled their eyes at Noah.

When he'd suggested we tell Jax the truth because we might need someone to vouch for us in the future, I was reticent. The more people involved in a lie the easier that lie could be found out.

Then I gave Jax permission to tell Tanner.

Both guys were close to Noah, and they'd have our backs. It also helped that neither seemed to take him too seriously.

Noah took the window seat and buckled up. "Look at me. A month ago, I had never flown premium economy. Now I'm on a private jet. Knowing you certainly has its perks." He turned to face me. "You know the night you were drunk? After you asked me to marry you, you said you'd even make me happy. I'm pretty happy."

"You're ridiculous," I said, almost reaching out to hold his hand but stopping myself. Noah was openly affectionate, and I didn't mind when he got close, but I had to keep some distance to remind myself why I was going along with this crazy plan.

"Guess who bagged an invite to the mayor's ball," I said.

Noah perked up. "No way."

I nodded. "They must have issued the invite before my father passed away, so when I received it in the office, I called them and changed the names. I know my mom doesn't want to attend any functions for a while."

"Did you say we were getting married?"

"Yes."

He leaned his head on the headrest. "Wow, someone out there already knows me as Mr. Van Stern."

"Are you changing your name?"

"No...I mean, not unless you need me to. With the agency being named after us, I kinda like being a Spencer. Besides, I'd have to change it back when we divorce, and that's too much paperwork."

"Yeah."

"It's just a figure of speech, you know?"

"Of course." It made complete sense for him to keep his name. Was I disappointed? I had no right to ask him to make such a monumental life change.

No, you just agreed to marry him. Not monumental at all.

Once we reached cruising altitude, I got my notebook out, and we went through our plan. While organizing the wedding had been a breeze, everything else wasn't.

We were both concerned about lying to our families, but telling the truth wasn't an option. Then, there was the press statement, which would go out as soon as we told the partners at VSE. But before we did that, I needed to consult with Mr. Hoffman. It was a chain reaction that couldn't be stopped once it was in motion.

Noah was on board with everything, but I worried all the time that it would be too much for him. He wasn't asking much of me at all, which then made me question his motives. Was it possible that his feelings matched mine?

No, that was ridiculous. He came up with the plan to help his friends. It was a business transaction, I thought to myself, and I'd do well to remember that.

"I can't wait to get to the hotel. We're going to have the best bachelor party," Noah said.

"What do you know?" This was my worst nightmare. Enforced fun to meet a ridiculous tradition that you had to get stupidly drunk and make bad decisions before you got married.

We were already making one very bad decision, so it couldn't get any worse, could it?

"No clue. Individually, those two are bad enough. Together? I'm terrified to find out, but I hope there will be strippers."

"Fuck, no," I pleaded. Noah just laughed.

"It's okay, old man. If it gets too much for you, I'll take you back to our room for your gentle bedtime routine."

I quirked a brow. If he knew what I'd do to him, given the chance, he wouldn't consider it that gentle.

The car I'd booked to take us to the hotel was waiting for us on the tarmac. Traveling in luxury wasn't cheap, but it was certainly convenient.

"Fuck me. This is a palace," Tanner said as we walked into our four-bedroom penthouse suite. "I wouldn't have minded sharing a room with Jax, but this is another world."

"I figured it would be easy if we were all together, and this way, everyone also has their own private room."

Jax's gaze was on Tanner as he opened all the doors and picked a room.

"I guess I'll take this one next to Tanner's," Jax said before he took his bags away.

"Well, that's the kids sorted," Noah said. "Let's see what we got."

"We don't have anything, remember?"

He pouted. I walked up to him and pinched his chin. "Pick one."

"I want the one you want."

"Then I guess we're sleeping on the couch."

He gasped. "You wouldn't do that to your loving husband."

"Don't make me consider divorce before we're married."

"No divorcing until I've had wedding cake," Tanner shouted from his room.

Noah's eyes opened wide. "Good thing nothing's really happening between us. Those kids have elephant ears, and only you and I need to know how much I love it when you—"

I covered his mouth with my hand. "Don't finish that

sentence for the love of all that is holy. Go get changed for dinner."

"Yes, sir…" he purred.

Fucked. I was fucked.

If I managed to get through this weekend unscathed, how would I survive the next few months, possibly longer, with Noah by my side?

17

———

NOAH

I TOSSED and turned all night, and in the end, I just sat in bed, staring at the beautiful view outside the hotel.

The fountains stayed on all night. Who'd have guessed?

Not that I could hear anything. The windows must be soundproofed and everyone else was asleep, leaving me wide awake with only my thoughts for company, which was never a good thing.

When I wasn't looking out of the floor-to-ceiling windows, I focused on the carpet pattern. The longer I looked at it, the more it looked like it was moving.

I watched the sun rise from behind the buildings in front of our hotel. It was its own show of light and color.

A knock sounded on the door.

"Come in."

The door opened, and Lior came in. He was already dressed. A three-piece suit, no tie, with the top two buttons undone. His hair was perfectly styled. He was a walking dream.

"Hey."

"Hey."

He dropped down on the bed facing me.

"You couldn't sleep either?"

I shook my head. "I never thought I'd get married. It was a decision I made a long time ago. Last night, I was thinking this is the only time I'll ever get married. I should be angry with myself for breaking my promise to twenty-two-year-old Noah."

"Are you?"

"No. I'm fucking scared of messing up my lines, of making you look like a fool, of not looking like I'm a good husband. I'm scared of not being good enough, even as a fake husband."

Lior leaned forward and wrapped his arms around me. "Oh, Noah. You really don't know how special you are, do you?"

I shrugged, but in his embrace, it wasn't much.

He pulled back until our faces were just inches apart.

"I want to make a deal with you. We can call it the fake husband deal. We have each other's backs no matter what. Our relationship will be based on loyalty and honesty. If there is something we need to talk about, we will. No matter what. I already respect and care for you far more than I do men I've considered marrying in the past. If this all gets too big, we'll talk to each other and figure a way out. Deal?"

"Deal."

"Good."

He placed a chaste kiss on my lips and held one of my hands open. He dropped two cufflinks on my palm and closed my fingers around them.

"These belonged to my grandfather. He made them as a gift for my father when they opened their first office. My father gave them to me when I graduated from college, and I can't think of anyone else I'd want to pass them on to."

"Lior." I shook my head. I couldn't accept the gift.

"If you don't want to keep them beyond our marriage, you can give them back, but while we're married, they're yours."

I opened my hand. The cufflinks were a little larger than usual and circular. Encased in the circles were two pieces of glass: red and yellow.

"They're beautiful. Thank you. I don't have anything for you. No heirlooms or beautiful things."

He caressed my face with his thumb. "You're giving me my whole world, my history, my legacy. That's so much bigger than old cufflinks."

"Hey, don't talk like that about my cufflinks. My future husband gave them to me."

He laughed. "That's the Noah I know and…care about."

My heart stopped for a second when I thought he would say something else.

"I'll get ready quickly, and then we can go. Are Jax and Tanner out already?"

"No, I haven't seen them. There's no movement coming from either of their rooms."

I got up from the bed and ran to the other side of the suite where their rooms were. I knocked on Jax's door, but there was no answer. I opened the door carefully in case he was in the shower, but the room was tidy. As if he hadn't been in it at all.

His bag was on the floor and his suit hung from the closet door.

Lior shrugged. "Maybe he's in Tanner's room?"

We rushed to the other room but found exactly the same thing.

"Fuck. Where are they?"

Last night, after our bachelors' dinner and the disappointing lack of strippers, they said they were going out to stretch their legs from the flight and explore a little. Had they not come back at all?

"Okay, let's stay calm. Why don't you call one of them and see if they're together?" Lior suggested.

I ran back to my room, my little breakdown already forgotten because losing my friends in Vegas was not on my Bingo card for this year.

Then again, marriage wasn't either, so…

Jax answered on the third ring.

"Hey, man," he answered, almost like he wasn't really paying attention to the fact he'd answered his phone.

"Dude, where are you?"

"Um…breakfast…" There was noise in the background, and I swear I heard a shhh.

"Oh. Why didn't you say? We can join you. You know Lior was going to have breakfast sent up, right?"

"Yeah…um…I, we didn't know. We're not actually at the hotel. Look, can we meet you at the chapel later?"

"Sure."

"Okay, bye."

I looked up from my phone at Lior. He had to have heard it.

"Was that the weirdest phone call ever, or what?"

"Yeah, a bit."

I got dressed in my suit, and we shared breakfast in the suite. By ten o'clock, there was no sign of either Jax or Tanner, so we had to assume they'd do what they said.

"If they don't show up, we'll get witnesses from the chapel," Lior reassured me.

I knew that was an option, but I wanted my friends. After getting used to the idea that I was getting married for real and it would probably be the one and only time, I kinda wanted it to count. I had my best man and Tanner would act as Lior's best man. We'd even ordered cake and champagne to be sent to the suite so we could celebrate before going to the airport to fly back home.

"This is surreal," I said in the car on the way to the chapel. "Tomorrow morning, not even twenty-four hours from now, I'm going to walk into my office a married man."

"I just hope my mother doesn't try to set me up with someone else who turns out to be an ex she didn't know about."

"She better not. I can get very jealous. Bones will be broken."

He laughed. "Noted."

My hands started shaking as we approached the chapel. Holy shit, I was getting married. "We're really doing this."

"For the kids," Lior said.

"For your legacy."

He held my hand and placed a kiss on the knuckles.

When we got out of the car, relief washed over me when I saw Jax and Tanner waiting for us outside.

They wore matching suits, but not the ones they'd brought with them.

"You two took ten years off my life with your disappearing act this morning," I said as we walked inside.

"We didn't disappear," Jax said.

"We were just…misplaced," Tanner added.

I glanced at their hands. No new rings. Phew. No crazy Vegas weddings other than mine. They also didn't look hungover, so maybe they just went out to enjoy the city and stayed out.

They both had jobs with weird hours, so it wasn't surprising to see them looking this fresh after being out.

The wedding celebrant explained how the ceremony would go while another couple was getting married. We were told to sneak into the back toward the end and wait our turn.

"Are you ready?" Lior whispered as he held my hand when the celebrant called us.

"As I'll ever be."

We walked up the aisle together with Jax and Tanner behind us. "Welcome, friends and loved ones. We gather here today to celebrate the union of Lior Van Stern and Noah James Spencer…"

We turned to each other and held hands.

Before I knew it, it was time for the part I'd dreaded the most.

"Lior and Noah, vows are a personal and meaningful promise to each other, symbolizing your commitment, love, and respect. Lior, please share your vows with Noah."

Lior squeezed my hands tight.

"Noah, the first time you spoke to me, I was spellbound by your confidence and audacity. When I saw you on that stage in Atlanta, you showed everyone how smart and capable you are. You do everything with a passion and determination I can only aspire to. You are generous and selfless. I still don't know what's in it for you by marrying me, but I know I'm the luckiest man to call you my husband."

A shiver ran up my spine at the words *my husband*. They held such power. My parents had been husband and wife for thirty-five years. This promise meant something to them.

The vows I'd prepared were perfect, but I couldn't bring myself to say them, not unless I really expressed the meaning behind my words.

My brain scrambled to come up with something.

"Thank you, Lior. Noah, please share your vows with Lior."

I took a deep breath.

"Lior…you have a fine butt." I turned to the celebrant. "Can I say butt in here?"

She nodded, barely containing laughter.

"Yes, Lior, I love your butt. It's a fine, fine butt. Unlike what you might think, your butt isn't too old for me. Your butt understands me and sees what no one else does. It's simply a perfect butt. I promise to cherish and worship your butt every day for the rest of our life together. Even when it sags."

"My butt's not going to sag," Lior said in outrage before he caught himself. The way his gaze burned into mine, I wished the no-sex rule was banned so he could punish me for my ridiculous vows.

"Oh dear," the celebrant said, looking at Lior. "Gravity comes for us all. Well, that has to be a record for how many times the word butt has been used during a ceremony."

Jax and Tanner, who'd been quiet up till now, doubled over with laughter.

"Let's keep this show on the road, boys. I have a feeling someone's gearing up for the kiss." The celebrant pointed at me while looking at Lior.

"Can you blame me?"

After exchanging rings and a final word from the celebrant, we were given the heads-up to kiss.

The plan had been a single chaste kiss for the photos.

The execution was…flexible. As soon as we had permission to kiss, I jumped into Lior's arms, wrapped my legs around his waist, and kissed him like it was the last time I ever would.

I was barely aware of the sound of clicking cameras. Lior had his hands on my ass to keep me steady while I claimed his mouth. I was hungry for him, but I knew I couldn't have more, so while he couldn't do anything about it, I selfishly took advantage.

"Save it for the honeymoon," Tanner joked.

There wouldn't be a honeymoon. In just a few hours, we'd be back to our old lives with a huge secret—for now.

After signing the paperwork and getting our copies, we exited the chapel into the sunny Vegas morning.

"Guys, congratulations. That has to be the most entertaining wedding I've ever been to," Tanner said. "Now let us have cake and champagne and celebrate in style."

Our driver took us back to the hotel, where a buffet of food and desserts had been set up.

"We'll be right back," Lior said. "I just need a quick word with my husband."

18

LIOR

I DRAGGED my new husband to my room. He didn't even know how much trouble he was in.

As soon as I shut the door, Noah stepped closer, narrowing the distance between us in a few heartbeats. "Are we going to consummate our marriage?" he asked, his tone teasing yet laden with want.

Without another word, I pushed him back against the wall by the door. My hands found his waist, pulling him closer until there was no space left between us. He tilted his head up, our breath mingling, our lips inches apart. The anticipation built to an almost unbearable intensity.

"Did you think that kiss was a good idea?" I asked, my voice a low rumble.

"Yes…no?"

"Yes or no, Noah?"

I pinned his hands behind his back and held them there. With him having to look up to meet my gaze, it left his throat exposed.

His Adam's apple bobbed and his blue eyes became almost black.

"Yes or no, Noah?"

"Yes. Fuck, I'd do it again and again. I don't like the no-sex rule. I'm going to attempt to break it until you give in."

I chuckled, running my nose up his neck until my lips reached his ear. "You underestimate my willpower."

When my eyes met his again, I saw sheer determination. "You underestimate me, dear husband."

A breath of air whooshed out of me at the way he called me his.

We were playing a dangerous game where both players were on the same team with orders to not play together.

We were bound to lose.

"I'll give you one," I whispered.

"For now…"

Then, with a passion that felt like it could ignite the air around us, our lips met in a kiss that was the culmination of the tension and chemistry between us. It was heated and urgent. We deepened the kiss, both of us pouring every emotion into it.

The more Noah struggled to free his hands, the tighter I held them.

He moaned and his body shuddered against mine.

When we finally broke apart, gasping for air, our foreheads rested against each other's. I opened my eyes slowly, meeting Noah's. Outside, the sounds of the celebration started with the popping of a champagne cork.

"Come on, let's have some cake," I said.

Noah coughed. "Um…I'm gonna need a moment."

I pulled away from him, my eyes widening at the wet stain on his pants. There was so much that some of it had come through the thin fabric.

"I'll use the connecting door to my room to get changed."

I was left staring at his back as he exited the room. I

leaned against the wall with a thud, trying to process information.

Noah had come from the kiss, from having his hands held behind him, and probably because he knew he wasn't supposed to.

What should I do with that information?

A knock on the door made me jolt.

"I'll be out in five." Five seconds was all it took for me to spill my own load all over my hand with just a few strokes of my cock.

After changing into jeans and a polo shirt, I joined the guys.

Noah was already out, wearing jeans and a T-shirt. My change of clothes didn't go unnoticed, but I just said, "I didn't want to get the suit wrinkled on the flight."

"Yeah, same," Noah said with a snort.

Jax and Tanner shared a look.

We weren't fooling anyone, which was probably a good thing, considering we were supposed to be playing the part of loving husbands.

"Let's get some photos of you guys cutting the cake," Tanner suggested.

"Doesn't look like you're going to have to work hard to sell your relationship, and with photos to prove it, everyone will have a hard time not believing you," Jax said.

We posed for the photos and even fed each other cake.

That tension between us was back, but now it was different, although I couldn't pick out why or what it was.

Noah was a little quiet on the flight back, and eventually, he fell asleep. Tanner and Jax picked the same seats as before and spent the flight engrossed in conversation.

After watching Noah sleep longer than I should have, I opened my laptop and sent the email that triggered the chain of events leading to me taking my father's place in the company. If our plan worked out, of course.

My wedding ring felt heavy on my finger as I typed.

I'd never worn rings before.

"It feels odd. Doesn't it? Like it's not supposed to be there, but it's a comforting weight," Noah said when he caught me staring at my hand.

This man. He was the most authentic person I'd ever met.

"Yeah, it's going to take a while to adjust."

He looked at his own band. I liked seeing it there.

"Anyway, I saw you typing. I assume you've requested the meeting to tell your board about us."

"Yes. Have you thought how you'll tell your family?"

He pursed his lips. "I was hoping to introduce you as my boyfriend first and tell them it's really serious. Then, one weekend, we got impatient, flew to Vegas, and got married. I mean, it's not entirely untrue, is it?"

"Not, it's not. Are you worried about telling them?"

"A little. My family is very close. Most will say we're too close, considering we work together and see our parents every week, but it's just the way we are."

I took his hand and held it between mine. "I think it's wonderful. I've always had a great relationship with my parents and grandparents, but I think it's because the business brought us closer by default."

"It'll be fine. Let's face it, is this or is this not a Noah thing to do?"

His smile didn't do a good job of proving he believed what he'd said. There was nothing I could say to take away his worry, but for him, I'd do my best to make our relationship believable.

His family might not be happy when they find out about us, but they won't question why we're together.

That was my unspoken promise to Noah.

"Do you want to come over tonight? I have to be in the office tomorrow, so I can give you a lift back into the city."

He gave me a sideways glance, the corners of his lips curling up into his signature smile.

"Careful, Lior, I'm gonna start thinking you like me."

I did like him, probably more than I should.

"I take it back."

"Nope. Not a chance, hubby. You're taking me home with you."

And just like that, lightness returned between us.

I arranged a car to take Jax and Tanner home, so we separated at the airport.

Jax sent me a questioning look, especially because they lived in the same building, so it would have been natural for them to ride home together.

I kept a neutral face. Noah and I were friends. We could hang out. Besides, if we were going to sell the married thing, we needed to get to know each other better.

Noah's playful self was in full gear all the way out of the city. By the time we reached the road to the museum, our driver was convinced we'd been together for years and still in the honeymoon phase.

"I hope you guys get to have a real honeymoon," he said.

"Hear that, Lioreo? We need a honeymoon. Somewhere really romantic where we can walk on the beach at sunset, make out under the stars…"

"You'll never get these years back, my friends. Especially when kids come along."

I coughed. "What?"

Noah's smile turned into laughter when he saw my reaction. "My Lioreo isn't sure about kids, but that's okay. As they say, we'll have fun trying."

The driver let out a hearty laugh.

"You can leave us here," I said as we reached the museum's parking lot.

"All the best, boys. May health and happiness be with you always," the driver said as his parting words.

"Aww, he's sweet," Noah said.

I grabbed his bag and mine and started walking to my place.

"Wow, I didn't know you live in the actual museum. This was your family's home?"

"I don't live in the museum. Come on, I'll show you."

The museum gardens were by far one of my favorite places in the world. Whenever I looked out my office window and saw visitors admiring the sculptures and using the many benches to appreciate the art, it made all the hard work worthwhile.

What many people didn't notice, even though there were countless photos of it circulating the internet, was the gate with the intricate design that led to my grandfather's old workshop, which was now my home.

"I bet this place is magical in the daylight," Noah said, following me up the gravel path.

"It is. You'll get a chance to see it."

I made sure to close the gate behind us. Charlie loved to tell me off when I forgot because it left my home vulnerable to curious eyes when the museum was open.

It wasn't a problem if I worked in the museum office, but these days, I spent a lot more time in the city and drove out of a secret private entrance.

"This was my grandfather's workshop, so it's not a huge place," I said. "When we moved his stuff to the museum, this place was left empty. It made sense to convert it into a home because I spent all my time here anyway."

Noah walked in after me, taking in all the glass panels and the skylight that illuminated the open-plan living space during the day. When I'd worked with the architect on the conversion, I hadn't wanted to lose it. Instead of having a separate kitchen and living room, I had a single door at the back where an extension had been built for the bedrooms and the bathroom.

"Your home is nothing like I imagined. When I first met you, you were so composed, so in control. I made you for the kind of man who lived in a minimalist apartment."

"You mean clinical?"

He chuckled. "Yeah."

With piles of books on the coffee table, furniture that had belonged to my grandparents, and old photos of my grandfather working, this place was anything but minimalistic.

"Let me show you to your room, and then I'll make us something to eat."

"Okay."

While Noah got settled, I took some bread out of the freezer and put it in the oven to warm. I also got out a container of homemade tomato soup and started defrosting it in the microwave.

"It's a shame we need to set off early tomorrow. I'd love to see all these windows in full light."

When I turned around, I saw that Noah had changed into a pair of sweatpants and an old college T-shirt. He was barefoot. Not a single inch of him looked out of place in my home.

He leaned against the door, his crossed arms over his chest, raising his T-shirt enough to show a line of skin and hair that trailed down to what I knew was a stunning cock.

"Having a moment there?" he teased.

I bit my tongue and didn't reply. If I was as honest as Noah was with all the thoughts that crossed my mind, we'd be naked in my bed already.

"Do you want grilled cheese with your soup or buttered bread?"

"Surprise me."

He directed his attention to all the books on the shelf. My grandfather had made that too, out of the wood from a fallen tree he found on the property.

"You like cooking."

"Yeah, I find it relaxing. I also spend far too much time working, so unless I cook in batches when I have the chance, I'd be eating nothing but takeout and crap."

While I stirred the soup in the pan to make sure it was piping hot, Noah scoured through the cabinets to find plates and cutlery to set the table.

The only man I'd had in my space was Pierce, but he hadn't liked it here. He'd said it made him feel like my grandfather's ghost was still here.

I knew it was an excuse for us to spend more time at his place. Now *that* was the definition of cold and clinical, with his black leather couches that gave you back pain if you sat on them for too long.

Noah was nothing like Pierce. Was that why I found him so captivating?

"What are we doing after dinner?" Noah asked, wiggling his eyebrows.

"We're sitting on my couch with a drink and getting to know the things we need to know to pass as a real couple."

I hated to be the one to remind us of what we were doing but having Noah in my space felt too comfortable. If we were going to stick to the plan, we both needed that reminder.

"You're no fun." He pouted.

"I think you've already had enough fun today."

His cheeks reddened.

"You're right." He stood and took our plates to the sink. "Come on, hubby. Let's get to know each other."

19

———

NOAH

"Come on," I muttered under my breath. The old clock on the wall of Lior's guest room ticked on, a silent reminder that I needed to hurry.

Soon, the eyes of Cliffborough's elite would be upon us. I needed to get every detail right.

Right now, the sleek, silky fabric of my bow tie was my nemesis. Each attempt to form the perfect bow seemed more futile than the last as the fabric slipped like water between my fingers.

"Why didn't I get a clip-on?" I groaned.

"Because that's not the way of a gentleman."

I sagged, meeting Lior's amused gaze in the mirror. "This is impossible."

"Come here."

I dragged my feet over to him. He was already perfectly dressed and looking like a dream. A sexy fucking dream.

"How do you always look so good?"

His salt-and-pepper beard was groomed, his hair styled. I would waltz into the mayor's ball on the arm of a man who

135

was put together and sexy beyond belief. Someone who belonged there.

Him? He'd be dragging a fucking hot mess.

Wasn't I the one who broke deals? Brought in new clients to the agency?

But how would I win the hearts of the people I needed to influence to help West and Drew when I felt so discombobulated?

"You need to take a deep breath, Noah. You look great." He pushed my hands away, and in a New York minute, my bow was tied and straightened.

Lior turned me around and pushed me toward the mirror.

"See? Stunning."

I studied his gaze for a moment. His dark eyes rarely gave him away, his emotions sealed in a vault.

Not all his emotions. Just the ones I so desperately craved.

In the weeks since our wedding, Lior had fast become one of my best friends.

I didn't need to pretend with him because he knew to call me on my bullshit, but he also let me be myself.

It had been weeks since I'd felt the need to go out to a bar to connect with people.

It never was just about sex for me. I craved connecting with people on an intimate level.

Well, as intimate as you could get in a bar restroom. But my point was that I needed to see someone's eyes glazed over as I sucked their cock or stroked them to completion. I needed the gasps, the trembles.

Connection.

What was disconcerting about my relationship with Lior was that while I knew he could give me what I needed and more when it came to sex, even though we weren't having any, just being his friend was enough.

I'd never had that with anyone.

"I don't want to add to your anxiety, but my mom is on her way here. She wants to meet you."

I turned around hastily. "She, what…what?" I yelped. "That is not how you don't add to my anxiety."

"I know, but you had to meet her at some point. I promise she's gotten over the initial shock, and apparently, all I talk about is you, so she's curious."

Okay, that got my attention. "All you talk about is me?"

He raised his brows. "Of course that's what you'd hear. Yes, Noah, all I talk about is how insufferable you are. How you leave your socks everywhere—"

"I do not."

He pointed at the floor near the bed.

"I was going to grab those in a minute."

"Sure you were." He kissed my cheek. "Once you do, join me in the kitchen."

That was another thing he'd started doing whenever I was being "insufferable." He'd say something sweet and kiss me on the cheek.

He was the worst husband ever.

I finished getting ready and tidied my room a little. After my first night here, we decided that I'd come stay here on Saturday and Sunday nights, and during the week, Lior would stay with me if he was working in the city office.

Even though the museum was only an hour outside the city, Lior worked long hours when he was in the office, so he'd gotten used to crashing at the hotel.

Staying with me meant he wouldn't have to stay in the hotel, which could blow our secret.

His mom would probably not come to the back of the house and see the rooms, but there was no guarantee. I made it look like the spare room was just an extra space for me to get ready rather than the room I slept in.

By the time I walked out, I heard voices.

My heart galloped as I prepared to be face-to-face with my mother-in-law. My very legal mother-in-law, who I'd never met before.

"Noah. Oh my goodness, I'm so happy to finally meet you."

I'd never seen someone so small move so fast, and before I knew it, I was wrapped in her petite arms.

She smelled like flowers and rain showers. It was different from my mom, who mostly smelled like baked goods, but her hug was just as warm.

"Um, nice to meet you, Mrs. Van Stern."

She had the same dark eyes as Lior, but her hair was now all white and in a tidy short haircut, which gave her a very distinguished look.

"Please call me Mathilda. I guess since I didn't know about you until last week, it's probably a little too early to ask you to call me Mom."

I smiled, unsure of how to reply.

"Mom!" Lior warned.

"What? You can't expect me to not say anything, Lior."

"We've talked about this already."

She went back to her seat at the table. I was still unsure of what to do, but Lior, as put together as always, came over to me, placed a kiss on my cheek, and said, "You look amazing tonight, my dear. Ignore her. She's just jealous I got you all to myself first." The second part was definitely loud enough for his mom to hear.

We sat at the table next to each other. Lior put a protective arm over the back of my chair. There were three cups of steaming coffee on the table already. While it was probably unwise to have caffeine when I was already on edge, I still drank the coffee to occupy my hands and mouth.

"Noah, Lior said you run the PR agency working with him and the museum."

"Yes, I own it with my brothers. It's a privilege to support the museum. I haven't visited yet, but my brother spoke highly of it."

She turned to Lior.

"You haven't given your husband a private tour of the museum?"

I bit my lip. She looked more upset over that than the fact we got married in secret.

Lior let out an amused sigh. "I thought you came over to help us, not to play the role of evil mother-in-law. It doesn't suit you."

She rolled her eyes at him and sipped her coffee. "Right, let's talk business."

I glanced at Lior. He winked and nodded toward his mom.

"What kind of business?" I asked.

"The business you're doing tonight, my dear. Okay, listen carefully. Cara and John McMartin will be your allies. They adopted their three children—gosh, they're adults now—from the foster care system. Back in the day, in the social circles, that was seen as shameful."

She frowned. "Imagine taking three siblings from the foster care system to give them all the love they need and to make sure they stayed together, and then get shamed for it because you didn't push them out of your... Anyway, they've donated money to many charities throughout the years. I'm sure they would love to connect with your friends."

"Thank you," I said with a lump in my throat. "I'm so grateful for the information."

"You're welcome, dear. Also, word on the street is that

Prince Kristoff of Lydovia and his husband, Prince Charlie, are also attending the ball because they're in the country for a personal event. Their son was also adopted from the foster care system in Lydovia and they haven't hidden the fact they like to support charities in both countries."

I snapped my head toward Lior. "A prince? Christ, I was already nervous. I'm not sure I can go now."

"You will go, and you're going to be amazing. I'll be right there by your side, okay?"

Lior brought his hand to my cheek and caressed it gently. I became lost in his warm gaze, my belly doing little flips from nerves. I nodded.

"Awww."

We both turned toward Lior's mom, who was staring at us with heart-eyes.

"I'm still angry with you both for not giving a mother the chance to throw a good wedding party, but I can see you're happy together. You did well, Lior. Your father would be proud."

She reached her hand out to Lior, who took it, but I felt him tense at her words.

"Thank you for your help, Mom. I'm afraid we need to get going if we don't want to be more than fashionably late."

Lior walked his mom to the door, where her driver was waiting for her.

"She's scary," I said when we were alone again.

"Nah. She's a marshmallow. Now, I wasn't kidding. We have to go." He tapped my ass to lead me to the door. "Come on, sexy. We need to charm some people tonight."

"Careful, Mr. Van Stern. I'm going to start thinking you're with me just for my body."

"It is a fine body."

I groaned but followed him out, taking a deep breath as I

took in the fresh evening air. I hoped it would give me the level head I needed to network like a motherfucker tonight.

20

LIOR

I'D HEARD stories from my parents about how incredible the mayor's ball was. My mother's words had been enchanting and magical.

She wasn't wrong.

From the moment we walked onto a red carpet of dancers and performers to when we entered the large ballroom at the botanical gardens, it was like we'd stepped into a different world.

The glass ceiling was filled with hanging lights that made it look like the night sky. All around the room, the trees were lit from beneath, making them glow.

"This place is… I have no words," Noah said, looking over the room around us.

"I agree." I pulled him closer and snaked an arm around his waist. "Tonight is going to be magical," I whispered in his ear.

"You're making promises again, Mr. Van Stern." He ran a hand up my tuxedo jacket, stopping below my shoulder blade.

"Sometimes I look at you and wonder where you've been all my life," I said.

"Probably in high school or college, you know." He shrugged. "Being young and stuff."

"And sometimes I look at you and wonder if spanking you would work that attitude out of you or if you'd enjoy it."

"Enjoy it. Definitely enjoy it." He took my hand and pulled us away.

"Where are we going?"

"The bar. I need a drink before I drag you out of here and make some husbandly demands."

I laughed. "Husbandly demands?"

"Yes."

"Okay. Let's get a drink."

He didn't need to keep holding my hand while we waited in line to get closer to the bar, but I liked that he did.

We were playing with fire, and I was going to get burned if I didn't stop flirting with my husband.

"Can I ask you something?" I'd wanted to bring it up in the car, but he'd spent the ride asking questions about my mom and my childhood, and I hadn't wanted to interrupt him.

"Of course."

"At the conference in Atlanta, you commanded a room full of strangers. You were confident and self-assured. Why are you so nervous today?"

He shrugged. "I don't want to fail West and Drew."

I understood him now. For Noah, these were the highest stakes. The man who barely batted an eyelid at getting married put more pressure on himself to perform in his area of expertise because he couldn't bear the thought of letting anyone down.

I wrapped my arm around his shoulders and pulled him

close. He wasn't alone in this, and I'd make sure he knew that.

"Lior, how great to see you here."

I doubted that. I winked at Noah and turned to face one of my dad's business partners. It was show time.

Noah held out his hand. "Good evening. I'm Noah Spencer. Lior's husband."

Disapproval gleamed in his eyes as he took Noah's hand.

"Noah, this is Anderson Getty. He's on our board, overseeing the international division for houseware products."

"Very nice meeting you, Mr. Getty."

"Likewise, Mr. Spencer. How's married life treating you?"

Noah leaned into me with an adoring gaze that would melt the coldest of hearts, just not Getty's. "It's the best thing that's happened to us. When you meet the love of your life, everything just falls into place. You know how it is."

I bit my tongue. Getty didn't know how it was because he was currently divorcing his fourth wife.

"Well, I look forward to seeing you two at the next meeting."

He dipped his head in a quick nod and left.

"He had a bad aura," Noah said.

I almost doubled over in laughter. "Is that Noah speak for, *he's a spineless dickwaffle?*"

"And then some. What's this about a meeting?"

It was our turn at the bar, and I ordered us drinks. There were several standing tables nearby, so I set the drinks on one and turned to Noah. "I didn't want to tell you until after tonight. The meeting with the partners when I announced our wedding didn't go too well. They demanded to reconvene the meeting to include my dad's attorney and you. They want to meet you."

Noah's eyes widened. "Do they think we're faking it?"

"Possibly."

"What do they want? For you to bend me over the conference table and fuck me right there?"

I tucked his chin between my thumb and pointer finger and tilted his head up a little. "Now you're giving me ideas."

"And you're making more promises. One day, I'm going to collect them all in one go."

"We'd need a week."

"I'm due some vacation time, and we haven't had a honeymoon."

His eyes held mine hostage, daring me to break first.

"Lior, darling." Pierce's voice cut through us like a sharp knife.

My heart sank when I turned to him. My eyes landed on Cara and John McMartin, who were by his side.

He took a step forward and gave me an over-the-top kiss on the cheek.

I gripped my drink so tightly that I thought the glass would break.

"What a surprise to see you here."

"I didn't know you'd been invited, although I wished for it. In fact, I was only just telling Cara and John how I'd enjoyed attending these events with you."

I ignored his words and turned to the couple we'd hoped to see tonight.

"Cara. John. How wonderful to see you. Mom was over earlier and telling me how grown up the kids are."

Cara beamed. "Time passes far too quickly. We're wondering how we'll keep busy when our youngest goes to college next year. We'll be like two Ping-Pong balls rattling around that big house."

I nodded. "Oh, how rude of me. Please let me introduce you to my husband, Noah Spencer. Noah, this is Cara and John McMartin."

Pierce's shocked gasp was silenced by Cara's happy shriek.

"Your mom didn't say you were getting married. Congratulations. So nice to meet you, Noah."

"It's really lovely to meet you too, Mr. and Mrs. McMartin."

"Please call us Cara and John," John said.

Pierce touched my elbow. "Could I have a word?"

"Of course." I turned to Cara and John. "Could I leave my husband in your care for a moment?"

Cara waved me off. "Of course, dear."

Noah gave me an imperceptible nod. Pierce's interruption hadn't been part of our plan, but it came in handy.

I followed Pierce to a space between two trees that seemed away from prying ears.

"How can I help you, Pierce?"

"The question isn't how can you help me, but what can I do to help you. The answer is, I'll go all the way."

I snorted. "We've already gone all the way, Pierce, and the problem was that you were going all the way with a few other people too."

"Why do you always have to bring that up? I'm trying to help you here."

His discontent wasn't my problem. "I bring it up to remind you that what happened was your fault, even though you seem convinced of the contrary. And what exactly would I need your help for?"

"I can marry you."

I laughed. "And why would I do that?"

"To get your father's share of the company, of course." He now looked exasperated. "Look, I know about the will conditions. You don't need to pretend to be married to that guy. No wonder the partners don't believe you."

His words made me do a double-take. "I'm sorry, what now?"

He sighed. "I know you don't want to lose your family's

company, but resorting to lying is beneath you, Lior. Getty told me you announced your fake marriage at the meeting a few weeks ago. I didn't get in touch because I had the feeling you didn't really want to see me after Atlanta. Besides, I didn't think you'd actually show up in public with him, but this is going too far now. You even have a wedding band."

"Oh, you think we're faking it?"

"I know you're faking it. You were so opposed to marrying me when I asked, and now you've met a guy five minutes ago, and you're *married?*"

"Fortunately for me, I don't have to prove my relationship status, or anything else, to you, so I don't give a crap if you believe it or not, but our marriage is very real. More real than anything you and I ever had." I walked away from a stunned Pierce.

Noah beamed when I joined them. He opened his mouth to say something, but I couldn't resist swooping in for a kiss. It was quick and, by anyone's standards, very understated.

When I pulled away, his cheeks were flushed and his pupils were dilated to the point his eyes almost looked black.

"Hey. Good talk?" I asked, turning to the McMartins.

"You too are so adorable," Cara said. "Where have you been hiding this delightful young man, Lior?"

I smiled, keeping Noah tucked under my arm. He seemed to recover from the kiss quickly.

"Did you know Cara and John know West and Drew?"

"I did not."

Cara shook her head. "I'm going to have to pay those boys a visit. How did I not know they were hoping to take over the old hospital?"

She weaved her arm through Noah's. "Lior, I'm going to take your husband away now. We're going to have a word with the mayor."

"Be my guest. Just bring him back in one piece," I joked.

I gave Noah's shoulder a little squeeze of encouragement before I let him go.

"She's relentless," John said, staring lovingly at his wife's parting figure.

"Our country needs more people like them."

He raised his glass. "I'll drink to that and also to your old man. He's missed."

"Thank you, John. It's hard stepping into his shoes when so many people knew and liked him."

"If you want the advice of an old man, just be your own self. Your father always spoke very fondly of you." He leaned closer. "I don't have a stake in your company, but I used to talk to your dad a lot. If you ever want to workshop an idea with an independent party, I'm here for you."

I raised my glass. "Thank you. I appreciate the offer, even if you might end up regretting it."

We talked about business and family while keeping an eye on Cara and Noah, who seemed to have gathered a group of people around them. There were a lot of flying hands while they talked.

I'd learned that Noah's nature for being so animated when he talked about something he cared about came from his Portuguese side. I wanted to know more about it, but he still seemed worried about telling his family about us.

He glanced in my direction, and our eyes met. My heart thumped a little faster. At my age, I didn't need anyone to point out that I was rapidly falling for my husband, but I wasn't stupid enough to let it happen.

"We'll never get them back now," John said, laughing. "We better get another drink."

"What do you mean?"

"That couple joining them? That's the prince of Lydovia and his husband, Charlie. Cara met them at a charity function a while ago. You can bet good money that my wife and your husband won't be back until they've made sure the prince's pockets are a little lighter before they go home tonight."

"I'll have another drink to that. The kids from that community deserve all their efforts."

By the time we got to the front of the line at the bar, we'd decided to get a round of drinks for the group.

Noah's hand sought mine when we joined them. His energy was electric, and I'd never seen him so happy before.

Watching him do his thing, all I could think about was how I wanted to do everything in my power to make Noah happy.

21

___

NOAH

I WAS STILL RIDING the high of the ball days later when I strolled into the office with a coffee and a muffin after an early morning call with West and Drew, who wouldn't stop talking about the visit they'd had from Cara. She'd brought along Prince Kris and Charlie.

I still couldn't believe I'd mixed with royalty. Talk about feeling like Cinderella, and I'd even gotten to take my own Prince Charming home.

Coming back to reality was a total downer. Although I'd been relieved that with the amount of press at the event, I hadn't seen any photos of us from that night.

My sore muscles complained when I sat down.

"Someone's been having too much fun," Adam said, poking his head through my open office door. "You know hooking up isn't a competitive sport, right?"

I bit my tongue and waited three seconds before I said, "You know I like to lean on my strengths. Anyway, what can I do for you? We don't have a meeting booked, do we?"

"No." He came in and sat on the chair in front of my desk. I took that as a sign that I was going to be dumped with a new client or we were going to have a bro moment. "Is everything okay with you?"

"Of course. Why wouldn't it be?"

"I don't know? Because you've missed the Spencer Weekly for the last month? Or maybe because you run out of the office every evening like your ass is on fire?"

"I'm getting my work done and more. What are you getting at?"

He scrunched his brows. "How about the missing Sundays?"

"I've been busy."

"Right."

"What's that supposed to mean?"

"Nothing. Just wondering where my older brother is because I feel like I haven't seen him since he practically ran out of the family brunch a month ago. Even Victoria has noticed."

I turned my computer on and busied myself getting paperwork out of my drawers so I wouldn't have to look at him.

It broke my heart to not see my family as much as I used to, but at the same time, I couldn't handle being around them while I was keeping such a big secret.

"I'll make an effort this weekend."

I glanced at him. The hurt on his face hit me in the gut.

"Don't do it on our account." He stood up.

"Adam."

"If it's an effort to spend time with your family, then maybe it's right that you're not around as much. Even if Mom keeps asking about you and Avó is one skipped Sunday lunch away from breaking into your apartment and dragging you out by your ears."

He was by the door when he turned around.

"For what it's worth, it would be nice if you could attend

the wedding rehearsal weekend at Mabel's Vineyard on Peet Island. It was booked weeks ago, and you said you'd come. Victoria emailed you the details for the second time a week ago, but you haven't RSVP'd. Usually, I'd take your word for it, but considering your recent absence, we'll need actual confirmation."

He walked out before I could say anything.

"Fuck." I'd really messed things up.

A message popped up on my phone.

LIOR

The meeting with the partners is scheduled for Friday afternoon.

NOAH

I'll be there.

Another one followed straight after.

JAX

Dude, you need to hang out with your brothers. I saw them at Tanner's on Friday, and they asked about you. Why are you avoiding your family?

NOAH

You know why.

JAX

Just tell them already. What's the worst that could happen?

NOAH

I don't know. I could be disowned by my family and end up alone after Lior divorces me?

JAX

Trouble in paradise already?

NOAH

Ha.

JAX

Dude, if there's one thing you don't need to worry about, it's Lior divorcing you.

I didn't want to think why Jax believed that. The terms of our marriage were clear. Marry. Help the kids. Help him keep the company. Stay married. Divorce.

NOAH

Unless you know something I don't know, the plan hasn't changed.

JAX

All I'm saying is, if you want to stay married to Lior, you just need to show him how good it can be to remain married. Starting a shift now. Over and out.

I stared at my phone, unable to move. And not just because Lior insisting on us working out together every morning before breakfast was killing my poor body.

The more time we spent together, the more I fell for him, but despite the way he teased me, he hadn't given any indication that he felt the same way. Not beyond struggling to fight his attraction to me.

We flirted with each other all the time, and I was going through lube like it was going out of fashion and risking a repetitive strain injury, from jacking off daily to thoughts of Lior. But there was nothing else between us.

I'd even stopped asking for sex because he hadn't given in once since our wedding day. My confidence was taking a hit.

I finished my coffee.

Could Jax be right? Would I give up this easily, or could I do as he suggested and show Lior how great we could be together for real?

I walked to my brother's office. He was pacing the small room, talking to his phone like he always did when brainstorming copyedit ideas for campaigns.

He stopped the recording when I knocked.

"Can I bring a plus one?" I asked.

"What?"

"This weekend. Can I bring someone?"

He leaned against his desk. "Is that why you've been AWOL? You're seeing someone?"

"Maybe."

He quirked a brow.

"Okay, fine. I am."

"Is it serious? It must be if you've ditched us. Is it Tanner? Is this why you haven't been out on Fridays with us? Because it's hard to hide how you feel for each other? You don't have to keep it a secret. We like Tanner."

I laughed. "I like Tanner too. Just not like that."

"Okay. I guess we'll meet him… Wait, sorry, I'm making assumptions here. Is it a woman?"

I chuckled. "No, you guessed right." I tucked my hands in my pockets. "This isn't easy for me, Adam. I don't want to hurt anyone."

He released a breath. "This is a good thing, Noah. I'm glad you found someone who's rattled that cage you've locked yourself in."

I returned to my office, waving at Lex who was swaying to the sound of his radio while he worked.

He was finally truly happy. The last Spencer Weekly I'd been to was after Lex and his boyfriend had gotten together for good.

Just like with Lior and me, Lex's second chance with Emery had been based on a lie. But they were happy now. I could see it in my brother's eyes and the way he smiled again. I think it also made Adam happier.

Four days later, as I met Lior outside his office, I wondered if we could also overcome the lies.

I'd worn a suit to disguise how nervous I was. I felt like I was about to take the most important exam of my life, which I expected to fail.

"Hey," he said with a warm smile.

I wound my arms inside his suit jacket and around his back. "Tell me this is going to work," I said against his chest.

He kissed my hair. "It's going to work. Leave it with me, okay?"

Because we were so openly comfortable with each other, I hoped selling our marriage wouldn't be impossible.

We had Lior's mom on our side too. She had joined us for dinner at Lior's place a few times, and as he'd promised, she was a true marshmallow. A pushy one, though, since she was determined we needed a *real* wedding.

Thank god for parents who fell in love at first sight and expected everyone else to experience the same. I just hoped my parents would react the same way when they found out the truth.

"Come on up." He held my hand and guided me through reception, getting me registered so I could always just walk in without being verified.

"You own the whole building?" I said in awe as I saw Lior's name on the wall by the elevators.

"Yes and no. Technically, that's my dad's name, but it'll save us money in the future when the company is officially mine. But the building belongs to the company."

"You could take my surname and change it on the wall to

Lior Van Spencer. Ooh, that has a nice ring to it. Makes my name sound very exotic."

He laughed. "You're ridiculous."

Ridiculously in love with you, I thought. At least that was something I didn't have to sell to the partners.

I wanted to laugh at the thought that I was walking into a meeting where I had to convince Lior's business partners of my true feelings for him, while to him, I had to sell the fact I didn't want more than friendship.

How fucked up was that?

Lior's mom greeted us outside the large conference room.

"Christ, you could fit my whole office in that room."

Mathilda laughed. "It needs to be big enough for their egos, my dear."

"Mom," Lior chided.

"I never lied to your father. I'm certainly not lying to you. Half of those men think they're God's gift to the world, but given the chance to do what they brag about, they'd shit their pants and go home crying to their wives who do a lot of the business negotiations for their husbands behind their back while doing downward dog in a hot yoga class."

"I suggest you keep those thoughts to yourself, Mom. Their fragile egos won't handle that much truth."

"I'm sitting next to you, Mathilda," I declared. She'd have my back.

We walked in together while twelve suited men stared at us as we took our seats.

I recognized Anderson Getty from the mayor's ball. I didn't expect a smiling face from him, but downright antagonistic was a surprise.

"Good afternoon, everyone," Lior started, standing. He had such a big presence with his tailored suit and groomed appearance. It made me feel a little hot under the collar.

Whose idea had it been to wear a tie? I hadn't even worn a tie to my own wedding.

"Thank you for taking time from your busy schedules to be here today. I know my recent wedding has come as a surprise to all of you, and as expected, there have been a few questions. Before I let Mr. Hoffman lead the meeting, I would like to introduce you to my husband, Noah Spencer."

I stood up next to Lior. "Thank you. It's a pleasure meeting you all." I gave a brief professional introduction similar to what I'd done in Atlanta. It had been Lior's suggestion. He thought they'd appreciate knowing I was a respected professional. He followed that by saying it was all bullshit, but unfortunately, we had to speak their language.

When I sat down, Lior took my hand. I didn't miss a few glances in our direction, but this part was easy. Wanting his hand in mine, feeling it ground me, and looking at him like I was in love? Easy.

Mr. Hoffman stood to address everyone.

"Thank you all for the questions you've submitted since the announcement of Mr. Van Stern's nuptials."

Lior squeezed my hand a little. This was the part he was really nervous about.

"A few partners expressed a desire to buy Mr. Van Stern's shares. The regulations around that have been emailed through by my team, so I trust they are clear. The bottom line is, until I finalize the completion of the will according to Mr. Van Stern's wishes, there won't be any negotiations regarding the shares."

It was my turn to squeeze Lior's hand. He relaxed a little, but we weren't out of the woods yet.

"All partners submitted a request for my consideration." Mr. Hoffman turned to us. "They expressed a concern that your marriage might be one of convenience. While it's not my place to make a judgment on that, I agree that the request placed by the partners is reasonable."

"What is that request?" Lior asked.

"You will need to remain married for the period of a year. During that time, you are expected to attend functions together and appear in relevant publications, just as Mr. and Mrs. Van Stern have done in the past."

I felt Lior shift in his seat, but Mathilda stood up first.

"I have something I'd like to say."

Everyone stared at her as if they'd just realized she had a voice.

"My husband and this company served you well. You've sent your children to private schools, and your wives are able to spend their time doing charity work instead of taking a paid job. Your wealth is intrinsically connected to the success of Van Stern Enterprises. As much as you are each responsible for the success of your areas, you cannot deny the company has stayed together and thrived with my husband at the helm. I am very aware that before my husband passed away there were doubts over Lior's suitability to take over because he hasn't been as involved in the company as you believe he should have been. Let me tell you something. You think anyone but Lior's son should run this company? Be our guest, but remember he's seen two generations of Van Sterns grow this company from nothing. No one else will care about the success and viability of this company as much as he does. I have seen my son and my son-in-law together, and trust me when I tell you, I know what it looks like when two people are in love. Lior has met his father's condition. He is married, and he did it within the stipulated time period. Any further requests may be reasonable, but they shouldn't be what the final decision is based on. Ultimately, you need to choose who is going to be the person you believe will take this company into the future."

I wanted to cheer at her speech but managed to hold it together. Lior didn't move a muscle until everyone was out of the room, and then he stood and hugged his mom.

My throat closed a little, seeing them like that. In the fight for the company, it was easy to forget they'd just lost someone really important to them.

When they pulled apart, Lior's eyes were red. I couldn't hold my feelings in any longer. I narrowed the space between us, stood on my toes, and kissed him.

He wrapped his arms around me tight.

"Thank you," he whispered against my lips.

"Your mom is a rock star."

"Damn right I am," she said, reminding us she was still in the room. Oops. Maybe I shouldn't have kissed her son like that.

"And now we're going from the fire into the frying pan." He let out a tense chuckle.

"Actually, I thought we should stay in a hotel near the ferry port tonight and check into the vineyard hotel in the morning. It's been a tough day, and I'd like to not see my family right now."

"Sounds perfect."

22

———

LIOR

Silence reigned in the car on our way to the small coastal town of Cape Mary. I wanted to put the meeting and the new requirements from the partners behind me.

Noah's quietness indicated that he didn't want to talk about the impending family weekend either.

I'd tried to talk him out of introducing me to his family this weekend, but he was determined.

His brothers had both worked with me, and now that I'd delegated a lot to Charlie as I spent more and more time in the office, I no longer had a working relationship with Adam and Lex.

How would they feel about their brother being in a relationship with a man who was seventeen years older?

"Do you think our age gap is too big?" I asked.

From the corner of my eye, I saw Noah turn his head away from the window.

"Why do you ask?"

"Just wondering…"

"When I'm with you, I don't think about our age difference. Never have."

"Even the first time we met?"

He laughed. "Especially the first time we met. You don't want to know the kinds of thoughts I had about you then."

I risked a quick glance and found him staring. An easy smile graced his lips.

"What?"

"What's made you think of that? Are you afraid my family won't like you because you're older than me?"

Yes…maybe… "No?"

"That means yes." He chuckled. "Don't worry. If they're going to be upset at anyone, it'll be me."

I wasn't so sure about that. A man with graying hair and pushing fifty was probably not the partner his parents had imagined for their eldest son.

"Why do you think that?"

"We're a close family. Weekly lunches, regular calls. Hell, we all work together. Adam gave me a hard time this week about not being present for the family lately. He was pacified when I told him I was bringing someone with me this weekend." He sighed. "But I know they'll be pissed off that it's you—not because it's you, but because you're a client."

"Was a client," I clarified.

"When they find out we're actually married, my parents are going to be upset. I never wanted to hurt them or my brothers. I just…"

"I know…" I took his hand and brought it to my lips, planting a kiss on his soft skin. He wasn't the only one with feelings of guilt when it came to family. My mother's actions this afternoon weighed on my conscience. She truly believed Noah and I were happy and in love. She would be heartbroken when she found out the truth.

The hotel room turned out to have just one bed instead of the two I'd requested because, apparently, a family had needed a last-minute stay and the receptionist made the swap without asking.

"It's not a problem. Is it?" Noah asked as we dropped our bags on the floor of the small room.

"It's only one night."

He scrunched his face. "I got us a room with one bed only at the vineyard. Adam had a room block booked, and I didn't want to ask for a different room in case anyone asked questions."

I took him to the bed and made him sit down. I kneeled in front of him between his legs.

"Hmm, you look good there."

"Focus, Noah Spencer."

He rolled his eyes. "How can I when you're inches away from my…inches…"

"You'll live." I held his hands and took a deep breath. "I need you to know that you have the option to not tell your family about us."

"How can I hide from them for the next year? I don't want to lie to them, but pretending this hasn't happened is freaking me out."

"That's okay. I just wanted to remind you that you have options. I hate that you're stuck in this mess."

Noah let go of my hands to run his fingers through my hair. I closed my eyes, enjoying the smell of his cologne and the feel of his fingers on my scalp.

"I'm so fucking horny for you all the time, Lior. How do I make it stop?"

"I wish I knew."

I opened my eyes to find his staring back at me, smoldering with heat. How easy would it be to give in? But then, where would we stop? I knew I couldn't. I'd had one small taste of Noah, and it had landed me in a fake marriage. If I had more, I would lose my heart to him and get it back broken.

Or would I? What real reason did I have? We had a whole year. Could we make something of it? Was I ready to risk it all for something real with Noah?

He threw himself on the bed with a groan. "Let's grab dinner."

"Yeah. Let's do that."

We didn't talk about our marriage, my business, or his family again until we were back in the room, brushing our teeth.

"We should probably take our wedding bands off," he said, holding his hand up. There was nothing special about the band. It was made out of gold and unpretentious, but it still glistened in the light of the room. He took it off and placed it in a small, zipped pouch inside his toiletry bag.

"Yeah, you're right."

My hand felt immediately naked when I took the ring off, and there was even a tan line. He took my band to keep them together.

It dawned on me that this was the first time I'd taken my wedding band off since our wedding day.

Noah gasped. "When did that happen?" He traced the white mark around my finger.

"Don't know. Maybe I caught the sun?"

His eyes met mine. "Is it weird that I like it?"

I wanted to say no, it wasn't, but the swirl of feelings inside me stopped me from replying.

"It's weird," he declared with a chuckle and went back to the room, tucking himself under the bedsheets.

"You better not be naked," I said, turning the lights out.

"Why don't you come over and check?" He wiggled his eyebrows.

I didn't know if I was disappointed or relieved to find him in a T-shirt and underwear.

He turned to face the wall. "I like being the little spoon. Just so you know."

I pulled the sheets up to my neck. My dick was rock-hard and more than willing to break all the rules.

Sweet relief came when I heard soft snores from the man beside me moments later. I was reaching my breaking point, and if Noah had pushed an inch, I'd have given him everything.

Sleeping in the same bed and no sex? We had the most real marriage out there. It was comical that we had to prove it.

By the time I woke up the next morning, Noah was already up and getting dressed.

"Morning," I said, taking an appreciative look at the way his ass looked in his jeans. He hadn't put a shirt on yet, so I also got to explore the curves of his back.

"Stop perving or I'll call my family saying I have the flu and then book this room for the weekend," he said, throwing his shirt on.

I got up, and ten minutes later, we were ready to go. The plan was to join his family for breakfast at the hotel on the island after we checked in, so we just grabbed a coffee to take on the ferry.

The hotel grounds were stunning. It was such a contradiction that on a day without a cloud in the sky, it felt like a storm was brewing.

We shared a glance and walked into the hotel lobby.

The reception desk didn't have a line, so the receptionist welcomed us with a smile as soon as she saw us.

"Welcome to Mabel's Vineyard. Are you here to check in?"

"We are," Noah said. "The reservation is under Spencer. Noah Spencer."

"Oh, you're with the wedding rehearsal party. Most of the guests arrived last night, but we made sure all the rooms were ready, so once you're checked in, we can take your bags up and you can enjoy our luxurious breakfast with the other guests."

She took our IDs and started to type away on her laptop.

"Nervous?" I asked Noah.

"It's too late to back out now. Better face it head-on." He steeled himself and grinned.

I took in our surroundings while we waited. The hotel was stunning. It had an old-world feel, but the number of windows and skylights made it bright and airy.

For a moment, my grandfather popped into my mind. He would have said the hotel needed several stained-glass windows to make the brightness colorful. *You can never have too much color in your life*, is what he always used to say.

I'd never understood those words so much until now. Having Noah in my life had certainly added a new palette.

"It really is you. Mr. Van Stern?"

I turned toward the young voice calling my name.

"That's me, and you are?"

The girl must have been in her teens. She had light-green eyes and bright-red hair.

"My name is Emily. My mom took me to visit your museum last week. It's so pretty. I loved all the colors, and… everything is so bright. My favorite was the gardens. I made my mom promise we'll go there again before school starts. I want to spend a whole day in the garden. Are we allowed to bring a picnic?"

I chuckled. "You certainly are allowed to bring a picnic to the gardens. You know where my favorite place is?"

Her eyes bugged out and she smiled like she was trying to control all the energy inside her.

"Find the giant caterpillar. When you stand next to it and look to your left, you'll see a row of trees. Go to the trees and look very carefully. You'll see a small gate. You can open it. It's allowed. Inside, you'll find a secret garden. Only our very special guests know it exists."

She gasps. "Mom, did you hear that?"

A woman who was the spitting image of the girl came closer. "I hope she's not bothering you, Mr. Van Stern. She's been obsessed with your museum. She probably recognized you from the museum website. She… Last year, she was bullied at school for having red hair. I wanted to show her that bright and different things can be beautiful and magical."

"I couldn't agree more," I said.

"Who's this?" the girl asked as Noah stood beside me with the room keycards.

"I'm his husband, Noah. Nice to—"

"Excuse me?"

My gaze moved from the girl to the interrupting voice. Noah was frozen still, staring at a very confused Adam and a woman I guessed was Victoria.

I turned back to Emily. "It was very nice meeting you two. When you go back to the museum, ask to speak to Charlie and tell him I said you could have a VIP ticket."

"For real?"

I chuckled. "For real."

I drew a business card from my wallet and gave it to Emily's mom. They thanked me and left.

"What's going on, Noah?" Adam asked. "What is Lior doing here?"

Noah stared him down with a defiant look. "You said I could bring a plus one. He's my plus one."

Adam's gaze shifted from Noah to me.

"Why did you say you're his husband?" Victoria asked, her voice definitely too loud for a hotel lobby.

"That's because I am. Lior and I got married a month ago in Vegas."

"Noah James Spencer."

Noah groaned and said between his teeth, "Time to meet the parents." He took the proverbial pin off the grenade and said, "Lior, this is my mom, Carla, my dad, Jack, and my grandmother, Jacinta. Mãe, Pai, Avó, I'd like you to meet Lior Van Stern…my husband."

I held my breath when suddenly, an explosion of words broke out, with everyone talking over each other in Portuguese with some English mixed in.

Lying, husband, scandal, joking, and *insane* were just a few of the words I picked out.

They talked over each other like air was a commodity rather than a necessity. I wanted to interrupt them and ask them to take this somewhere private. A few people slowed their pace as they walked past us to watch what was going down.

"I can't believe you'd do this, Noah," Victoria shouted. "I know you don't like me, but to do this to your family and me is disrespectful. This is all everyone's going to be talking about." Tears ran down her face as she ran off with Adam at her heel.

"We all have to calm down," Jack said.

"Calm down? Don't tell me to calm down," Carla said. "Your son got married without telling his own family. Who are we? The people that raised him and loved them, or nobodies?"

His grandmother stared at me like she wished she could whip out a machete from under her skirt and slice me into pieces.

"Noah, I suggest you speak to your brothers and sort this mess out. Then come to our suite with a reasonable explanation for your actions," Jack said before he practically dragged his wife and mother-in-law toward the elevators.

Noah's eyes were red-rimmed. He was on the verge of breaking down, and it was all my fault. Why had I accepted his ridiculous proposal?

I couldn't think of a way in which this could have gone any worse.

"Hey." I tucked my hand under Noah's chin to make him look at me. "What do you need? We can go. We can stay. Hell, I don't want to leave you on your own, but if it's what you need, I'll go."

"We're staying," he said, steeling himself.

"Are you sure?"

He opened his bag and took out his washbag, opening the little pouch where he'd kept our rings. He slid his band on and grabbed my hand, sliding mine in place.

"I'm not hiding my husband."

23

NOAH

"I AM NOT HIDING MY HUSBAND," I repeated. My fists clenched against Lior's chest. "I can understand their hurt over being lied to, but it doesn't excuse some of the things they said or what they thought but didn't say."

"Tell me what to do, Noah. I hate seeing you like this."

Lior's gaze was frantic like he was searching for any clue that I might crumble into a messy pile at any moment now.

"Can you take our stuff to the room and wait for me there? I'm going to speak to my family." And possibly destroy our relationship, but I was fed up with being treated like I was less than just because of their warped sense of how life should be.

He cradled the back of my neck and pulled me in for a kiss. "Come back to me in one piece, okay," he said against my lips.

I nodded, swallowing the lump in my throat.

Armed with everyone's room numbers, thanks to the receptionist, who was happy for the scene to disperse, I headed up to the only place I knew there was a chance of finding someone to have my back.

Lex's room.

On my way out of the elevator, I bumped into Victoria's sister, Ellie.

"Dude. Congrats," she said, holding her hand up for a fist bump. "For what it's worth, that's how I'd do it too if I ever found someone crazy enough to tie themselves to me legally."

"Um, thanks?" Word got around fast.

She looked at both ends of the hallway before saying, "The wicked queen is having a tantrum because God forbid life happens to other people. It may be the first time in her life something hasn't been all about her. Don't let anyone make you feel guilty for living your life and seeking your happiness. Her problem is not your problem." She sighed. "I wish your brother saw that, but I guess love is blind and all that."

"Thank you, Ellie. That's weirdly reassuring."

She grinned. "I'm just gutted I didn't get to set you up like I did Lex and Emery—the second time, at least. I didn't think you were in the market for love."

I chuckled. "Neither did I."

She excused herself to go have a sexy date with the break-fast buffet and disappeared into the elevator, leaving me in the hallway.

I followed the room numbers until I found Lex's. The door wasn't closed all the way, so I heard the voices inside.

"He didn't bring a date. He brought his fucking husband," Adam said in a raised voice.

"I'm sorry, what?" Lex sounded like he'd choked.

"What I said. Mom is crying in her room because she's hurt. Victoria is crying in our room because she's upset. Avó may or may not have gone down to the hotel kitchen to borrow a butcher's knife, and Dad...well, Dad is trying to keep everyone happy and failing miserably. It's not even nine o'clock in the morning. All because, apparently, our big brother went and got married."

Lex laughed. "You have to be joking. He wouldn't do that."

"He wouldn't? Lex, he's the practical joker. The one we can count on to lighten the mood. He never takes anything seriously. I wouldn't be surprised if he did it just to get back at Victoria."

"That's not fair, Adam. Okay, maybe not entirely inaccurate, but he wouldn't do that to you," Lex said. "Who did he marry? Tanner? He's protested so much about not hooking up with him that he's the only person who comes to mind."

"Worse. Lior Van Stern."

Bile bubbled up from my stomach. I slid down the wall and sat on my heels with my head between my knees.

It was finally clear what my family thought about me. It didn't matter that I was there for them whenever they needed me. All the times I'd dropped everything to help my brothers. The two years I'd worked with barely a break, saving money so we could open the agency as soon as they graduated. Being there for Lex when he was conflicted about lying to Emery about their relationship prior to him losing his memory.

It was all worth nothing.

I was nothing but a fuck boy to my brothers.

"Hey, Noah, what are you doing out here?"

I looked up to see River standing there.

"I'm surprised you don't know yet," I scoffed.

"Know what?"

"The fuck up that I am."

River kneeled. "Dude, you're not a fuck up. You're one of the most capable people I know. What happened?"

"I got married."

He let out a surprised gasp at the same time the door to my brother's room opened.

Emery poked his head out. "I thought I heard something. Do you want to come inside? Adam is here."

We stood and followed him inside.

River went straight to Adam, who looked like he wanted to punch me when we walked in.

"What are you doing here?" Adam spat. "Haven't you done enough? Victoria doesn't deserve this. I don't deserve this. Why don't you just go and leave us?"

"Adam," Lex said. "Let's hear him out."

"Why? I think I've heard enough."

I stood my ground, trying to portray a calmness I didn't feel. "You've heard nothing, Adam, but you've made plenty of assumptions, haven't you? God forbid your whore of a brother actually falls in love, right? Who'd be the butt of your jokes then?" I paced the small space by the door. My instincts told me I should leave now, but I was too angry and keyed up. "This is a fucking circus, Adam. You've been walking on eggshells around Victoria since the day you met her. I'm already the black sheep of the family, so I don't care if you hate me any more than you already do, but you have to hear this."

He took a step forward, but River held him back.

"Don't walk on eggshells for the rest of your life," I continued. "At my wedding, we didn't try to impress anyone. There were no choirs or string quartets. It was just us. Our reception was cake and champagne in our hotel room. You know what's been the best part so far? Knowing I had him all to myself. That no one else's judgmental stares or comments came between us."

Tears started running down my cheeks. Every word out of my mouth was a realization that the only fake thing about my marriage was the agreement to make it fake, at least for me.

"You know what was the worst? Not sharing my happiness with the most important people in my life. But look at what happened when you found out? No one thought I got so caught up in love that I couldn't wait to get married. No one. But everyone thought I messed up big time, and now I'm ruining someone else's celebration. I think that says more about you than it does about me."

Adam was stunned into silence. Lex and Emery looked at each other.

I turned around to leave.

"Have you seen these?" Adam pulled out his phone and turned it to me. "You went to the mayor's ball. You hung out with fucking royalty. It's like we don't know who you are anymore. You have a secret life. Why? Have we been so bad to you that you couldn't tell us you were happy?"

I fell on a nearby chair like a deflating balloon.

"When I told you I saw Lior in Atlanta, you asked me straight-up if I'd hooked up with him. That's the opinion you have of me. That I would do that, even with a client. How could I tell you that even though we didn't hook up, we spent the whole weekend together as friends? We talked about business and ourselves, and for only the second time in my life, I made a true connection with another person. Something so precious that I didn't want it tainted by my reputation."

Lex crouched beside me. "Can you tell us your story with Lior? I like him. He helped Emery when he had the flashback on the side of the road. Emery could have been seriously hurt, not to mention he was confused over regaining some of his memories that included us. Lior found him and made sure he got home safely. That meant a lot to me."

I'd forgotten about that. It had happened before Atlanta

and the wedding. I'd kept my life so segregated in the last few months that I'd forgotten about the tenuous connections between us.

"I met Lior by chance at Tanner's. We hooked up." I looked at Adam. "I'll give you this one." And then I turned to Lex. "It was a one-time thing. We didn't even exchange names. Weeks later, I got his contact information about the museum. That's when I found out who he was. I didn't want to miss the opportunity for us to work with Van Stern Enterprises so that's why I sent you to meet him. I didn't see him again until Atlanta. We hung out. I didn't lie to you at our meeting. We had a connection, but he was working with us, so we decided to not pursue anything."

"But you must have," Lex said.

"I bumped into him at Tanner's when I was meeting up with Jax. He was on a date." I smiled as I remembered how possessive I'd felt of him. "I kinda stopped the date and made him come home with me."

"Awww."

We all looked at Emery. He blushed and tucked his curly hair behind his ear. "Sorry."

I chuckled.

"And then what?" Adam asked. "You tripped and landed on the first commercial flight to Vegas? You sneezed and fell face-first into The Little Chapel of Love? Don't insult our intelligence, Noah."

I sighed. "I'm sorry. We…Lior took us away for the weekend. Jax and Tanner came with us. We got carried away, and it seemed like a good idea. I know it was fast, but…" I looked at Lex and then Emery. If anyone would understand my connection with Lior, it was them. Even if I was only telling my side of the story.

"What was your plan for bringing him here this weekend?" Adam asked.

"I was going to introduce him as my boyfriend. I honestly didn't mean to upstage you and Victoria."

"Then why did you tell that girl he's your husband?"

My cheeks heated. "Because he is, and… even though I wasn't ready to tell you all, I didn't want to lie."

"Not if you could help it, right?"

I stood. "We can go around in circles. It doesn't change the fact that I'm married. Or that my husband is probably worried sick in our room, wondering if I'm okay or if we've beaten each other to a pulp. It's not going to change the fact I lied. You can believe me when I say I regret everything but marrying him. Or you can choose to not believe me."

Adam narrowed the space between us in just a few steps, with River hanging right behind like he'd stop him from punching me if he tried.

"I don't know how I feel about this," he said. "I'm hurt, and I don't know what's worse. That my own brother kept something so huge from me or that the truth has come out this weekend, of all times."

He walked around me. "Now, if you'll excuse me, I have to check in on my fiancée." The door closed behind him before I could react.

I released a long breath. My body was shaking, and I needed…Lior.

Lex wrapped his arms around me. "This is a mess, but I'm happy for you, Noah. Adam will come around."

I nodded.

"I should go back to Lior. If you see Mom and Dad, tell them I'll speak to them later. I can't…right now."

24

LIOR

I TRIED everything I could to stop myself from going to the reception desk and asking for the room numbers of Noah's brothers.

Every little sound from the hallway caught my attention, from people walking past to the ding of the elevator.

I would have unpacked our bags, but from the tension earlier, I couldn't be entirely sure Noah wouldn't want to leave after speaking to his family.

Part of me understood exactly why they were upset. I'd never downplay Noah's feelings, but his family was angry because they cared. They loved him and, quite rightly, were shocked that he would get married in secret to someone they'd never met.

But I'd also gotten to know Noah really well in the last few months. Family was everything to him, and he struggled with not telling his family the truth for fear of how they might react.

After waiting for fifteen minutes, which felt like an hour, I ordered a selection of breakfast food up to the room.

Even if Noah wasn't hungry because of the high

emotions, he would be at some point. The hotel was accommodating when I asked that the coffee come in a thermos so it was warm when Noah got to the room.

Breakfast came with no sign of Noah.

Finally, the click of the key card sounded at the door.

I rushed to my feet as Noah barreled into the room and jumped into my arms, wrapping his legs around my waist.

The door closed behind him with a bang as his mouth sought mine, locking our lips in a brutal kiss. There was no exploration, no tasting. This was raw and desperate.

His teeth grazed my lips until he trapped them between his and sucked hard, leaving my mouth burning with fire.

When he pulled away, we were both panting.

"I don't wanna talk. Not yet. I just need you, Lior. I need you so much. Please."

I set him on his feet and cradled his face between my hands. His eyes were wild, fire burning within his gaze.

I'd never seen him like this before.

"Are you sure you want to do this?" I wasn't sure if giving him an out was for his benefit or mine.

"Yes. I need you to make me feel good. To just make me…feel."

Oh, my sweet, kind man. What wouldn't I do for him?

I nodded. "We can stop at any moment, okay? You're frantic. I can help you calm down, but I need to be sure you won't let me hurt you, okay?"

"I promise," he said with determination.

"One word, and I'll stop."

"I understand." He nodded.

"On your knees."

It was such a simple command, but the moment I uttered the words, Noah surrendered. The restraint he'd been holding on to evaporated.

He fell to his knees and looked up. His blue eyes were deep pools of desire, trusting me to do what he needed.

"You look so beautiful like that."

A proud smile parted his lips.

I searched my bag for the small travel-size bottle of lube I'd packed at the last minute. Even though it was a foregone conclusion that we'd end up in this position at some point, I hadn't expected it to happen now or like this. I had only packed it because lube and my left hand had become best friends since I'd been spending so much time with Noah.

There was way too much chemistry between us.

When I turned back, Noah had his shirt half unbuttoned.

I put my hand under his chin and tilted it up. "Who's in charge here?"

"You."

"Did I say you could take your shirt off?"

He huffed, dropping his hands by his sides. "You're too slow."

"Do you want a reminder of what you asked me to do?"

He shook his head.

"Good. Now take me out."

Since the night at the hotel, I'd made a mental list of the ways I wanted to fuck Noah, given the chance. Now we were here, and I wanted them all. I couldn't pick.

Staying dressed was hot but uncomfortable. Besides, I wanted to take a shower with him afterward. I didn't know how I knew it, but my gut feeling told me there would be a crash.

Noah was feeling way too much and struggling to process it all.

"Your cock is so big." He cupped it over my underwear, leaving open-mouth kisses all over until he reached the head and sucked over the fabric.

"Fuck, Noah."

His eyes never left mine as he explored. I groaned when he exposed just the head and then wrapped his lips around it, licking the slit and then sucking.

All my sensitive nerves were firing. Pleasure coursed through my body. He hooked his hands over the elastic of my boxer briefs and pulled them down together with my jeans.

"Lift your feet," he asked.

I watched him as he undressed me with so much care. I took my shirt off, making me the one who was fully naked this time.

Noah swallowed my cock to the back of his throat. His hands gripped the backs of my legs, pushing me into him.

"So good, Noah," I gasped. "You love sucking my cock, don't you?"

When he moaned, the vibrations from his throat traveled all the way to my spine. Fuck, I shouldn't be so close. This wasn't about me.

I already knew this wouldn't be the last time we'd be together, so I could take my time and make it all about him.

I pulled my cock out of his mouth, rubbing my leaking head over his lips. His tongue followed the trail, licking every bit of my salty precum.

"On your feet," I commanded.

He groaned, pushing his eyebrows close together.

"As much as I'd love to come down your throat or all over your face, I'm not thirty anymore, Noah. You're going to do exactly as I say so I can give you what you need. Right?"

"Yes." He sprung to his feet.

"Remove your clothes and get over to the window. Face the desk, hands on top. Legs spread wide."

I hadn't finished before his shirt flew across the room. His jeans and socks followed. He must have kicked his shoes off when he jumped me.

He assumed the position. I inhaled a deep breath at the sight in front of me.

"Look at you, Noah." I bridged the gap between us and ran my hand down the middle of his back. "You can't wait to have me inside you again, can you?"

"No."

I leaned against him, pushing my dick between his thighs. "Can you feel how hard I am for you?"

His breath caught in his throat. "Yes."

I planted open-mouth kisses all over his shoulders, neck, and behind his ears, relishing in the sounds he made as I sucked until there were small marks all over his skin.

Even with bare touches, he was already taking himself into that space where only pleasure mattered. I quickly applied some lube to my dick and pushed it between his thighs again. This time, it glided in easier.

"Look outside the window. What do you see?" I asked, desperately holding on to my control.

"There's…a flock of ducks by the pond."

I pulled back and pushed again, knowing I would hit that spot between his hole and his balls.

He gasped.

"What else, Noah?"

He pushed back against me, his head falling forward. I gripped his hair and pulled his head back up, exposing his throat.

I wrapped my hand around it, pressing just enough to feel each gasp as I thrust against him.

"Noah."

"A couple," he said quickly. "They're walking and holding hands."

"Do you think they're on a vacation? Maybe a honeymoon?"

"I don't know. Please, Lior…"

"Do you think he fucks her like I'm about to fuck you?"

He closed his eyes, swallowing a breath. With my free hand, I managed to get some more lube out of the bottle to cover his hole. I pressed a single finger inside him.

"Yes," he gasped. "No…no, you're going to do it better. Fuck…"

I pushed a second finger inside him.

"Tell me, Noah, do you think she's begged for his cock until he filled her up. All. The. Way." I pressed down on his prostate with each punctuated word.

"Lior!"

"You're not ready yet, Noah."

"Fuck, I am!"

I chuckled in his ear, getting the third finger ready. "Who's in charge here?"

"Oh god. You. You're in charge."

"Then tell me. What do you see?"

"She can't take his eyes off him. She wants more. She can't get enough. He's staring back like he can see through her clothes. This walk is a waste of time when they could be fucking right now."

I laughed. "Is that what you think? This is a waste of time?"

My three fingers were doing a good job of opening him for me. When I got inside him, I wasn't going to be gentle or take my time. He was going to soar.

"No. Lior, please, I need you."

"Relax, Noah. We have time."

"Time? You've been edging me for months. It's fucking time."

I licked a path up his neck, tasting the sweat and shower

soap on his skin. "I've been edging you? I'm not the one who walks around my house or your apartment in nothing but underwear and a semi."

"What do you think happens when you come back from your run in those criminal gray sweatpants, and the first thing you do is take your sweaty T-shirt off?"

"I have a shower?"

"No, Lior. *We* have a shower because I have to leave whatever I'm doing to go give myself some relief if I don't want to have a painful erection all day. And you know what happens after?" he asked between gritted teeth as I continued to fuck him with my fingers.

"Tell me."

"It doesn't go away. There must be a connection from my brain directly to my dick. I think *Lior*, and it just pops a boner."

"Sounds inconvenient."

"The other day, I was in a meeting, and Lex mentioned something you'd said a few weeks ago. Bam. Boner."

I chuckled, but the joke was on me when he clenched his hole and pushed his ass onto my fingers. I needed to regain control of the situation before he found his own relief.

"Keep your eyes on them, Noah. Do you think they'll look up and see us like this? See your half-lidded eyes? The lust on your face?"

"Yes." His breath was becoming shallower as he got closer to orgasm. I pulled my fingers out, massaging his rim.

I turned him around and pushed his ass onto the desk, lifted his legs up around my waist, and aligned my cock with his hole.

In a single thrust, I filled him as deep as my cock would let me.

25

NOAH

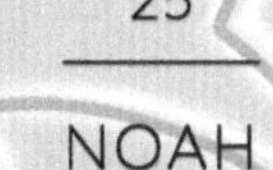

I LET OUT a shuddering breath as Lior sank into me, filling me up. It shouldn't feel this good, but I couldn't think of anything else that took my breath away like this.

He groaned, "Noah," as he pulled out and thrust back inside me again.

My cock leaked onto my stomach, leaving a trail of precum.

"It's so good. Please don't stop."

"I don't intend to. This is it." His voice was gravelly and thick with need. He needed me as much as I needed him.

"Do it."

My eyes fixed on the point where his cock disappeared into my ass. It was a beautiful sight, and combined with the feeling of fullness and the relentless pace, it caused shivers all over my body.

"What have you done to me, Noah? I can't get enough of you, of your body, your mind…"

I felt the same way, but I was too scared to voice it, so I cradled the back of his neck and pulled him into a kiss.

Some things were better shown, not told.

He took hungry possession of my mouth, his tongue laving over mine in a sensual but demanding dance.

My ass burned from his thickness. The desk banged against the wall under the windowsill. There was no way people walking on the path outside below our window wouldn't know exactly what was happening in here.

"Argh…I need…"

"What do you need, baby?" he asked, his deep voice going straight to my heart, wrapping me in a warm blanket. "I'll do anything, Noah. Anything."

"I want you to fuck me so everyone knows I belong to you. Make me come, Lior. Make me fly."

Our eyes met. His deep, dark orbs were so full of passion.

He didn't answer my plea, but he gave it to me anyway.

Harder. Faster. Deeper.

All I could feel was him. My husband. So I chanted his name repeatedly until he fucked my orgasm out of me. My body shook uncontrollably until I wasn't myself anymore.

My eyes caught a mirror in the room I hadn't noticed before. Even though I wanted to close them, to pass out from the pleasure, I couldn't.

The mirror offered a view of Lior's back as he plundered my ass, holding on to the control I'd thrust onto him.

"I want to see you let go," I whispered.

With my permission, he thrust into me a few more times before I saw the muscles on his back clench as he let go and filled me with his cum.

I didn't think it was possible to feel any more pleasure than the high of an orgasm, but watching Lior's body release, his teeth bite his bottom lip as he came, his eyes closing as he filled me up? It was heaven.

He rested his forehead on mine, breathing heavily.

When he opened his eyes again, I was afraid of what I

would see there, so I closed mine. I raised my head for a kiss, this time a lot gentler and less frantic.

"Fuck, Lior. If married sex is like this, I want to speak to the manager. Why haven't we been doing this the whole time?"

He let out a stilted laugh but didn't reply. Instead, he placed his hands under my ass and, with his cock still inside me, walked us to the bathroom.

I felt the loss as his softening erection slipped out of me.

Was it weird that I wanted to plug my butt so I could keep his release inside me for the rest of the day?

Yeah, it was weird and gross.

He turned the faucet for the hot water in the shower, and we stepped inside.

"Ooh, I get aftercare too. Nice."

I wanted to tell myself to shut up, but I didn't know what to do now that it was all over. A shiver ran through me, and not a nice one.

Was this a one-off? Now that we'd both relieved of all the pent-up sexual energy that had bubbled between us, would he suggest we go back to not having sex?

"You're thinking way too hard about something, Noah. Don't."

He tempered the hot water with cold and pushed us under the spray.

"Noah Spencer doesn't think. He does," I joked.

"Don't do that to yourself." He grabbed the small bottle of hotel shampoo and drizzled it into his hand, lathering it before applying it to my hair.

I closed my eyes as he massaged my scalp. If I hadn't just had the most intense orgasm of my entire life, my dick would have rallied up for more.

"Can you do me a favor?" Lior asked.

"What?"

"Can you use me?"

I looked up at him. His eyes were on my head where his hands worked their magic. He massaged my scalp, my neck, and my shoulders.

Something bubbled inside me, getting stuck in my throat.

"I don't know what you mean."

"I'm here for you, Noah. All the things you're feeling inside? You can let them out. I'll catch them for you."

Damn the man. Now that permission had been granted, a well opened and my eyes flooded with tears. I held on to him as he let me sob all over his chest.

I couldn't even bring myself to joke about his sexy salt-and-pepper chest hair, his tight abs, or the *V* that led to the most beautiful dick I'd ever seen, even soft.

By the time my crying subsided, he was wrapping me in a fluffy towel. Suddenly, I felt exhausted.

He took me over to the bed and lifted the covers.

"Sit up. Let me grab you some food, and then we can take a nap."

I nodded.

Lior opened a thermos and poured fresh coffee into two mugs. He put one on my bedside table and one on his side. Then, he filled a tray with a few pastries and some fruit.

When he came back to the bed, he sat with his back against the headboard and positioned me between his legs with my back to his chest.

"I don't know what to say right now."

"You don't need to say anything. Let me just look after you."

I so desperately wanted to let him do that, but I was also afraid I would become reliant on it and terrified of what I was about to ask of him.

"I need to tell you something I've never told anyone," I said.

He grabbed a strawberry and brought it up to my mouth. I took a bite of half of it, and he had the rest.

It was sweet and juicy and perfect for a post-sex cuddling and feeding session. Shame I was going to ruin it all.

"You can tell me anything. You know that."

"I wasn't always the person my family thinks I am." I paused, waiting for Lior to ask me what person that was, but he just grabbed a piece of mango and brought it to my lips.

I ate the mango and then took a sip of coffee, letting the caffeine filter through my brain.

"I fell in love in college. She was beautiful, smart, funny, and she had two sisters. I used to think she was the other part of me, down to her family setup. I fell so quickly that I didn't have time to question it. It just felt good."

Lior remained quiet but continued feeding me pieces of fruit before breaking a cinnamon roll into pieces and feeding me those too.

I waited for him to stop me and tell me he didn't need to know this story, but he never opened his mouth other than to eat or sip his coffee.

I sighed. "I decided to propose to her just before a road trip we'd planned for the summer. She said yes. I was looking forward to the rest of our lives together. I could see it so clearly. My mom and dad holding their first grandchild, my grandmother helping us pick a name, my brothers being, well, bro uncles." I laughed. "It would have been perfect."

I closed my eyes when Lior peppered my neck and shoulders with small kisses.

"It turned out she'd been seeing another guy while she was with me. She decided she wasn't ready to get married and left with him on *our* road trip. At least she had the decency to only take her half of the money we'd saved, but she may as well have taken it all alongside my heart."

Lior put the breakfast tray on the bedside table and snuggled back, wrapping his arms around my waist.

I turned to him, but all he did was kiss me gently before settling back against the headboard.

"I put the money away for the agency start-up capital and spent the summer working. Every day, I'd work twelve or fourteen hours, and in the evening, I'd go out. I didn't want to spend money, so I'd go to a bar and find someone to hook up with before I had a chance to get a drink. It became my new normal. I didn't have a heart to lose, so I had fun instead."

"Do you think that's all anyone sees in you?"

"That's all there is."

He cradled my cheek and turned me to face him. "It's all you let them see, Noah. But it's not all there is because if that's the case, how do you explain what I see?"

I swallowed dry. "What do you see?"

"I see someone who's incredibly generous with his time. Someone who loves his family and friends, someone who isn't afraid to put himself out there. You're smart and funny and so fucking gorgeous, Noah. That's what I see."

That lump in my throat threatened to make a return, but I swallowed it. "Can I ask you something?"

"Sure."

"Would you…would you pretend you're in love with me so my family believes we're…you know…real?"

26

———

LIOR

Pretend had never before sounded like such a dirty word as it did out of Noah's lips.

How many layers could a single word have?

Could I pretend to pretend I was in love with my husband? I guessed that made it a two-layer word because I didn't have to pretend to feel something I already felt. I was in love with Noah. No pretending needed.

"It's okay, you don't have to do it," he interjected before I could say anything.

I claimed his lips in a gentle kiss. "Noah, I will do anything for you, you hear me? Anything." And it was as much as I could confess to.

His eyes searched mine, but I was too scared they'd tell the truth, so I slid us down the bed. "Let's have a nap, you have to be exhausted."

"I am," he said, yawning.

"I'll even let you be the little spoon."

He turned his back against me and pushed back until his ass cuddled against my front.

Do not get an erection now, Lior, I thought to myself. Not

197

that it was likely my poor dick would rally so quickly, but I was naked and so was Noah. We'd had sex twice, but this was the first time we were both naked in bed.

He already had power over so much of me that I couldn't be sure he also wouldn't get my dick to harden on demand.

"Hey, Lior?"

"Hmm?"

"Is sex on the table for us now? It's just…my ass really likes your dick."

Dammit-fuck-goblins.

He chuckled as he pushed back into my erection. "I take that as a yes."

I sighed. "Okay, I agree we can add this new clause to our agreement. I'm not immune to you, Noah. The things I want to do to you should probably be illegal."

"I'll bail you out."

"Ever the romantic, huh?"

"You know it." He yawned again.

After a moment of silence, I heard his cute snores. I focused on his breathing until sleep took me too.

I jumped awake to a loud thumping on the door.

"What the fuck?"

Noah had turned around in his sleep to face me. His erection pressed against mine as he woke up and moved. Our dicks rubbed together, making me hiss.

"What's that noise?"

"Noah Spencer, open the door or else."

I recognized it as Lex's voice.

Noah groaned.

"What's happening?"

He sat up. "My guess is they're coming to beat our asses, or they decided to initiate you."

I coughed. "I'm sorry, what?"

He got up from the bed and walked to the door.

"What are you doing?"

"You better cover up, dear husband," he said.

I sat up and pulled the blankets over my privates. While my dick had gone down from the prospect of seeing Noah's siblings while naked, his was still fully erect.

He opened the door and turned around, coming back to bed but not before giving his two brothers, Emery, and River a good eyeful of his junk.

"Ew, dude," River complained, putting his hand over his eyes.

Noah covered himself, leaning against me under the sheets. "What did you think you were going to find here? Us braiding each other's hair? Painting toenails?"

"Why does it smell like sex in here?" Adam grumbled.

Lex, Emery, and River stared at him.

"Oh…oh! Ew. I'm leaving."

River grabbed Adam's arm to stop him.

Lex raised his hand. "I'm just going to put this out there. Lior, I'm glad my working relationship with the museum is through Charlie. Thanks for the chest visual, but—"

"It is a nice chest, right?" Emery asked.

Lex stared at his fiancé, his mouth hanging open before he recovered. "Anyway. I'm happy to work with Charlie, and this won't change our relationship with VSE. That's all."

"And you better get dressed because we have a game of soccer outside in half an hour," River said.

"Soccer?" I asked.

Adam sneered. "Yeah, it's a friendly game, but the stakes are high. We all had to put some money into it. There will be bets, and the winning team gets to pick the charity the money goes to. Don't worry. We can run you through the rules of the game quickly so you won't get lost."

"Sure, thanks."

They turned to leave, but then Adam turned back

around. "I'm still mad as fuck at what you've done, but…" He waved at our covered junk. "I guess I can try to get my head around it. Just apologize to Victoria and mean it."

"Of course," Noah said straight away. "I'll speak to her. Adam, I really didn't mean for it all to come out like this."

Adam stared at Noah, but I couldn't read him.

"Just get dressed. I can't wait to kick your ass at soccer."

When they closed the door behind them, Noah straddled me, looking down at our cocks between us. He licked his lips suggestively.

"No," I said, placing a finger under his chin for him to look at my face. "We're in hot water with your family. We're getting dressed, and then we're going to kick your brother's ass on the soccer field."

He raised his brows. "You're confident."

I kissed the tip of his nose. "Baby, you're not the only one with European blood in your veins. I actually went to school in Europe and played soccer for eight years throughout high school."

He laughed and jumped off my lap. "Then what are we waiting for? We have a game to win and money to raise for the Star Finders Youth Network."

The bride's and groom's families were all under a gazebo set up with tables, chairs, and drinks. There were more people than I expected.

All eyes were on us as we approached.

Noah's mom walked right over to us. "We still need to talk, Noah James Spencer, but I don't want to ruin your brother's weekend. Victoria has put a lot of work into organizing it, and she deserves to have a good time."

Noah gave his mom a kiss on her cheek. "I'm so sorry, Mãe. I know I messed up, but please don't be mad at me. I can fix it."

"I'm not mad, Noah, estou desapontada."

"It says something when you can upset your mother in two languages," Noah said, and I groaned. He really did know how to poke a bear.

"Mrs. Spencer," I said, holding my hand out. She took it with hesitance. "I'm also very sorry about the current situation. We…got carried away and didn't think of the consequences. I promise I have the best intentions with your son. I just want to make him happy." I turned my gaze to Noah and smiled. I wasn't lying there. "I hope we have a chance to get to know each other, and I'd love to introduce you to my mother at some point."

"I would very much love that. Lior, is it?"

I nodded.

"How about your father?"

Noah squeezed my hand and spoke for me when my throat seized at the unexpected question.

"Mom, Lior's dad passed away recently."

"Oh dear. I'm so sorry to hear that," she said. Her eyes were honest and full of sympathy.

"Thank you. That means a lot."

"Hey, are you coming or what?" Lex shouted, throwing the soccer ball in our direction. I caught it with my chest and let it fall to my feet, where I passed it back and forth a few times and then kicked it to Lex.

"I'm on his team," River shouted.

"Come on, husband. Let's go kick some Spencer ass," Noah said, running toward the grass field.

I could swear I heard his mom gush.

"Does that mean I get to kick *your* ass?" I teased when I caught up with him.

"In sickness and in health, in family feuds and friendly soccer games with asshole brothers."

I laughed. "Funny, I don't remember that being in the vows."

"I've just added it."

He squealed when I grabbed him by the waist and twirled him around. His laughter made everything better.

"What else are you going to add to it?"

He held on to me, wrapping his arms around my shoulders. "In the bathroom or the hallway, in the living room or on the kitchen table, until death do us part."

I snorted.

"Come on, love birds. We have some ass to kick." River and Adam flipped a coin to pick their side of the field.

Our team was me, Noah, River, Victoria's sister Ellie, and their cousin, Thatcher, who they called Meatball.

The opposite team was Lex, Emery, Adam, their cousin Harrison, and his husband, Fletcher.

"You heard him." I slapped his ass. He ran over to the other side of the field, throwing me a smile over his shoulder.

I glanced at the sidelines, particularly at Noah's family and Victoria.

While his mom was smiling and chatting to her husband, Victoria had a sour expression. Even when Adam waved at her.

27

NOAH

CONSIDERING she'd been the one to put together the schedule of events, Victoria couldn't have looked more disinterested in the soccer tournament.

She didn't seem the type to get involved in group sports unless it was a girls' group massage while sipping champagne.

Okay, I was probably being a little unfair to her, but why go to the trouble of doing something if you weren't going to enjoy it?

Cada um por si, as my grandmother would say. Each to their own.

My eight-year-old cousin, Megan, and her stepbrother, George, blew the whistles.

"Players to the field," George shouted, and Megan followed with, "Please."

George grumbled. "Please."

"Just because we're in charge doesn't mean we can't be polite," she said.

I glanced at my cousin Harrison and his husband, Fletcher. Both were trying to suppress their smiles.

Meatball and Adam flipped a coin to see who kicks off the game.

"Hey, Spencer, are we going to kick some ass, or are we going to kick some ass? I'm still salty Victoria wouldn't let me bring a plus two," Ellie said, jogging past me. "I should have done a Noah and brought Libby and Ten anyway."

I laughed. "It would have taken some heat off my back."

"Doubt it. Not unless Bridezilla caught us making out in the hotel lobby."

I hissed. "I bet that'd be hot."

She rolled her eyes to the back of her head. "You have no idea. Libby and Ten are…" She bit her lip.

A tap on my ass made me jump. "Hey, don't you get any ideas. I'm not sharing you."

I caught Lior before he could run away from me. "I swear to God, husband. If you make me pop a boner in these shorts, I'll never let you get anywhere near my ass."

He laughed as he jogged to his spot. "Liar."

With all of us in position, George and Megan distributed armbands. We were the blue team, and Adam's team was red.

The early afternoon sun was high in the sky. A bead of sweat ran down my forehead, and we hadn't even started playing.

"Are you ready?" the kids shouted excitedly.

"Yeah," we all shouted back.

They blew their whistles, and the game started.

Adam passed the ball to Fletcher, who maneuvered it with precision, passing it back and forth to Emery, trying to find a gap in our defense.

"You're going down, Spencer," Fletcher said between gritted teeth. "I've got my eye on that prize."

I tried to defend the best I could, but soccer wasn't my sport, so I fought back the way I knew best.

"Did you borrow those shorts from your kid?"

"Yep, my husband likes staring at my ass. Sue me," he said without skipping a beat.

I glanced at Harrison, who was staring at Fletcher's ass.

"Sucker." The bastard saw my distraction and got past me.

Thankfully, the dynamic duo that was River and Lior countered with their seamless coordination, intercepting the ball and saving Ellie from having to defend a shot.

If I didn't know better, I'd have thought River and Lior spent hours playing soccer together.

As the game progressed, both teams showcased a great lack of skill but willingness to take a fall, as demonstrated mostly by my two left feet. Hand sports were more my thing.

"Baby, I'm going to have to carry you up to the room if you can't stay upright," Lior said.

"The fucking ball is round," I complained. "And I'm better with my hands."

George and Megan whistled at the halfway point.

"Is anyone else confused by the two-whistle situation here?" Emery asked. "I'm not sure if I've done something wrong or if I should do my cheerleading routine."

"Baby, you're showing me your cheerleading routine later," Lex said, draping his arms over Emery's shoulders.

"Keep it in your pants," Adam said.

Did I detect some tension from Adam? What was his problem?

Our loyal spectators lined the makeshift sidelines, their cheers and encouragement adding to the fun. Even my grandma was shouting for us, picking one team to cheer for at a time.

The only person not joining the fun was Victoria, who'd moved to a lounger, her phone in one hand and a cocktail in the other. Adam bypassed the drinks table and went to sit with her.

"Well done, boys and girl," Mom said cheerfully. "I never knew my babies were so talented."

I snorted. "I've always been good at going from vertical to horizontal in no time, as I demonstrated to my husband five minutes after we met." It was a joke, but my mom, ever used to my crude teasing but rarely accepting it, cuffed my head.

Lior grabbed my waist from the back and whispered in my ear, "If I remember correctly, we remained vertical throughout."

I turned around in his hold. "We better sit down for this break if we don't want to scare the children in the second half of this game."

He grabbed two glasses of soda, and we took one of the free loungers. I sat against his chest, with my knees pulled up to my chest.

"This is fun," he said.

"Maybe for you, Ronaldo. Some of us are simply trying to make it with all our teeth in place." I shifted to face him sideways. "Would you stay married to me if I lost all my front teeth in the tragedy that is this game?"

He brought his hand up to his beard, stroking it. "Hmm, I don't know. You'd probably talk funny, which could be entertaining. I'm not interested in public life so that's that. Oh, blowjobs could be awesome. Yeah, I'd keep you."

"I want a divorce. I don't feel respected in this relationship," I grumbled like I meant it.

He tightened his hold around me and said in a low voice, "Would you rather I said it doesn't matter what you look like, I'd still want you?"

I rested my head in the crook of his neck. Did I want him to say that? Yes, I did, but also not.

Every time he was sweet to me, it was the greatest thing ever, but it also reminded me this was temporary. A year at most, and I didn't know if it would be long enough to make him fall for me for real.

At least I could be thankful that sex between us was on now.

Not that I was in any way inclined to have sex with anyone else right now, but not having any at all would've been a total mood-buster.

Our two little whistle masters called us for the second half of the game.

The score was tied, so we still had everything to play for.

We gathered around. Meatball looked at all of us. "I hear the other team wants to donate the winning fee to an animal sanctuary in Chester Falls."

"Awww," Ellie cooed.

"Focus, Eleanor," I said, snapping my fingers. "There's a local charity to us that I think should get the money."

"What's that?" River asked.

"The Star Finders Youth Network. They help out kids in the system, giving them a community—"

"Yes," River interrupted. "I want to help them."

Lior held my hand and squeezed it gently. "If we win, I'll match the value of what's been raised."

"I'll do the same," River said. "I've been looking for a charity to support, but with the work at the restaurant, I haven't had time. I'd love to know more about this one."

"Let's do it," I said.

We high-fived and returned to the game with renewed energy and a purpose.

The start of the second half was pretty much like the first. I lost my footing twice, ending up on the grass with a scuffed knee and a rapidly growing bruise.

Ellie shouted from her position as our goalie, and Meatball tried his best, but with me aiding him on the defense, a dream team we were not.

In a pivotal moment, Lior, our team's unofficial captain, intercepted a pass intended for Emery. With a quick glance, he found River open on the left. The pass was perfect, and Lior, with a burst of speed, broke away from his marker.

I held my breath. He was going to score. I just knew it. Lior made his move, sending a powerful shot toward the net.

Harrison, the red team's goalkeeper, leaped with an outstretched hand, but the ball was just beyond his reach. It hit the back of the net with a satisfying thud.

Everyone cheered. Our team came together in a group hug.

Our young referees went to their parents. From the gesticulating, I couldn't be sure if they were telling Harrison and Fletcher to do better or trying to comfort them.

Those kids were adorable. The last time I'd seen Harrison, Megan was only three, and they were still living in Boston. So much had changed since.

The game resumed, but the score remained the same. When our referees whistled the end of my torture, we all gathered to celebrate the win for our chosen charity. In the end, with everyone's matched donations, we decided to split the money between the Star Finders Youth Network and the Chester Falls Animal Sanctuary.

Adam clapped me on the back, "That was one hell of a game. We'll get you next time," he said with a smile that reached his eyes.

I returned the gesture. "Looking forward to it, little bro. You guys gave us a run for our money."

"Meh, we underestimated Lior. Are you sure he's in his forties?"

The Noah my brothers knew would have made a crude joke, but after everything that had happened this morning, I was just thankful my brother seemed to have gotten over the shock. Shame that the same couldn't be said for his bride.

"Hey, is everything okay with Victoria? I will apologize as soon as I can have a moment with her."

"I appreciate that. Sports aren't her thing, but she knew with so many guys around, she needed to get us to expend some energy. I sure could do with a nap now."

"Same, dude. Same."

I was relieved that Adam seemed to be a little calmer about things. I met Lior's gaze and gave him an imperceptible nod. Would he be disappointed to know how quickly I'd put the things I'd heard from my brother behind me?

Did it make me weak? I hated fighting with my brothers, and even through the hurt feelings, I couldn't blame Adam. I was the one who lied. About everything.

While we'd been playing the second half of the game, the hotel staff had put together a table with light snacks.

We filled up and rehydrated before, one by one, everyone retreated to their rooms.

When we got to our room, Lior practically dragged me to the bathroom, ripping my sweaty clothes off.

"I love it when my husband goes all caveman on me."

He pushed me against the shower wall. The cold tiles made me hiss.

"I love it when you call me husband." His deep gravelly voice went straight to my dick.

"Is that so...*husband?*" I ran my hands up his chest, feeling the hairs under my fingers. Lior was the fucking sexiest man I'd ever seen.

His nipples peaked under my touch. His breath caught and his eyes darkened. He licked his lips and sank to his knees.

As he engulfed my dick in his mouth, hollowing his cheeks as he sucked me to the back of his throat, my mind went blank.

All I could do was stand there and take it. I spilled into Lior's throat a moment later.

He stood up and kissed me. I moaned as I tasted myself in his kiss.

"My turn."

He stopped me from going down. "Save it for later."

"Hmm, will we make it to the bed this time?"

He chuckled, sucking a mark on my neck. "We'll see."

28

LIOR

NOAH WAS RELAXED throughout dinner with his family. The tension from this morning seemed to have vanished, which was a relief.

There were still some looks thrown our way from Victoria's family, but it was more important to me that Noah's family accepted me as his husband. And even better, that they'd forgive him for keeping it a secret.

Ellie sat next to us, with Emery and Lex.

She couldn't be more different from Victoria. With her colored hair and bright clothes—Emery mentioned she made them herself—she was a ray of sunshine.

The kids also loved her, asking her a bunch of questions about all kinds of things, which meant our table was a rotation of people coming over to chat. Even Adam stopped by for a bit while he was doing the table rounds and being attentive to Victoria's family.

"I'm going to send your cousin an invoice," Ellie said when Megan and George left us for the third time after drawing pictures of Ellie's dress and asking her to pick the best.

Emery rolled his eyes at his best friend.

"What for?" Noah asked.

"For having to engage with little terrorists while off duty."

"She's an elementary school teacher," Emery said for my benefit. "I don't know why she moans so much when I caught her lesson planning in the bar earlier."

"Snitch."

"Who's up for hitting the local bar?" Adam asked when he returned. "With all due respect, Ellie, your family is hard work. I need a drink."

"Why do you think I'm sitting with *your* family? No one told you to pick the wrong sister, mister."

Adam laughed. "You'd break me by the third date."

She nodded smugly. "You wouldn't last that long."

"Hey, I'm sorry Victoria was a bit difficult about you bringing someone. I get why you didn't want to have to choose. You know how it is in these situations. The groom doesn't get an opinion."

Her smile had an undertone of resignation. It reminded me of Noah in all the times he thought he wasn't the person his family wished he was.

I was starting to see that he was so wrong. Not that he'd believe me if I told him.

"I called a cab," River said, joining us. "I don't want to think about your parents' restaurant catching fire while I'm not there, so please, let's get some drinks in me."

"I'm not drinking, so if anyone wants a lift with us, be my guest," I said since Meatball had joined us. Harrison and Fletcher had already gone up to their suite with the kids, much to their arguing about it being a party and that granted a later bedtime.

Ever since I'd sucked Noah off in the shower earlier, I'd been counting the minutes until I could be inside him again.

But I'd happily admit that going out with Noah and his brothers and being free to put my hands on him gave me ideas.

Twenty-four hours ago, we'd been skirting around each other, knowing we wanted something we couldn't have.

Now? I was addicted.

"I just need to pop up to the room quickly, and then I'll be ready to go," Noah said.

By the time we arrived at the bar, River and Adam were already finishing their first drink. I got a round of drinks for everyone but kept mine a soda, so I didn't have to worry about driving back to the vineyard.

"River, look. That bartender you were eyeing yesterday is here," Adam said, elbowing his friend.

"I wasn't eyeing him."

"Oh, come on. When was the last time you dated someone?"

River frowned. "Can we not have this conversation here?"

"Sorry, I didn't mean to embarrass you," Adam replied.

"Oh, trouble in paradise," Noah joked.

River walked up to the bar and sat on a stool. The bartender Adam had pointed at zeroed in on River straight away. The guy was definitely interested.

"I'm going to talk to him," Adam said.

"Sit down. You're not cockblocking him on my watch," Noah said, holding Adam's arm and pushing him down on his seat.

Adam sulked. He finished his drink and then turned his attention to Victoria. "Babe, get off your phone," he said, sounding frustrated.

"I'm working, Adam. Someone needs to make sure things get done."

"What are you doing?"

"Writing my vows."

"In a packed bar?" He narrowed his brows.

"The wedding is in three months. Have you written yours yet?"

"No!" he screeched. "I'm in a bar."

He seemed to become aware they weren't alone when he grabbed his beer and brought it to his lips. When he realized he'd already finished it, he went to the bar. I noticed he made sure to stay clear of River but didn't take his eyes off him.

He came back with a round of drinks for everyone.

"I know!" he shouted. "We never got to hear Noah and Lior's vows because, you know, we weren't there." He pointed at Noah. "You, big brother, robbed me of seeing you get all smooshy over someone else, so I want you to do it now."

I hadn't engaged with Adam as much as I had with Lex, so it was hard to tell if he was challenging us or being genuine.

"I'm sorry, what now?" Noah almost spit out his beer.

"Yes. Do your vow…thingy."

Noah looked at me with panic in his eyes.

"Adam, it's not the right place," I said.

"It's perfect," he replied. "Most of us won't remember this in the morning anyway, but I want to hear them."

I tried to think of something to change the subject, but everyone else was looking at us expectantly. I held Noah's hand and brought it to my lips.

Shrugging my shoulders, I stared into his big blue eyes and started, "Noah, you came into my life with unmatched confidence, refusing to take no for an answer. I gave in once, but even then, I knew I'd give in again and again. When you asked me to marry you, I thought you were joking, but that turned out to be just another one of those times when you chase life, guns blazing, fearless. You are the most selfless, caring, and generous man I've ever met. When I thought I was going to spend the rest of my life alone, bitter and wondering why I couldn't find someone on my level, you came, and you stayed. I am so proud to call you my husband, now and forever."

My heart thumped. Noah's eyes became red with unshed tears. This had not been the plan. Our vows had been personal, but they hadn't told the whole story because our story had barely started. Now, I couldn't look into his eyes and repeat them. Not when there was so much more between us.

He took a deep breath and stroked my beard.

"Lior, my sexy silver fox."

"You did not say that," Adam said, interrupting his brother.

Noah smiled but didn't take his eyes off mine. "The moment I laid eyes on you in that bar, I knew you were different. Before you even spoke a word to me, I knew you'd change me. Getting to know you has been one of the best adventures of my life. With you, I can be myself because you see through my bullshit. And while I know you find it adorable, I also know that when I take it too far, you're there to guide me back to myself. If I'd placed an order for my ideal partner, I wouldn't have gotten you because, before I met you, I didn't know someone like you could exist in my world. Certainly not for me to keep. I hope you're comfortable because I'm not giving you up. Ever."

Our mouths met in a kiss that echoed every single word we'd just said to each other.

Around us, a loud cheer sounded. We smiled into the kiss.

My heart was so big I wasn't sure how it was still contained within my ribcage because Noah hadn't just told me what was in his heart. He'd said it aloud in front of the people he cared about the most.

I stood. "If you'll excuse me, I need a moment outside with my husband."

Noah followed me, holding my hand as we navigated the crowd in the bar. I spotted the sign for the restrooms. Someone went into the men's room, so I took us into the all-gender single stall.

"What are we doing here?" he asked, his expression turning heated.

"I think you know." I flipped the lock shut and turned him around so his face was to the door. I pulled his jeans down, exposing his ass. "You make me so fucking horny all the time, Noah. But when you open your mouth, you take it to a new level. I need to be inside you so fucking bad. Please tell me I can." I ran my hands under his shirt, feeling for his nipples and pinching them into peaks.

"I thought you were too old for restroom hookups," he said, releasing a sharp breath.

"Desperate times call for desperate measures."

"And you're desperate?"

I growled in his ear. "You have no idea, dear husband."

He pushed his ass into my crotch. I took my dick out and stroked it, rubbing the head against his skin and leaving a trail of precum.

"You look so good like this." I took a small packet of lube I had in my wallet and coated my cock. When I ran my finger down his crack, I found an unexpected…

"Surprise…" he sang.

"Am I ever going to not be amazed by you, Noah Spencer?"

He chuckled, but it turned into a moan when I moved the butt plug inside him, pressing against his prostate.

"Where did you get this?"

"I've been wearing it occasionally because you drive me

insane with need. Pretending it's you inside me when I cum is my favorite fantasy."

He gasped when I moved the plug. "This is the reason you went up to the room before we came here?"

He nodded, his eyes already glazed over with the need to come.

"This is going to be quick and dirty, baby," I rasped in his ear.

"How dirty?"

"I'm going to fuck you until I come, and then I'm going to put the plug back in you. Do not come, you hear me?"

I removed the plug and, in one go, stuffed him full again with my cock.

"Lior."

"I'm serious, Noah. Do not come right now."

"Fuck."

He hissed as I fucked him right against the door. The pent-up sexual energy from the blowjob earlier, the words he'd just said to me in his mock vows, and knowing that he'd been wearing a plug to get ready for me were enough to make my dick hard enough to pound nails.

The heat and tightness of his channel, his moans, and the smell of his cologne did the job of getting me ready to blow.

"I'm so close, baby."

"Do it, Lior. Fill me with your cum. I want to wear you for the rest of the night."

I pumped into him three more times, and then I was coming like I hadn't orgasmed in a week. I replaced my cock with the butt plug sooner than I wanted to leave his body.

"That was the dirtiest, best fucking thing I've ever done in my life." He turned around and kissed me, consuming my mouth, tasting me, and sucking hard enough that my lips would be bloodshot for sure.

We laughed as we pulled ourselves together. Our eyes met in a complicit gaze.

I couldn't help stealing one last kiss before I opened the restroom door slowly. The coast was clear, so we walked out.

We were barely clear from being caught when Victoria turned into the hallway. Her face was red, but it was hard to tell if she was upset, blushing, or angry.

"Hi, Victoria. Are you okay?" Noah asked.

She looked around. There was no one else in the hallway leading to the restrooms. "I'm glad I've caught you both."

"Actually," Noah said, "I was hoping to catch you anyway to apologize."

"Save it."

I didn't like her tone, especially the way she clearly wasn't interested in hearing Noah.

"How can we help? If you're worried about things getting out of hand out there, we can make sure everyone gets back to the vineyard in one piece," I said, hoping my helpfulness went somewhat toward reducing her permanent frown.

"Thank you. I am more than capable of controlling my future husband."

Noah tensed next to me so I placed my hand on the small of his back to settle him.

"Then what can we do for you?" Noah asked.

"You can start by toning this"—she waved in our general direction—"down. I know you're faking it, although, for the life of me, I don't understand why. Maybe you're going through a rebellious phase or something. I don't know and don't care. You ruined the weekend I've worked so hard to organize. If you ruin my wedding, I swear to everything holy, I will end you."

She plastered the fakest smile I'd ever seen on her face and turned around.

Noah shook beside me.

"Hey. You okay?" I cradled his face, caressing his cheek.

His expression went from red-hot murderous to amused.

"It's funny she's calling us out as fake when I have a bucketful of your cum in my ass."

I groaned. "Noah."

"What? Am I lying?"

I sighed.

"How about we go back to the vineyard?" I suggested.

"Let's go. I have a boner to pick with you."

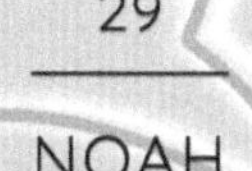

29

NOAH

Married sex was the best thing in the world, I thought as I stretched out in our super comfy bed before turning around and snuggling into Lior's chest.

"I know you're awake," he said, running his fingers through my hair.

"I'm not. Totally sleeping." I pretended to snore.

"That's not how you snore."

I opened my eyes and raised my head to stare at him. "I do not snore."

"Oh yes, you do."

I grabbed a pillow and threw it at him. The audacity! I so did not snore.

My phone lit up with a notification, so I reached for it and got up to go to the bathroom.

"Damn, is it really this late?" We'd missed the hotel's breakfast. Thankfully, there was a brunch before everyone left to get back home.

"Well, someone exhausted all my energy last night, and I'm an old man. This"—he pointed to his naked and drool-worthy chest—"doesn't come easy."

I leaned against the bathroom doorway, staring appreciatively. "You are one fucking sexy silver fox, Lior." I moaned and went into the bathroom.

After washing my hands, I checked the notification on my phone, squealing when I read the news.

When I returned to the room, Lior already had his underwear on. Shame, I would have loved a quickie. Then again, I was getting hungry.

"Good news?" he asked.

"The best. West says the McMartins have come through, and the mayor agreed to lease the old hospital to the foundation. They're getting the paperwork sorted this week and the keys before next weekend."

Lior crossed the room and lifted me off the ground. I wrapped my legs around his waist. The man was strong.

"Well done, Noah. I knew you could do it."

"It was all because of you and your mom. Her tip about the McMartins was invaluable. If I hadn't been at the ball, none of this would have happened."

He shook his head. "You can be in the right place at the right time, but to succeed, you need more. You need charm, perseverance, and passion. You have all of those and more when it comes to helping those kids."

"Thank you," I said, smiling as I stroked his beard. "That means a lot."

He slapped my naked ass. "Now go get dressed so we don't end up missing brunch too." He glanced down at my hard dick pressed against his belly.

"Can we be a teensy weensy bit late?" I gave him my best puppy eyes.

He took a couple of steps back to the couch and sat. I ended up on his lap. His strong hand wrapped around my cock.

"Fuck, yes," I hissed.

An orgasm and a quick shower later, and we were on our way down to the lawn where we'd played soccer yesterday.

Most of the family was there, filling their plates with fresh fruit and pastries.

"Bom dia, Mãe, Avó. Olá, Pai." I greeted my parents and grandmother.

"Bom dia, sweetie. Did you have a nice time last night?"

I raised a brow. Did she really want to know?

"We did. Now, where's the coffee?"

Lior followed me to the food table. I grabbed two plates while he went on coffee duty.

We sat with Lex and Emery, who were deep in conversation with Ellie and Meatball. Adam joined us shortly after.

"I don't know about you guys, but I'm getting too old for this shit," Adam said, dropping onto an empty chair with a single cup of coffee.

"No one told you to get smashed off your ass last night," Lex said. "Where's River?"

Adam shrugged. "My guess is in bed. Maybe in the bartender's bed. He didn't come back with us."

"Go River," I chanted.

"Where's Victoria?" Emery asked. "She wasn't drinking last night."

"She has a meeting with the catering chef. He wasn't supposed to be here this weekend, but he popped in, and she didn't want to miss the chance to talk to him about menus or something. To be honest, I only heard half of what she said and understood even less."

Lex stared at his twin like they weren't even related let alone had shared a womb. "Dude, no wonder she's always annoyed. You're doing nothing for this wedding, and she's picking up your slack."

"In my defense, I keep offering to do stuff, but she doesn't want me to. It's not like I'm forgetful or unreliable.

She knows if she gives me a job, it'll get done. It's her choice to control everything."

"You should do something for her, like take her on a weekend away, just the two of you," I suggested. "I don't know the slightest about planning a wedding—case in point, we got married in Vegas—but for a woman, this is the most important and stressful event of their life. They want it to be perfect and get every detail right. Take her away. Do something romantic."

Adam sipped his coffee, a little color returning to his face.

"You're right. I'll get on it as soon as this hangover leaves the station." He pulled a pretend train horn.

"Change of topic," Lex said, stuffing a piece of fruit in his mouth. "Yesterday's game got me thinking about how we can get more involved in charity work. So far we've worked mainly on helping people in the industry and other startups, but I can see how that's a privileged situation. How about those who really have nothing?"

Lior leaned closer to me and placed his arm over the back of my chair. I glanced at him, and he pointed to my phone.

It took me a moment to realize what he was trying to say.

West and Drew would need all the help they could get to get the foundation headquarters up and running.

"I have an idea." I raised my hand. "I've been volunteering with the Star Finders Youth Network for a while now."

"The one we raised funds for yesterday?" Adam asked.

"Yes. I don't do much, just go play basketball with the kids on Saturday mornings and then we do some coaching. It's fun, and I get a workout out of it too."

"Wait," Lex said. "Is that why you were all sweaty when Adam changed the Spencer Weekly that one time?"

I nodded.

"Why did you let us believe you'd just fallen out of a random stranger's bed?"

I looked at Lior. "That was the day we met."

"So you did get into a stranger's bed." His lips curled into a teasing smile.

"We never got to bed if you remember."

"Ahem…" Adam coughed.

"The truth is that Star Finders is my thing. I know it's stupid, but you two have this connection between you, and I never got it. Having this little secret was my way of having something special too." My face heated as I made the confession. Now that it was out, I knew how stupid it was to not say anything.

Adam and Lex looked at each other. They stood from their chairs and came over to mine. I tried to hold on to Lior when they grabbed me and lifted me, but he let me go.

Worst husband ever.

My brothers dropped me on the grass and wrestled with me, trying to tickle where they knew I was super sensitive.

"You want to be our triplet?" Lex asked, tickling the backs of my knees.

"No, that's River's job," I said, fighting back by holding Adam down.

"You can be our quadruplet. I can already feel the connection," Adam said. "You want to turn vegetarian and eat grass."

He tried to push my face into the grass, but I was stronger and managed to worm out of his hold.

"Boys!" Mom shouted. "I thought you grew out of that a while ago. Don't make me grab my slipper."

We all split apart. "Not the chinelo, Mãezinha. We'll be good."

We doubled over in laughter. I couldn't remember the last time my brothers and I messed around like this.

I'd forgotten we weren't just close. We were tight. Maybe I let myself create that distance. I'd blamed Lex for it because of the time when he was sad that Emery was gone, and I'd blamed Adam because spending time with Victoria had taken him away from us. But I was equally to blame.

And now I had an even bigger secret.

I looked at Lior, who was smiling back at us. That man made me feel so much it wasn't fair.

"What happened?"

We turned to Victoria, who looked like she'd swallowed a rotten piece of meat.

"That's just boys being boys, my dear," Mom said. "You'll have to get used to it if you end up having boys. They run in our family. Twins too."

Victoria's eyes bugged out, and she suddenly looked ill.

"Adam, can I have a word?"

The three of us were still sitting on the grass, so I said under my breath, "Someone's in trouble."

30

LIOR

NOAH

Whatever you're doing this weekend,
cancel it. West and Drew have keys, and
we're going to start clearing the hospital.

LIOR

I had planned on doing you, but since that's
canceled, I guess I could lend a hand.

NOAH

Wait! Don't need to go *that* far. I'm sure
they can cope. West has muscles and Drew
has West.

LIOR

Nope. I'm committed now. Gotta help the
kids.

NOAH

Ugh. Charity sucks.

I LAUGHED AT THE SCREEN, knowing exactly how excited he was to get his hands dirty and help his friends.

He would be handsomely rewarded for his big heart. I'd make sure of it.

I turned in my chair to face the street. From my office, I couldn't see farther than the building on the other side of the street, but knowing Noah was in his office less than a mile away made me want to break the rules and be reckless.

My phone buzzed with a message. I unlocked the screen to find a selfie of him holding his shirt up to show his stomach. His jeans were partly undone, showing a trail of blond hair that disappeared into the waistband of his boxer shorts.

I saved the photo and put the phone away. If I replied, this slippery slope would turn into a slippery slide, and the next thing I knew, I'd be barging into his office to fuck him over his desk.

I didn't even know what his desk looked like, and I was already imagining bending him over it and sinking deep inside him.

Working on the expansion into a new market with an online gift store dedicated exclusively to stained glass kept me busy all morning and then I did a quick visit to our closest factory.

My granddad would turn in his grave if he knew there was any kind of mass production of our products, but as a business, we had to do what it took to survive.

Our factories boosted local employment and we still used his techniques to produce our glass products. We just couldn't afford to do it all manually, or we'd never meet the demand from retailers.

By the end of the day, I was eager to get home and hang out with Noah.

Tina, my dad's secretary and general lifesaver, was busy typing at her computer when I walked out of the office.

"Tina, I'm heading out. Is there anything from today that I need to look at before tomorrow's meetings?"

"Nothing today, Mr. Van Stern. You might be interested to know Mr. Dellcourt is with Mr. Getty. His secretary let me know earlier."

What was Pierce doing here?

"Thank you, Tina. I hope you're wrapping up soon to go home."

"I am, sir."

"Good. See you tomorrow."

"Goodnight, sir."

I would never get used to the formality of this place, but it was too soon after my father's death. Hopefully, we'd transition out of it at some point, and everyone would just call me by my name.

Seeing Pierce wasn't on my list of things I wanted to do today or any time soon, but as they say, keep your enemies closer.

Not that he was an enemy. Or at least I hoped he wasn't. Him hanging out with Getty didn't leave me with fuzzy feelings.

The elevator door opened on Getty's floor and Pierce came in as I was about to get off.

"Lior."

"Just the person I was looking for. Can I buy you a coffee?"

His expression went from lukewarm to happy. He looked at his watch. "Do you want to catch dinner instead?"

"No. I can't stay long."

"Oh. Okay, coffee it is."

The coffee shop on the first floor of the building was closing down, so we went to another one across the road.

Pierce picked a table while I grabbed us a coffee each.

"No muffins?"

"Like I said, I can't stay long. I just wanted to know how you've been."

He stared at me quizzically. "I've been…managing. Why are you so concerned all of a sudden? Last time we talked, you couldn't wait to get rid of me while you flaunted your new young husband around."

Was this what people thought when they saw me with Noah? That he was my trophy husband?

"You seem to have an issue with my life choices, which is your problem, not mine. What concerns me is the company you're keeping these days."

He frowned. "What do you mean?"

"Getty isn't trustworthy. I take it he was the one who told you the very confidential terms of my father's will. If he's the kind of person who'd do that to the CEO of the company he has a huge stake in, imagine what he'd do to someone disposable. I just don't want you to get involved in something you'll regret."

"Don't worry about me. I know what I'm doing."

And that was the crux. "What exactly are you doing?"

Pierce's business had no affiliation with mine. When we'd dated, my dad had been fond of him, and they often met when Pierce came to join me for lunch if I was in the city office. But now? I was worried Getty would use Pierce to get to me and that Pierce was angry enough with me to let himself be used.

"Getty has business contacts I'm interested in."

"Just be careful with him, okay?"

He stood up straight. "Like I said, I can take care of myself. Was that everything?"

"Yes."

He stood, but before he left, he looked me straight in the eye. "You might want to listen to yourself at some point."

"What's that supposed to mean?"

"You're putting an awful lot of trust in people you don't know."

And with those parting words, he left.

I thought about his words for a moment. Did he mean Noah?

Yes, I wouldn't disagree with him entirely. I'd put a lot of trust in a man I'd met as a one-night hookup.

Noah was also more than that. He was a businessman, a family man, a caring and generous person.

Pierce thought I had to be careful with my business when it came to Noah, but I was more worried about my heart.

My phone dinged with a string of messages from Noah.

NOAH

> I had a super stressful day. Adam. My soon-to-be-married loving brother…

> I'm saying this because I have to remember I love him.

> He made me sit through five different versions of his wedding vows.

> FIVE!!!?!!!?!!!?!!!

That was a scary amount of punctuation for a single-word message.

NOAH

> May I remind you Adam is the word man in this company. If he can't get the words out about how he feels about marrying Victoria, then no one else can.

> I certainly can't *grin emoji*

> Anyway, I'm temporarily emotionally damaged and need repair.

What followed was a photo of his sad face.

NOAH

Come kiss me better.

And then a photo of his hard cock with a cock ring. I put the phone down as I looked around, hoping no one had seen it over my shoulder.

I looked again, and there was a new message.

NOAH

Junior also misses you and is sad. No one has paid attention to him aallll day.

LIOR

One, please don't give it a name. It's weird.

Two, I sure hope NO ONE has even had thoughts about him, let alone paid him attention.

NOAH

Oh, so you're alive. Why aren't you on your way home?

Wait, you're on your way home, right?

Because I may be in a little…predicament.

LIOR

Oh lord. I'm scared to find out what the hell you're talking about.

Also curious.

On my way.

I disposed of the coffee cups and made my way to his apartment.

The benefit of staying downtown was that I could walk to the office. Saving the environment, saving on gas, and exercising a little when I spent most of the day sitting down were huge benefits.

Having to walk when I wanted to be there with Noah right the fuck now was a huge drawback.

By the time I got out of the elevator and unlocked the front door, my mind had raced from a million different sexy situations to Noah accidentally killing himself while buck naked.

The lack of any follow-up messages also made me worry.

His apartment being open-plan meant I walked straight into the kitchen-living area where Noah was impaled on a dildo stuck to the fridge door.

"I needed a snack," he said, gasping for air. His eyes rolled to the back of his head as he slowly fucked himself.

My dick went from dormant to NASA spaceship immediately. A bottle of lube was conveniently placed on the kitchen table.

"Sometimes I don't know what to do with you, Noah Spencer." I didn't bother getting undressed. I undid the button and zipper of my pants and got my dick out.

"There's a list on the table. I also have a spreadsheet if you run out of ideas. I know how you old guys can forget things."

"You're playing with fire." I lathered my cock with lube.

"Burn me, Lior."

I pulled him away from the dildo and the traumatized fridge door and bent him over the kitchen table. I aligned my cock with his hole and thrust in all the way.

"Was this what you wanted?" I gasped, loving the warm heat of his channel.

"Fuck, yes!"

As I fucked him into oblivion, I wondered who was really in charge here. I didn't need special intuitive powers to know it was not me.

31

NOAH

WHAT I HAD NEVER CONTEMPLATED when the only sex I had was through hookups once a week were the consequences of having sex available on tap.

I had never considered myself an exclusive bottom. Mostly because I'd been on the giving and receiving end with both women and men.

The problem now? My greedy ass.

Nothing to do with me. I swear, Your Honor. It's my ass. He's the problem.

Oh, and Lior being so fucking sexy that my ass couldn't get enough.

"You all right over there?" West asked as I squatted to grab a box and groaned like an old man.

"Peachy."

I managed to lift it and take it out of the room into the industrial trash container outside.

"You look really stiff. Is your back still hurting from the game last week?"

Yeah, sure, let's go with that. Nothing to do with the

creative positions I'd put myself in every day this week while waiting for Lior to come home.

I didn't know how to ask for sex now that we'd agreed we could have it, which made no sense to anyone else but me.

Lior was addicting, and I wanted more. I wanted to cuddle with him and kiss him and snuggle and wake up in his arms every day, but we had a deal, and wanting affection wasn't part of it.

"Yeah, I think I overdid it."

"You should probably book a massage to relax your muscles. I had this pain on my left side, and Drew kept at me to do something about it. I went to that place on the edge of town and they sorted me out real quick. Two sessions and some physio was all it took."

I helped him with his box. "Yeah, I think I'll do the same. I know which one you're talking about. I've been there before. Just haven't had time recently, you know?"

He slapped my shoulder. "What, with having the fucking sexiest husband in the city and all? Don't blame you."

"I want to say it's not all it's cracked up to be, but I'd be lying."

"Okay, Mr. Smug. Some of us aren't getting it on the regular."

Drew walked past us carrying a few chairs. He frowned as he caught West's words.

When he was out of sight, I turned to West.

"Are you ever going to do something about you and Drew?"

"No, dude. He's my brother."

"He's not your brother."

He sighed. "He's as close to a brother as I'll ever get. I can't mess with that. If I lost him, I…I can't even imagine how I'd cope. So, no. I'm never going there."

"I'm just saying—"

"Leave it, Noah. I know you have good intentions, but it's not gonna happen."

I raised my hands in defeat. "Come on, help me with the mattresses."

I'd never noticed how big the hospital building was until now. The new hospital had more floors, new equipment, and a bigger parking lot, but the old one wasn't exactly small.

After talking to my brothers about supporting the foundation, they created and launched a social media campaign to recruit people to help clear the old stuff from the building.

Much of it couldn't stay, but the sheer number of chairs and bedframes would be handy for Star Finders' future plans.

"Hey, Lex, how's it going on the western front?" I shouted to my brother, who was coordinating the deep clean of the cafeteria.

"Going great. Mom and Dad should be here in a couple of hours with supplies.

"Oh, man. I hope they bring pastéis de nata. I need a sugar boost."

"Stop. I skipped lunch."

My belly rumbled. "Dammit."

I went back inside to focus on my job. The building had been inspected to make sure it was fit for West and Drew's plans. It needed some work and a paint job but the cafeteria was by far the area that needed the least amount of work because it didn't need to be repurposed.

A deep clean and stock up, and we'd be able to offer simple refreshments to the troops.

"Sorry I'm late. Lex sent me over here."

I raised my head over the mattress I was trying to lift to see Adam standing there in an old pair of jeans and a college T-shirt.

"Help me here."

He came from the other side, and together, we got it out to the trash.

"This place is huge. I don't remember it being so big when we came with Mom to the doctor when we were kids," he said, looking around.

"Right? This is going to be a perfect space. Imagine the community the guys can build here. All the kids from the neighborhood, those in foster care or from low-income families can hang out here. It's going to be great."

"You're really passionate about this."

I smiled. "Yeah, I am."

"I owe you an apology."

I paused on my way down to grab another mattress.

"What for?"

"For using your behavior as a marker to judge you against. Actually, not really your behavior but your mouth. You talk some talk, bro. But I should have been paying attention to the way you walk."

I went around the bed and pulled him in for a hug.

"Now, if you put that kind of poetry into your wedding vows, you'll definitely get lucky on your wedding night. Victoria's pants will fly off faster than a can of Red Bull."

"You had to ruin the moment." He playfully punched my gut.

"What can I say, most of the trouble I get in is because of my mouth. You're not special."

He laughed.

"Where's Victoria? She come too?"

Adam looked away. "No, she had a trip."

"Where to? I thought she wasn't going away until after the wedding since it's so close."

"Yeah, me too. I was going to take her away next weekend. You know, do what you said and be all romantic and shit. I've just spent the morning canceling stuff and trying to get my money back."

He looked so deflated, which wasn't like Adam at all.

"Maybe we can all hang out next weekend at Lior's place. He has a deck with a grill."

"He? You mean you, as in you two."

I laughed. "Yeah, I do. It's not easy to think of his stuff as mine too. It's too early." I nodded to the mattress. We need to get back to work.

My mouth needed a filter. More than usual. It needed a filter for the filter.

By the end of the afternoon, we'd filled all of the containers, which would be collected during the week.

My parents came through on the pastry and refreshments front.

"I could eat these until I drop," West said, stuffing a second pastél de nata in his mouth. "It must have been amazing growing up having them all the time."

"You'd think, but the payoff was having to help out at the restaurant every weekend. Do you know how many miles you walk in a shift?" I asked.

He shook his head.

"Let's put it this way. None of us has picked it as a career."

"Apart from River," Lex said, "because he's a sucker."

West rolled his eyes and moaned, looking at the cafeteria entrance. "Damn, Noah, that man of yours is more than chefs kiss."

I turned around and watched as Lior walked toward us, his smile directed at me.

"Hey." He greeted me with a kiss.

"Hey."

"Swoon," West said.

Drew hit him in the chest.

"What?"

Lior laughed. "How's it been? I'm so sorry I had to pull out of helping at the last minute. I had to deal with something really important at the museum.

"It's okay. You can massage my tired muscles later because they worked a double shift to make up for your absence."

The look he gave me was a promise and more.

Dammit. And this was why my ass was permanently sore and I needed a massage to sort out my back.

"Are you ready to go home?" he asked.

"Sure."

I was let out early for good behavior and got in Lior's car.

On the way out of the city, I dozed off because I was so tired. He woke me as we arrived at the house.

"Come this way, I want to show you something," he said when we got out of the car.

Sometimes we walked in the museum's gardens, especially if the weather was nice. We would sit in the grass and chill. The house was surrounded by trees so there was less open space to do the same.

"Can we grab a shower first? I stink."

He pulled me closer, buried his face in the crook of my neck, and inhaled.

"You smell divine. I'd lick you head to toe if you weren't covered in hospital dust."

"Ugh, and now I feel even more gross. Come on, show me your thing so I can get clean. Then you can make me dirty again."

He took my hand, and we crossed to the gate to the garden.

I saw it before we got to it because it was majestic.

"What's this?"

"It's my grandfather's gazebo. It went away to be restored

because we don't have a big enough workshop here. Some of the glass broke during a storm last year."

I walked under it, the colors reflecting on my skin. My dusty white T-shirt was bathed in a rainbow.

"This is stunning. All the colors. Your grandfather made this himself?"

Lior put his arm around my waist, holding me close. "He did. It was a gift to my grandmother because she loved reading outside, but in the sunlight, she struggled to see properly. The glass helped, but it also made it a magical place. They used to have a couch under it, but with all the visitors we have, it's not practical."

"Maybe we should move it to your place, then we could sit under it all the time."

He smiled. "Maybe. It's always lived in the gardens, but I think you might be right. We'll give it until the rest of the summer so visitors can appreciate it, and then we'll find a place for it at home."

At home.

I sighed.

As if his place was also somewhat mine.

"Oh, I also spoke to my mom earlier. She's totally panicking about meeting your parents tomorrow."

"Why?"

He laughed. "You don't know how overwhelming your family is, do you?"

I raised a brow. "I live in it. I know how overwhelming they are, but she'll be fine. She just needs to bring a big appetite because my mom is a feeder."

"Come on. Let's go get you clean. You're going to chill tonight. Your husband is going to cook dinner for you, and then we're going to watch a movie."

"Oh...the perks of being married."

32

—

LIOR

I PUT an arm around my mom's shoulder and kissed her hair.

It was overwhelming meeting new people when you were recently widowed.

We'd talked about it when I told her about the invite to join Noah's family at their weekly Sunday lunch.

Stepping into a new place alone was different from doing it with your life partner.

Mom and Dad had always done everything together. From functions to attending my school events or birthday parties, they were always together.

"Give me the signal if you want to go, okay?" I whispered in her ear as Noah rang the bell.

The door opened, and Noah's mom beamed. "Welcome. You must be Lior's mother. Come on in. I'm Carla." She kissed my mom on both cheeks.

"Nice to meet you too. I'm Mathilda."

Mom glanced at me.

"Sorry, I forgot that's a thing for Portuguese people," I said.

Jack came out and shook her hand.

243

Carla led us to the kitchen, where a large old table was set.

"Noah, help our guests pick a seat and then get your brothers."

I chuckled at Noah's reaction.

"It's like I'm back in high school," he mumbled.

His dad lightly smacked the back of his head. "Respect your mother."

"Jack, go get your mom. Mass should be over by now."

He rolled his eyes at his wife's orders. I had to suppress a smile because he looked so much like Noah.

"Carla, I'm not great in the kitchen, but my late mother-in-law taught me to make these cookies, and to this day, they're still my favorite." Mom handed Carla a box.

"That's so lovely, Mathilda. We can have these with coffee later. Can't wait to try them."

Noah went over to the kitchen door and shouted his brothers' names.

"Mathilda, I'm sure you'll understand this as the mother of a boy. No matter how hard you try to teach them manners, they never learn. It's like I raised three wild animals," Carla said.

"Oh, I can imagine. Lior is an only child, but he made up for it in his teenage years."

"Which were a long, long time ago," Noah said, coming back and sitting next to me. I poked his sides, making him giggle.

After the introductions to the rest of the family, after Noah's grandmother, brothers, Lex, and River came into the kitchen, Carla started plating up the food.

"Mathilda, I hope you like our food. I forget that not everyone will like Portuguese food. This is a beef stew with peas and potatoes. There's also some rice there and vegetables."

"Double carbing is a thing in Portugal, Mathilda," Noah said. "Don't feel obliged to have it, although if you don't, Mom will be very upset."

"Noah," Carla chided.

"See? And you better finish your plate, or you won't be allowed to play games after dinner— Oh wait, that's just for us."

"I'll have extra vegetables, Mamã," Adam said. "I'm trying to be healthy for the wedding.

"Kiss ass," Lex coughed.

"Boys…" Jack threatened, although I wasn't sure what the threat was because after spending time with him at the vineyard, I knew he wouldn't hurt a fly.

"This food is wonderful," Mom said.

"Have some more, dear," Carla added.

"Oh no, I couldn't…"

"Oh yes, you can. There are no ceremonies in this house. We're all family here."

"Oh, go on then."

Noah and I exchanged a smile as he knocked his knee against mine.

Mom and Noah's parents found some common ground in the shortage of daughters in the family. For a moment, I thought Adam would speak up and mention Victoria. After all, she would officially be part of the family soon, but he remained silent.

Noah's grandmother, who only joined in the conversation in small bursts, turned to my mom. "Mathilda, what do you think of these two getting married? We didn't even know they were dating. I may be too old for the modern world, but that isn't normal."

Mom stiffened a little. She'd been around us a little longer than Noah's parents, so I understood their reluctance to understand or accept our marriage.

"Mãe, it's not the day to ask these questions," Carla said.

Mom waved her off and smiled, "I think you're right, Jacinta. I was quite upset when I found out. I get more upset now because I've come to know Noah quite well and love him like my own son. I wish I'd had the chance to be there for their special day."

Noah grabbed my hand under the table. I squeezed it to reassure him we were good.

"Can we not talk about this? It happened, and there's nothing we can do about it," Noah said.

"You could get married again," Lex said. "Or renew your vows or whatever people do when they're already married."

"Or you could shut up," Noah threw a piece of bread at his brother.

"Noah. Behave." Carla said. "Now, who wants chocolate mousse for dessert?"

"Me!" Noah, Lex, Adam, and River said at the same time.

By the time we finished dessert, there was nothing left.

Carla couldn't have looked more pleased at the justified success of her meal.

I knew Mom would come out of her shell eventually, and it happened during coffee when Carla shared her homemade cookies. The sign of acceptance made her open up, and before I knew it, the women were sharing stories.

"Hey, why don't you show me your room?" I whispered in Noah's ear.

"Because my parents say I'm not allowed to have boys in there," he whispered.

"Noah, why don't you show Lior your school trophies?" Carla asked. "Did you know he was great at sports? Well, maybe not soccer. He never liked playing sports that involved his feet. We always wondered if he'd ever pick one and go professional, but he just couldn't make up his mind."

I grabbed his hand. "It sounds like we've just got permission."

Noah took me upstairs, and as soon as the door closed behind us, he pushed me against the wall and fused his mouth to mine.

"Hmm, you taste like chocolate mousse and coffee," he said.

"I thought I was here to see your trophies."

"You've seen my biggest trophy already. The others don't compare."

I took him to the bed and had him straddle me. I couldn't remember the last time I'd made out with another boy in their childhood bedroom. I must have been seventeen at the time. When I went to college, I engaged in a mix of hookups and more serious relationships.

"If we stay here any longer, you're going to have to give me your jersey so everyone knows I belong to you," I teased.

He took my hand and rolled my wedding ring around my finger. "This is what tells people you're mine."

We made out a little longer. It was becoming harder to tell when we were acting about our relationship. It was even harder to tell if Noah felt the same as I did or if he was just a very good actor.

When Lex suggested we remarry to have a party with the family, I didn't recoil or feel like I was being pushed against a wall. The opposite, actually.

I pushed the thoughts aside as we joined the family downstairs.

We didn't need to tell anyone what we'd been up to because it was all over Adam's, Lex's, Emery's, and River's faces.

Thankfully, the parents remained oblivious.

When it became too late and Carla started threatening to

feed us dinner, we left and gave my mom a lift back to her place. She was quiet on the ride.

"Do you want us to stay over?" I asked as she unlocked the front door.

"Would you? I know it probably sounds odd to you, but after spending the day around so many people, the silence in this place is deafening."

"We understand, Mom."

Noah wrapped his arm around my mom's. "Mathilda, do you by any chance have photos of Lior as a baby? I'd love to see how adorable he looked."

"Oh, of course. I have tons of photos. He was the most beautiful boy. With his tan skin and dark eyes, he definitely inherited the European gene. We think there may be some Mediterranean blood on his dad's side. Of course we can't be sure because everyone's long gone now."

I couldn't help smiling at the two most important people in my life, even as they colluded to talk about me.

Resigned to my role as an outsider, I went to the kitchen to make a pot of tea for my mom and coffee for us.

We stayed up longer than I expected after Noah asked to see album after album of my childhood photos.

"I would definitely have dated you in high school," he said.

"My high school or yours?"

He thought about it for a while. "Oh. Yeah, maybe not. Besides, I think your silver fox look is by far the best of all."

"I aim to please."

Mom stifled a yawn. "Oh gosh, I think I better retreat. Will I see you boys in the morning?"

"We'll grab a quick breakfast before going to work," I said.

"Goodnight, boys."

She gave me and Noah a kiss and left for her room.

"Boys." I shook my head.

"It's kinda sweet, isn't it?"

"I'm forty—"

"Seven years old, I know." He rolled his eyes.

"If we weren't in my parents' house, you'd be in for a good spanking right now."

His lips curled into a smile. "What if I'm really, *really* quiet?"

"No."

"But I've been bad, so bad."

"No."

He sulked. "You're the worst husband. What happened to meeting all my requests?"

"That wasn't in the vows."

"In sickness and in health. Having regular sex is healthy."

I gave him a cursory glance. "If our sex life is any more regular, we'll need to check into therapy."

"What can I do? Stop being so goddamn addictive, and I might take a break. You could try being bad at sex, you know?"

I cradled his neck and brought him in for a kiss.

"Not in my nature, Mr. Spencer, but not in my parents' home. This is an old house, and everything creaks."

"Fine," he sighed. "Then take me to bed and cuddle me to sleep."

"I can do that."

33
___

NOAH

"Go, Hannah!" Remi shouted from the bench as she dribbled the basketball a few times and took a shot straight into the hoop.

He jumped up, whistling.

"Well done," I said to her. "You can be on my team any time."

She smiled, pushing her long braid behind her back.

"Thank you, Noah."

There was no time to celebrate because Joel was right on it. He stole the ball from Alma and then passed it to West, who was way ahead of the rest of us.

Before our defense could get to him, he passed the ball to Avi, who scored another point for the other team.

Remi blew the whistle for break time.

"This is so much fun," Hannah said as we walked to the benches.

"I'm glad you can join us. The guys needed some friendly competition."

She laughed. "You mean someone to put them in their place?"

"That too."

She jogged up to the refreshments table and joined Remi.

"Those two are getting cozy," Alma said.

"They're cute."

"All you see is love hearts now that you have a new man. At least her foster parents are here, so we can tag team. I can coach kids, but I'm not good with teenage hormonal breakups."

I bumped her shoulder. "You don't remember how it was? You never wrote Alma hearts Brad Pitt in your schoolbooks?"

She snorted. "Big difference. Brad never broke up with me."

Someone caught my attention on the other side of the fence.

"Hey, are you Noah Spencer?" the man asked.

I approached the fence. "Yes, and you are?"

"Richard, Daily Cliff. Would you be willing to make a statement for our news readers?" He pointed a small recorder at me.

"I have no idea what you're talking about, but you can't be here."

"This is a public space, and I'm only doing my job, man. Come on, give me a statement, and we'll both get on with our weekend."

"I don't talk to the press, and I have no idea what you're talking about. Knock yourself out if you want to watch a bunch of teenagers play basketball and have fun. While you're at it, make sure to name the Star Finders Youth Network so your readers can donate to support the charity."

I turned and started walking back to the group. Lior had said that eventually, news of our wedding would break out and I might get harassed a little by reporters.

He'd said not to worry because his life was never interesting enough for the press to become a hassle. If I ignored them, they'd go away.

"So it's not true that your marriage is a sham?"

I stopped. "What did you say?"

"Did you marry Lior Van Stern for money? Is that why you're cheating on him?"

I took two steps forward to confront the guy when West grabbed my arm to stop me. "Ignore it. Come on, let's go back."

"Did you hear what he said?"

"Yeah, I did. It's bullshit. You know it, and they know it. They're just trying to get to you so you do something stupid that gives them the real headlines."

Hannah's foster mom had a bottle of water for me when I reached the group.

"Thanks."

"What was that about? Can I help with anything? I have some contacts in most of the papers because of my day job," she said.

"I appreciate it, but it's okay. I knew this might happen eventually."

Drew came over, panting. "Look." He thrust his phone in my face.

The first thing I saw was the photo that had been taken of me, Lior, and the princes of Lydovia at the mayor's ball.

Then, my eyes landed on the headline.

I couldn't bear to read the article properly. A few phrases caught my eye, calling me a gold-digger, a fraud, and a cheat. As I scrolled down the article, it just got worse. I almost dropped West's phone when I saw photos of me and Jax at Tanner's bar.

Jax was leaning his head on my shoulder as I whispered something in his ear. He was smiling with his eyes half-lidded.

Without context or a time stamp, that photo looked incriminating. It was incriminating.

"I have to get out of here," I said.

"Let us take you home," Drew said.

"No. It's okay. I'm not far, and you still have half a game to play. I'm not letting the fucking press get to the work we're doing for the kids."

He nodded. "Please be safe on your way home. Text me when you get there."

"Thanks, man."

I grabbed my rucksack and made my way out of the court.

Thankfully, the reporter didn't follow me out, but it was clear why a few yards later when I was swarmed by dozens of reporters taking photos and shouting questions at me.

"Is it true?"

"Do you have an open marriage?"

"Does Mr. Van Stern know about your lover?"

"Did you do it for money?"

I sped up my pace and tried to ignore them, but they kept up with me. How was I going to get home with a bunch of people on my tail? The last thing I needed was for them to camp outside my apartment block.

My jaw ached from grinding my teeth to keep from replying to some of the stupid questions.

When I crossed the road, a car screeched to a halt right in front of me. I was about to call the driver some choice names when the window came down and I saw Pierce.

"Get in. Now."

Beggars couldn't be choosers, so even though I despised Pierce, he was currently my ticket out of this mess.

When I closed the door, he put his foot down and drove away.

He didn't say anything until we were clear of the reporters. He drove around the city for a while and then stopped in the parking lot of the city park.

"Thank you for…you know, getting me out of there."

"Sometimes one does what one must to put things in their rightful place."

I stared at him. Was he talking about me? Figurative things?

"Once again, thank you. I can walk home from here." I pulled the door handle to get out. Pierce grabbed my arm, gripping it tight.

"Not so fast."

The guy put me on edge. I couldn't wait to get out of his car, and I needed to get home, check my phone, and call Lior. His dark eyes and overly groomed hair gave me the chills.

"I know all about your deal with Lior."

"I don't know what you're talking about."

"Don't play dumb. It's beneath you. You're a smart man. If you weren't, you wouldn't have bagged the most eligible gay bachelor in the city, so you know where I'm going with this."

I narrowed my eyes. "Entertain me."

"I'm sure you're a good fuck, but there are more important things than sex. Van Stern Enterprises is the most important thing in Lior's life. He will do anything not to lose the company his grandfather started and his father built into a multi-million-dollar international enterprise."

"I know exactly how important VSE is to Lior. What's your point?"

"My point is that Lior's cute young new husband with the clean rap sheet is now a liability. What do you think the partners will do now that those photos are out there? Do you think they'll let Lior keep the company? They'll oust him faster than you can spell sham marriage."

"What do you care?"

He sneered at me. "I care because the wedding ring on your finger should be on mine. Our breakup was a mistake, but I wasn't going to make him stay with me after he cheated."

"What the fuck? You're the one who cheated."

Pierce deflated a little in his seat. He kept his eyes on the grassy field in front of us. He was the one who'd cheated, right?

"I found out Lior was cheating on me. I confronted the guy he was with, and someone got photos of us. Lior accused me of cheating because I guess it was a way of getting rid of both of us. What he didn't expect was for his dad to add that clause to his will. He was too proud to come back to me, so he set his eyes on you."

I laughed. "I was the one who proposed, so your theory doesn't hold."

He scoffed. "Yeah, so was I. Think about that."

This conversation was giving me a headache.

"What do you want me to do? We're married."

"Break up with him. Ask for an annulment. Let me help Lior save his company. I'm really sorry you've been dragged into all of this, but Lior and I have decades of shared history. I can forgive him for his transgressions. You don't have to, Noah. You have your whole life ahead of you."

A lump formed in my throat. Pierce was asking me to give up the only person I'd truly deeply loved in my whole life.

"I can't."

I exited the car and ran into the park, not stopping until I got home.

My phone was turned off. No doubt it had lost battery from all the notifications and calls. I put it on the charger and took a shower.

When I got out and turned the phone on, I braced myself.

JAX

> WTF, dude. We're in the papers. How did they find out? Call me.

TANNER

> Jax can't do his shift at the hospital because the press is camped out there. WTF is going on?

> He's at my place, BTW. Call us.

There was also a message from Lior, but it was from early this morning.

LIOR

Hey. Hope you don't get too sore from your game. I have plans for you. Have fun with the kids. See you tonight.

I dropped down on my couch. What was I going to do?

Pierce's words had gotten to me. No matter how much I tried to shake them off, I couldn't forget some of the things he'd said.

It was hard to separate the truth from Pierce's accounts of what may have happened between him and Lior. If I was going to bet on anyone, it certainly wouldn't be Pierce.

After all, I'd looked at incriminating photos of me with Jax that had a completely innocent explanation, so I had to take Pierce's account with a huge pinch of salt.

What worried me the most was what I couldn't deny.

I was a liability. I wasn't good enough for him. If Lior lost his company because of me, I'd never forgive myself.

My stomach churned while my limbs felt heavy and numb.

I couldn't see a way out.

34

LIOR

I CHECKED my phone for the hundredth time. Noah wouldn't be home yet, and he always left his phone at home, so why couldn't I leave it alone?

Whipped. That's what I was. Totally, irrevocably, insanely whipped by my husband.

A distraction was what I needed.

Leaving my office, I turned left to the door with direct access to the museum gardens.

It was a warm summer day. The museum was packed with visitors. Many of them were outside.

The educational treasure hunt Lex had suggested to us was working great. So many parents ended up in the gift store buying a little memento of the trip.

Sales had increased, which was always great, but inquiries for our workshops had increased too. I always knew sharing my grandfather's passion with people was a good idea, but with the help of the Spencer Brothers Agency, it was profitable.

As I walked around, I noticed some people sneaking in photos of me. It happened sometimes. People were always curious about the family that had once lived in the house with the magical glass windows.

I continued my stroll, leaving the gravel path for the grass. This place really was magical to me. As a child, I'd played hide and seek with my dad and learned to ride a bike here.

How many generations of children played here before me or my dad? My granddad had built the existing building from the footprint of the house that had stood on this location many years before.

At forty-seven, maybe for the first time in my life, I found myself wondering if I'd missed the boat on having children, someone to pass on the Van Stern legacy.

Once again, Noah intruded on my thoughts. Did he want children?

Why was I even thinking about it? In less than a year, we'd need to face the very real conversation about divorce and all that it entailed. We'd kept our lives separate to make it easier in the end, but the longer we were together, the more our lives weaved around each other.

Yes, in practical terms, he had his place and I had mine. We split our time, but we were always together. There hadn't been a night in the last month we hadn't slept in the same bed, tangled limbs, breathing in each other, which begged the question, did we even want a divorce after the year was up anymore? Because neither our behavior nor my feelings felt fake any longer.

"Mr. Van Stern."

Charlie's voice brought me out of my daydream. He was practically running toward me.

"Sir, we have a crisis."

"What happened. Someone got hurt in the gift store?" It wasn't unusual when the place was filled with breakable glass items. Usually, our first-aid team or calling the paramedics was enough.

Charlie held out my phone, which I'd left on my desk, and a newspaper.

I unfolded the paper and nearly dropped it on the grass. Charlie held my elbow and guided me away from prying eyes as I scanned the article.

"Fuck. How the hell did this happen?"

The things they were saying about us, about Noah. My hands shook as I tried to take in the accusations from the article.

"We can handle it, sir. These lies are preposterous. How can they print this kind of drivel? I thought the Cliffborough Press wasn't a tabloid."

I looked at Charlie. Concern was etched all over his face. I couldn't tell him the article wasn't entirely false, but how had they found out?

"I need to get to Noah," I said.

"Sir." Charlie stopped me. He flipped a page on the paper, and on the inside, there it was for everyone to see. Noah and Jax together at Tanner's.

My husband and a man his age were practically on top of each other in a public place. Or at least that's what the photo and the article made it look like.

I folded the paper and crossed the garden to my house.

"What do you want us to do here? I've heard people commenting," Charlie said, trying to keep up with my pace.

"We're not making statements if anyone openly asks about the article, but if they want to buy a gift from the store or make a donation to our charity of choice, then they're welcome. We may as well profit from this mess."

"Yes, sir."

I crossed the gate onto my property. Something was simmering inside me, but it was hard to tell what it was.

Disappointment that Noah let himself be photographed in that situation? Betrayal that somehow the story about our marriage had gotten out?

What I struggled to understand was how the news had leaked when no one knew about our deal.

Not even my mother or Charlie knew, and they were the closest people I had. I told them everything.

Tanner and Jax wouldn't tell, that I was sure of.

I took a deep breath as I opened my front door.

No, this had to be conjecture. Someone who didn't believe our wedding story.

I'd packed earlier for my stay at Noah's, so I grabbed my bag. I wasn't even sure I'd be staying at Noah's tonight, but at least I was prepared.

We certainly needed a good conversation.

A small brown envelope on the floor by the door caught my eye. I could have sworn it wasn't there when I came in.

I picked it up. It didn't have a stamp or address, just my name on it. I stuffed it inside my bag.

When I opened the door, I found myself face-to-face with Pierce.

"What are you doing here?"

"Can we talk?"

"As you can see, I'm on my way out."

"This is important," he said in the whiny voice that had driven me nuts even when we were together.

"Not a good time, Pierce."

I closed the door and walked around him to my car.

"For fuck's sake, Lior Van Stern, just fucking listen to me for once."

"What do you want?" I shouted.

He bridged the gap between us and leaned against my car. His was parked behind mine, so I couldn't leave until he did.

"I've seen the article," he said.

I hated the sympathy slash pity in his expression.

"And?"

"I just wanted to see how you're doing. Is this true? Please don't tell me you married a stranger just to get the company. I know your father's will stipulation was unfair, but god, Lior, I've been here all along. Couldn't you have come to me?"

I frowned. "No, because there's nothing between us. We are over."

"Do we have to be?" he asked with a tinge of hope.

"What do you mean?"

He leaned over to touch my face, but I stepped back.

"Look, I know what the stakes are. Ultimately, you need to end up with someone who can fit into your life. Your dad knew me. The partners know me. Why don't you annul your silly marriage and marry me instead? Together, we can make this work. The company will thrive with both of us working together." He took a step forward. "Do you remember when that was our dream? I'd take charge of the company while you focused on the museum? We could have our dream back."

How could I have had such dreams when staring into his eyes now did absolutely nothing for me? "Dreams change."

"Not like this. Tell me you're not worried about losing the company over this scandal."

I couldn't because it would be a lie. I wasn't just worried. I was terrified.

"What will your mother think of all of this? Does she know you married to save the company?"

"Pierce..."

"First, she loses her beloved husband. The love of her life. And now she's losing everything else? Come on, Lior, you have to do the right thing."

I clenched my fists. "You are about three seconds away from being punched. Please leave my home right now."

"Lior. Be sensible. I've come all this way to help you."

"What do you want? A medal?"

He shook his head. "I'm so disappointed. I thought the company and your family's legacy were the most important things to you. You used to leave me alone, waiting night after night when you were working late, and now you're ready to throw it all out."

"You are wrong, Pierce. Van Stern Enterprises isn't the most important thing to me. Noah is."

He scoffed. "You can't tell me you're in love with him."

"What if I am?"

"Are you joking?"

I stared at him.

"You could do better, you know?"

"Like what? You? That's where you're wrong. I couldn't do worse than you. Regardless, this isn't about who the best option is for me. I don't need an option. If things with Noah don't work out, being alone is a viable end game."

"What about the photos?" He pointed at the paper I still held in my hand.

"It's none of your business."

"Fine." He walked back to his car. "Come to me when you have no other way out. I'll be waiting because that's just the person I am. But I won't wait forever."

"Pierce," I called as he opened the door. "Please don't. Find someone to be happy with and live your life."

"I thought I already had. Clearly, I was mistaken."

I leaned against my car to steady myself. Pierce left my driveway without another word.

Was I making a mistake? My gut told me to trust Noah. I knew him. The sounds he made, the way he smiled, how silly he could be. He was my Noah. I had to trust that there was an explanation for the photos. Once I had that, we could figure out how to fight this.

I got in the car and put it in gear. The brown envelope poked out of the bag, so I took it out.

Inside, there was nothing but a bunch of photos.

My heart sank when I scanned through them. One by one.

I pulled out of my driveway, wondering how Noah would explain those.

35

NOAH

THE MORE I paced the wooden floor of my apartment, the fewer answers I had.

Things I knew: I was in love with Lior.

Things I didn't know: if he loved me back.

That meant I had to think about the current facts, and those were that Pierce was right. I was a liability.

The part of the article about our marriage would certainly raise suspicion with Lior's business partners, but who could prove it? We had a marriage certificate issued by the state of Nevada. We had two witnesses who would support us. We lived together.

If anything, the adjustment we'd made to our lives by splitting our living arrangements but remaining together proved the commitment we'd made.

Wherever we were, we came home to each other every night. We slept together. We'd had sex on top of or against every piece of furniture we owned. What did they want? Photographic evidence?

The only place we hadn't had sex yet was the bed, which

was a running joke between us, and like with everything else, it was just a matter of time before that happened.

So why was I so worried about the photos with Jax? They looked incriminating, but they could be easily explained.

I would fight for us, but I couldn't fight for something one-sided. I'd done that once, and it nearly broke me, but I loved Lior with far greater intensity than I'd ever loved my ex.

Which was why I would never forgive myself if Lior lost his family's company because of me, even if it wasn't directly my fault.

A person who went as far as marrying someone they barely knew to save their legacy wouldn't be happy having that legacy taken away.

The big question was, did Lior trust me implicitly? Or did he believe the photos?

Could we handle this together?

I stopped pacing when I heard the sound of the door unlocking.

Lior was here. I wanted to go to him. To hug him and kiss him and have him tell me everything would be okay. I wanted him to take all the anxiety away and then fuck me into the wall to show all the reporters and the doubters that what we had was something and it was real.

The first thing I noticed as he came inside was that he didn't have his usual bag with the suits he'd wear for the week at the office.

There was a tightness in his expression, and he held a newspaper in his hand, which I guessed contained the article.

He's not staying.

My heart raced as he made his way to me, but it sank when he dropped the newspaper on the coffee table and sat on the couch.

I had one decision to make. Tell Lior the truth and hope

we could fight this together or let him go in the hope that being away from me would help him keep his company.

I just hoped my decision was the right one in the long run.

Lior opened the newspaper to the page with the photo of Jax and me.

"Can these be explained?" His voice lacked emotion. He wouldn't even look at me. It was like he'd both believed and didn't want to believe what the article had printed.

I sat on the chair next to the couch because I didn't trust myself to not break down if I was too close to Lior.

"Yes."

"Favorably?" He looked at me for the first time since coming inside my apartment. There was a glimmer of hope in his eyes, but his lips remained tight.

"It looks like we were caught in the photos taken by people from another group at Tanner's. It was loud in the bar, and he didn't exactly want everyone to hear his *what happens in Vegas doesn't stay in Vegas* story."

"What do you mean?"

"It's not my story to tell. Two friends were having drinks. It was loud, so we were in each other's space."

He rested his elbows on his knees and ran his fingers through his hair.

Even in a moment like this, when I could see our whole short-lived relationship flash through my eyes, he was still the most beautiful man I'd ever seen.

"I don't know if I can fight this, Noah."

"I understand. It doesn't look good for you and no one will ever believe the innocence in the photos."

He leafed through the paper and removed an envelope that was tucked inside. He opened it and dropped the contents on top of the newspaper.

All my blood drained from my face, and I felt cold as I

stared at the stack of photos on the table. Photos of me hugging someone on the street, having lunch out like I was on a date, and the worst, photos of me in very compromising positions with other men.

"Where did you get these?" I asked, my voice trembling.

"They were dropped at my place when I wasn't home. Can you explain them?"

"No." They hadn't happened, but how could I argue with the visual evidence that I'd been having sex with other men while married to Lior? I even had my wedding ring on in all those photos. Whoever had staged them made them look like they were recent.

Lior stood and went to the window. In the distance, I could see our hotel. The place we'd hooked up that first unforgettable night.

"Lior, let's talk about this."

"Yes, let's talk about how it looks like you've been with a string of other men while you were married to me. I am such a gullible idiot." He turned around. "I thought I knew you. I thought I was the only one who did."

I wanted to say he was, but I didn't think it had even occurred to him that those photos were fake.

Words got stuck in my throat. I couldn't defend myself against these accusations when I stared at the photos, and all I saw was this person who looked exactly like me in the arms of another man. Someone who looked like me on the receiving end of a damn good fucking.

I wrapped my arms around my waist to stop my whole body from trembling, but it didn't work. I needed him to go so I could get my head around what was happening right now.

"Tell me you can explain these," he said, his voice breaking.

"I can't." And that was the truth. How could I explain

something I didn't understand myself? "You should have married Pierce. Maybe you still can." I removed my ring and placed it on the coffee table.

He walked to the door, ignoring the ring on the table and the photos.

"Do you remember when you said you would do anything for me?" I asked.

He turned around, and in a few steps, I bridged the gap between us. I opened the door for him. "I would do the same for you."

His eyes widened, and he looked like he was about to say something, but instead, he walked away. I closed the door and finally let all the tears I was holding in fall down my cheeks.

In the end, I didn't have to make a choice between keeping Lior or letting him go because he made that choice for me by believing that I was the kind of man who would cheat so openly.

Things I knew: I was disposable. I was still in love with Lior. Lior did not share those feelings.

Things I didn't know: where the photos had come from. Why Lior had believed them so easily. Was it really all over?

With nothing else to lose, I did the one thing I could. I pulled my phone out and messaged my brothers.

NOAH

CODE RED

36

LIOR

I BANGED my fist against the steering wheel of my car.

He didn't deny it. He didn't fucking deny it.

"Why, Noah? Why would you do this to me? To us. Was I not enough for you?"

I pressed the palm of my hand against my chest, but it didn't do anything to alleviate the pain and betrayal I felt.

I drove home in a haze of anger and pain. My suit bag was still in the passenger seat, and I wondered if I should just drive somewhere else and get away for a while.

Maybe being in a different place would give me clarity to deal with the fallout of the article, the threat of the other photos being shared, and the end of my fake marriage.

Despite everything, I didn't want those photos of Noah to get out to the public, which meant I had to find out who'd taken them.

As soon as I took the private driveway up to my place, I saw my mother's car parked while she sat on a bench I had outside my door.

She was the last person I wanted to see now, but she must have seen the story and rushed over.

Taking a calming breath, I parked beside her car and got out.

"Lior, I've been calling you all afternoon."

"Sorry, Mom, I've been busy."

She gave me a pitying look. "I can imagine. Let's go inside, brew some coffee, and talk about this. Where's Noah?"

The mention of his name made me flinch. "He's at his place."

I took my suit bag to my room while she went straight to the coffee maker.

It was time to come clean with her. She wouldn't be happy with the truth, especially as I knew she liked Noah, but she needed to know.

When I returned to the kitchen, she was leaning against the sink, waiting for the coffee to brew.

"What is this about a fake marriage? Where on earth did they get the idea that your marriage is fake? You got married in Vegas, and you have a marriage certificate, don't you?"

I released a breath. "Yes, our marriage is legal." I paused. "But it doesn't make it any less fake."

She brought her hands to her chest. "Lior Van Stern. What have you done?"

"Something really, really stupid. Epically stupid. No wonder Dad didn't trust me to just inherit the company. He knew I'd screw things up." I laughed. "He gave me a test to prove myself, and I just proved him right."

She came over to me and held my hands. "I don't believe it. You're a responsible and intelligent man. Whatever you did, you did it with the best intentions and with your heart on your sleeve. That's how you do everything, Lior. I am your mother, and I know these things."

She wrapped her small arms around me when I pulled her in for a hug. Her perfume was the comfort I needed. She hadn't changed it for as long as I'd been alive and it always made me feel like I was home.

"Let me grab a couple of mugs, and then we'll talk."

She sat at the table while I poured the coffee.

"Okay, tell me everything."

So I did.

I told her about meeting Noah at the bar on the day of Dad's funeral, sparing her the lewd details. I told her how we'd met by chance in Atlanta, which was when I'd found out about our work connection. How I'd accidentally told Noah about the will when I'd had a few too many drinks.

"And he proposed just like that?" she asked.

"Yes. Noah can be very persuasive…and he had a point. I could help him access the mayor's ball so he could network with the people who'd support his friends' charity. With a little bit of press and my connections, he could make sure his friends had the best chance of winning the bid for the old hospital building."

"And in return, he married you so you could meet your father's will demands."

"Yes."

She sipped her coffee with her contemplative expression that sometimes scared me.

"So, you're saying there was nothing in it for Noah, marrying you."

That was correct. Noah had insisted on it to help me, but he'd known I would have helped him regardless.

I nodded.

"But you still got married and, forgive me for asking this, but you two were more than friends who married for a deal?"

I pinched the bridge of my nose. This was not the topic I wanted to discuss with my mother.

"Yes. We…were intimate before the wedding. We decided to stop it because we didn't want that kind of intimacy involved in what would be a transactional relationship."

Mom laughed.

"What's funny?"

"You thinking that not having sex would make it less emotional."

"We tried, but…it was an impossible ask. Noah is so irresistible, and he presses all my buttons. Ugh, I don't want to be talking about this with you, Mom."

"Do you think I don't know what good sex is?"

"Mom! In my head, you don't know what sex is, period."

She laughed. "Yeah, let's go with that. Anyway, it didn't work for you, and you started a sexual relationship with your husband. I see how that was completely the wrong decision."

I gave her the side eye even though she was right.

"What I'm hearing is that you got married and—shock and horror—you were intimate with your husband. You also lived together. Can you explain to me how anyone would think your marriage isn't real?"

I shook my head. "That's what I'm trying to figure out. No one knew, not even our families."

"That photo of Noah in the paper…"

"That's his friend and best man, Jax. That was an innocent meeting."

Mom put her mug down on the table. "The press doesn't just print a story like that without being alerted by someone."

"I know, but I don't know who that might be."

She put her hand on my arm. "Why isn't Noah here?"

"Because the article isn't everything there is."

She sighed and took a brown envelope out of her handbag.

"You mean these?"

Bile bubbled up from my stomach. "How did you get that?"

"It was put through the letter box."

I opened the envelope, and it was exactly like mine. No messages, just my mom's first name on the front of the envelope.

"In case you're wondering, I did check the door camera, and it was a kid, probably no older than fifteen, who delivered the envelope. My guess is he was paid to do it."

"I'm sorry you had to see them. Wait— You knew about the photos? Why all the questions?"

"I wanted you to tell me what was going on, Lior. I may not be young anymore, but I know when my own son is hiding something from me. When you told me about him, I thought you'd hired him to pretend to be your husband, but then I met him, and I just knew."

"Knew what?"

"How in love he is with you."

I choked a laugh. "You're imagining things."

"Am I? The man enters a legal contract with you even when it helps you more than it helps him. He faces lying to his family. He turns up to a meeting with the board of a multi-million-dollar company to stand by your side and tell everyone how in love you both are."

I stared at her in shock.

"Lior, that man loves you. Maybe he didn't intend to. But the first time I met him, I knew."

I slammed my hand on the photos. "He didn't deny these. The evidence is right in front of your eyes. Although I am sorry that you had to see it."

"I'll admit the first time I saw the photos, I had to sit down. No one wants to see their son-in-law in these…types of positions. I'm just glad they don't show everything. But there's something off about the photos. I can't tell what it is, but I don't think they're real."

"What do you mean?"

She frowned. "My first question would be. Do you think he'd cheat on you?"

"I didn't think he would, but…" I pointed at the photos.

"My second question is about the timing of the photos and the article. Someone has planned this very carefully. Which brings me to suspect the photos might be fake."

I hadn't considered that.

"Oh my god, Mom. I didn't consider that, and I don't think he did either. If I was presented with these photos of myself, even I'd have admitted guilt."

"Let me guess, that's exactly what he did."

Noah lied. He put me first because he feared the fallout of the article and the photos would lose me the company. His words at the end said as much—"*I would do the same for you.*"

I groaned. "I'm an idiot."

"Funny, you did start this conversation telling me you were an idiot. I'm inclined to agree."

"Wow, thanks for the motherly support."

She shrugged. "I've been your mother for forty-seven years, as you so love to remind me. You should know me by now. My next question is, what now? I'm assuming you love this boy back."

I smiled. "So much, Mom. I've never loved anyone more in my entire life. He captured my attention the first time I met him, and he's had it ever since."

"Do you know anyone who could look at these photos to see if they've been altered in any way?"

I thought about it for a while until the obvious answer came to me. "Yes. Noah's brother, Lex. He's the graphic designer the museum has been working with for the workshop campaigns. I can call him."

"Sounds like a good idea."

I leaned forward in my chair, cradling the empty coffee mug. "What do I do about the company? There's no way the partners will believe me if I say the article is a bunch of lies. And what if these photos go public? Even after we confirm they're fake, the public might not see it that way."

"You need to call a meeting with the partners. For tomorrow if you can. In light of the article, I'm sure they'll make time. We'll fight this together. If they think they can get rid of you, they'll have to get past me first."

"Thank you, Mom. I'm not sure going all mama bear on that bunch of conservative greedy men will work though."

Her lips curled up in a confident smile. "Your dad was not the only one with expensive attorneys on retainer. I've spoken to my attorney and he had a look at the company bylaws. As your father's wife, and considering my role supporting him throughout his career in the company, I get first refusal on any shares that go on sale. That includes those of the partners. Only once I decline them can the partners make an offer. Guess who's just inherited her husband's vast fortune? Of course I wish I'd known all this when we were surprised with the new will. By the time I got the information, you were already married, and it didn't seem relevant to bring it up."

"Mom…" I had no words to describe my gratitude.

For the first time since I'd heard that I had to marry to inherit my father's shares of the company, I felt confident in the future.

"I'm going to get Noah back too."

"You better. He's a good man."

"He's more than that."

I was on my second glass of rum and Coke—hold the Coke —when my brothers, River, Emery, and Ellie all stormed through my front door using the key they had for emergencies.

"Oh great. We have a party," I said. "If you came for the food, you're shit out of luck because I forgot to go grocery shopping, and now I'm too drunk to drive to the store."

I pointed at them. "Did you know that there are no decent grocery stores within walking distance from here? Someone should open a grocery store in downtown. We're people too, you know?" I poured another two…maybe four, fingers of rum into the glass. Was rum measured in fingers? "How do you measure rum? Is it still a rum and Coke if you want it with Coke but don't have any?"

They all shared funny looks.

"What's wrong?" I asked.

"You called Code Red?" Adam said.

"Where's Lior?" Lex asked.

I scoffed. "Probably marrying Pish."

"Who?"

"His ex. Did you know they almost got married?" I pointed at my wedding ring but then realized I'd taken it off. I stared at my hand, wiggling my fingers. "I miss it. I don't like it naked."

Adam came around the kitchen island and guided me back to the couch.

"I'll order some food," Ellie said. "I think we're gonna need it."

"Maybe more booze," Adam added. "Noah doesn't do emotional crisis. This is very unsettling."

"Noah doesn't do emotions," I mimicked in a fake Adam voice. "Noah doesn't emote. Doesn't even emo."

"Sure, sure," River said.

They all pulled up chairs and cushions and sat around me like we were about to have a come-to-Jesus moment.

"What happened, Noah?" Lex asked.

"I fell in love with my husband. That's what happened."

"You say that like it's a bad thing." Adam chuckled.

"It is when you're not supposed to have feeeelings. It's not my fault, okay? He's just so, so…sexy and big." I leaned forward, wiggling my eyebrows. "Like *big*, big. And he always smells so nice I just want to crawl into his lap and take naps."

"Again, not a bad thing to feel for your husband."

"It's bad. Terrible. Catosphrotic. Catastrotic. Fuck, I've drank too much."

"Catastrophic?" Ellie offered.

"Yeah, that one."

"You'll be fine. There's a shit ton of pizza on the way, and I don't want anyone moaning about toppings." She kneeled by my chair. "What's going on, sweetie?"

Emery snorted.

"Shush you, I'm doing my best here," she said.

I looked into her eyes. She had that kind of inviting face like my elementary school teacher, where we'd confess everything we'd done before she even asked.

"I love him."

"You already said that. We need a little more context."

I reached over to the drawer on the coffee table where I'd stuffed the stupid newspaper and took it out.

A collective gasp filled my living area.

"Is this true?" Emery asked.

"It's the paper, baby. They don't know what the truth is," Lex said.

"It is…true," I said.

They all stared at me expectantly.

I sighed and reached for my drink, surprised they didn't stop me.

"Lior and I had a deal. He needed to marry to keep his father's company, and I needed someone with connections to help me help my friends at Star Finders Youth. We connected but decided this was a business transaction. It wasn't too bad spending time with someone you liked if we both got something out of the deal, right?"

"What does Lior think of this?" Emery asked, pointing at the paper.

I deadpanned. "He's not here, is he?" The sexy bastard had believed the lies a stranger had delivered in that brown envelope. And somehow, I still couldn't hate him.

"So everything you said about you two was a lie?" Adam asked, furrowing his brows.

I shook my head. "I loved him already when we told the family. I think I have for a long time. The reason I was so scared to tell you all was because it would make it too real. Having to pretend to be in love when I wasn't pretending at all was the hardest thing."

Ellie tilted her head. "Hmm, I don't buy it."

"What don't you buy?"

"I saw you two. You couldn't keep your hands off each other that weekend. The way he looked at you? No way there isn't more between you."

"We have insane chemistry, but that's it. He didn't catch feelings like I did because I'm stupid."

"How do you know?"

I opened the other drawer and slapped the photos on the table.

Adam grabbed them to look closer. "You cheated on him?"

"I'm so confused right now," River said.

"He believed those are real."

"They're not?" Adam asked.

"No! Do you think I'd be here drinking hard liquor and trying to hold it together while facing the end of my marriage to the man I love if I'd cheated on him?"

"Good point. Wow, this is like that book I borrowed from River by A. Lawton, except Lior isn't a prince and you're not his loyal secretary."

We all stared at him while River tried to contain a snort and failed.

"What?"

One of these days, Adam was going to discover that he liked dick, and I was so going to be here for it. Shame it was also unlikely to happen with Victoria in the picture. Also, I had my own crisis to deal with.

Lex stood and walked behind the couch. "We need to rewind a little. This article claims your marriage is fake, but you did get married."

"Yes. And the photo with Jax is a misunderstanding. It was loud at the bar. We were close so we wouldn't be overheard by people."

"So how do they know it's fake?" River asked.

I shrugged. "Beats me. We've been spending all our time together, fucking like it's going out of fashion—"

"TMI," Adam said.

"Our families have even met. There's no reason for anyone to suspect. The only people that knew were Jax and Tanner, and you know neither would say anything."

"Where's Jax?" Lex asked.

"He's with Tanner. The press knows who he is and camped outside his hospital. I think he's afraid the press will come here. We live in the same building. Can you already imagine the headlines?"

"Is he okay?"

"I haven't spoken to him yet. After Lior came here, I kinda lost it."

Lex paced back and forth like he was thinking hard about something. Then he took the photos from Adam's hand.

He stared at them for a while.

"These are fake."

"Well, duh. I know," I said.

"No. I can prove these are fake. Look." He pointed at a discolored spot on one of the worst photos. "Have you had any massages recently?"

"Yeah, I pulled a muscle playing basketball so I had a massage during one of my lunch breaks. It's the same place I always go to. They're great."

"Is there a chance someone could have taken a photo of you in the massage room?"

I had to think hard about it. It wasn't a place I usually paid much attention to. The staff were super sweet and professional, but the building was old and needed some renovations. That was all I— "Wait, yes. The windows in the room are covered with a matte film to let the light in but keep privacy. One of them is peeling off, which isn't a problem because the window is high up. You'd have to stand on something to look inside."

"I think someone has been following you," Lex said. "See this photo? That's my hand on your back when we grabbed a coffee together last week. Can you see my engagement ring? They clearly got a stock model and did a switch."

I sat forward with my elbows on my knees. "Someone was following me. Why?"

"Did you say you married Lior so he wouldn't lose his company?"

"Yeah. His dad made a stipulation in the will."

"That's insane," Adam said.

Lex stopped. "Could it be possible that someone in the company did this to get rid of Lior? They could have made up the fake marriage story and then backed it up with the fake photos."

Of course. "They don't know about the fake marriage deal. It's a coincidence." I stood up. "I need to talk to Lior."

"There's something else," Lex said. "Noah, is it possible Lior was hurt about the photos and not the company?"

"What do you mean?"

"What if he's in love with you? Did you tell him the photos were fake?"

I grimaced. "Not exactly. He seemed so sure of them. I mean, if he thinks I'm capable of cheating after everything that's happened between us, then what hope is there?"

"You're an idiot," he said.

"Excuse me?"

"You're an idiot. If you had stood your ground about the photos, what would have happened?"

"I don't know."

"In the face of the evidence, there's always a chance he'll lose the company, but he doesn't have to lose you."

I paced the room again, suddenly feeling a little less drunk.

If they were right, I needed to tell Lior how I felt about him. Between me and his company I was the consolation prize, but still a prize. Fuck, I'd take being second best any day if it meant being with Lior.

Lex's phone rang, so he left the room to take the call.

"Pizza's here," Ellie said.

Five minutes later, the newspaper served as protection for the coffee table covered in pizza boxes. It would end up in the trash later where it belonged.

Lex came back as we were tucking in.

"I have to go deal with something." He held the photos in his hand. "Can I take these? I want a better look at them."

"Sure."

Emery stood, but Lex went over to him and gave him a kiss. "Stay here and enjoy the pizza. I'll see you at home later."

I forced myself to eat some pizza and switched to water to sober up.

My head was a muddle of thoughts.

Things I now knew: there was a chance Lior loved me back.

Things I didn't know: why Ellie had ordered seven pizzas for six people.

When they all left, taking the leftover pizza, I called Jax and Tanner. I updated them on what was going on, and they decided it would be best if Jax stayed at Tanner's for now.

I was relieved to find out he wasn't mad at me. Just mildly inconvenienced about the work situation, but since he'd already built up a few days of vacation, he was happy to let it all die down. Hopefully, his absence from the hospital would get the reporters moving.

After speaking to Jax, I pulled my big boy pants up and messaged Lior.

NOAH

I know I said what I said, but can we talk?

Please?

LIOR

Of course we can. I'll come to your place tomorrow night.

When Lior canceled the next day, I called my brothers. Once again, they descended on my apartment and kept me busy. Lior reassured me he was trying to fix things and would be in touch, but patience was never my forte. I was going out of my mind.

My anxiety increased with every day that passed. Even after Lex told me he'd been helping Lior with the photos, I still couldn't understand why he wouldn't see me.

I scanned the online news to see if anything else had come out about us. Then, I started buying the actual paper. Considering the hassle the reporters had given me when the news broke, it was now dead silent.

Even Jax had returned to his apartment. We'd hung out, which was a way to stop me from driving out of the city to Lior's place.

Was this what Lior was doing? Managing the press?

I needed to see him, so after a meeting with Adam about a new client, I left my office and stormed into his building. The receptionist didn't stop me when I walked past her, which felt like a win.

The wind was blown out of my sails and into the water

when I got to the elevator and none other than Pierce was waiting there.

"This is going to be a painful ride up," he said.

"Afraid I'm going to punch you?"

He laughed. "I think I actually like you, Noah."

Huh? Was he on drugs? "The feeling is not mutual."

38

———

LIOR

I STARED at my phone and put it away again.

Noah hadn't contacted me since the weekend. I hadn't called him either.

Not speaking to him was killing me, but I wanted to fix things and prove to him that I would do anything to protect us. That meant getting the meeting with the partners out of the way first. Then I'd go to him, beg him to take my stupid ass back, and then kiss him until all the oxygen on the planet was used up.

I'd seen Lex earlier and thanked him for coming through with the photos. He'd taught me about all the points in each photo that clearly proved they'd been doctored. He'd even found the original source of a couple of the photos. Stock photography models had been used to make it look like Noah was being intimate with other men or had gone out on dates.

I was already feeling like a dick for how I'd treated Noah, but after talking to Lex, I felt a hundred times worse.

I liked to think the photos had been for my benefit only and would never have been made public because whoever had gone to the trouble knew they'd never get past the eagle eyes of the press.

"Mr. Van Stern," Tina called from the door.

I looked up. She seemed tense.

"What's up? Have the partners arrived yet?"

"Some of them, yes. They're being served refreshments in the conference room. It's um…you have visitors on the way up."

"Visitors?"

She bit her lip. "Mr. Dellcourt and Mr. Spencer."

"Lex?"

"Your husband, sir."

I stood, my pulse increasing at the thought of seeing Noah. Before I rounded my desk to meet him at the elevator, Tina's words sank in. Did she say Pierce was here too?

As I thought it, the elevator at the other end of the office opened. Noah and Pierce came out side by side.

"Oh fuck."

Noah didn't look happy. What had Pierce said to him? I would seriously punch him if he'd so much as suggested to Noah that anything was happening between us.

They both stopped in front of me, but my eyes were on Noah.

"Hey," I said.

"Hey." The corners of his mouth curled up a little, but then he glanced at Pierce, and the frown returned.

"What are you doing here, Pierce?" I asked, turning back and leaning against my desk.

"You wouldn't answer my calls, so you gave me no choice."

"You told me to divorce my husband and marry you. You can see why answering your calls was not only not on my priority list, it was way down on the *I will never again look at this list* list."

He deflated a little. "That's fair. I get it. Look, I don't understand this thing between you two. I guess I was jealous. When I saw you in Atlanta, you already looked like you had so much chemistry, and you'd barely met. In twenty years of knowing each other and five in a relationship, you never looked at me like you do him."

"I'm sorry." And I *was* sorry. Maybe I'd driven him away by not being present when we were together, but he'd ruined all chances when he cheated. He had to know that.

"Don't be. I can't force you to love me, and I guess… maybe I deserve someone who looks at me the same way."

"You do. What did you want to talk to me about?"

He glanced at Noah and then back at me. "I know about the photos, and I know who doctored them."

"Who?" Noah asked.

"Anderson Getty."

"How do you know?"

He looked away and then at me. "Your father was looking out for you when he asked me."

"Asked you what?"

"To get close to Getty. Your dad thought Getty would try to get his hands on enough shares to get the majority and take over. He asked me to keep an eye on him. Since I don't work for the company he figured Getty was more likely to collude if he thought I was on his side. He hasn't done anything noteworthy so far. He does throw some boring dinner parties. A few weeks ago, after a few drinks, he let it slip that he hired a personal investigator to follow Noah. He wanted to find out if your marriage was real."

"He did what? The fucking—"

Pierce raised his hand to continue. "I'm not going to lie. At the time, I was interested in that information too, so I didn't say anything. When the article in the paper came out, I thought that was my opportunity to get close to you." He turned to Noah. "I'm so sorry for what I said to you."

What did he mean?

"Pierce, you're going to have to speed up your explanation because I'm coming to some conclusions that are not very favorable to you."

"Yes, yes. After I left your place, I was angry, so I went to Getty's place. He was celebrating your departure from the company. I asked why he was so certain the article would do the job, and he said the article was just the start. He had photographic evidence that Noah had been cheating. He showed me the photos. I'll admit I believed it for a moment, but then, in his pretentious arrogance, he said that those things had never happened. The PI had taken photos of Noah, and he paid someone to change the photos to show Noah in those…scenarios."

Why was I not surprised Getty was behind this? It made sense that the photos never went public. He didn't want to damage the company's reputation any more than the article had already damaged mine and Noah's.

"You were so against us. Why are you coming clean now?" I asked.

"Because despite everything, I care about you. I cared about your father too."

I leaned back against the desk. "I know. He always talked about you and how you'd be a great asset to the company."

Pierce shrugged. "It wasn't meant to be." He pointed to the door. "I'll just…"

"Hey, Pierce, can you join the partners in the conference room? I'd like you to be at the meeting. Mom is there already. Keep her company?"

"Sure." He smiled and left.

Noah took a step backward. "I guess you know what I came here to tell you."

"Not so fast." I circled my arms around his waist, shut the office door with my foot, and pulled him against me. "We have to talk."

He swallowed and nodded.

"Noah, no words can convey how sorry I am for everything. I know you, and I should have known you'd put me first. After all, that's one of the reasons I fell for you so hard and fast. I failed you because instead of protecting you like I should have. I stood there and accepted what was clearly a lie. I am so, so sorry. Please forgive me."

"The photos looked so real. I was afraid if they came out, you'd lose everything because of me."

I shook my head.

"That's the last time you take the blame for something you didn't do. Got it?"

He nodded.

"You are not responsible for my reputation or the status of my company. Got it?"

He nodded.

"My company is not more important than you. Got it?"

Another nod.

"Now, do you have anything to say before I tell you that I've fallen stupidly in love with you and hope you feel the same because I don't want to give you up?"

He bit his lip, trapping the smile forming on his lips.

"I love you too, Lior. I've loved you since the moment your fat cock sank inside me. You left something behind that night, and it wasn't just your cum. Your whole energy is good. I need it. I need you to help me make sense of the world. I want to curl up in your chest and lick every inch of your sexy body."

"Shut up, you little shit." I silenced him with a possessive kiss that conveyed my feelings with every pass of my tongue over his.

He wrapped his arms around my shoulders to hold me there. My hands found his ass. He moaned into my lips, his cock thickening against mine.

My desk phone ringing made us spring apart.

I pressed the answer button.

"Yes?" My hands traced Noah's cheek as I looked into his blue eyes.

"Five minutes to the meeting. Everyone's here, sir."

"Thank you, Tina. We'll be right out."

I pressed the end call button.

"I didn't know they still made phones like that," Noah joked.

"If you're implying what I think you're implying about my age, remember we're in my office. The door locks, and five minutes is enough to spank your sexy little ass pink."

He pressed his hardness against my leg. "Please."

"Park that thought for later. We have a meeting to attend and some ass to kick."

He stood on his toes to kiss me. "Will you fuck me on this desk one day?"

"Yes."

"Then let's go kick ass."

I willed my dick to behave while I put my stuff away and shut everything down. There was no way I'd be returning to the office after the meeting.

"Lior," he said, stopping me.

"Yes?"

"Is this really happening? Are we really together, *together*?"

"As much as you want to be, Noah. From this moment on, it's you and me. No external voices, no more deals. I'm so sorry it took us so long to get here. The last few days were torture, but I knew if I saw you, I'd want to throw everything away. I just need one chance to fight for everything."

He drew in a breath. "I want us to stay married."

I leaned in and kissed his forehead. "You can bet your sexy little butt we are staying married."

Whatever was about to happen, afterward, I would stick to my original plan, except instead of going to Noah's office to talk to him, we could go straight to his place.

There was a blanket of silence when we entered the conference room together.

A few friendly faces smiled and nodded. Mom rushed to give Noah a hug, standing by his side. Pierce stood on Mom's other side. I almost wanted to laugh because we looked like the Four Musketeers.

"Good afternoon, everyone. If you could please take your seats, we have much to discuss, and considering the last-minute nature of this meeting, I'm sure you don't have time to waste."

Getty's face was a deep, angry red. I maintained my composure. If he was angry now, he was about to be furious.

"Is this meeting about the newspaper article from the weekend?" one of the partners asked.

"It is. As my business partners, we need to maintain an open discussion, especially considering the circumstances surrounding my inheritance of my father's shares."

A bunch of faces nodded.

I glanced at Mom, who smiled confidently at me.

"There are a few things to address today. The first one is the article. Noah and I got married in Las Vegas. That was our choice. We wanted a private ceremony. Two friends attended the wedding with us. One of them, the one that appears in the photo you'll have seen in the paper, is Noah's best man, Jaxon Mitchell."

I'd printed out two photos we took with the guys during our hotel suite reception. In one, I was feeding Noah wedding cake. We were both laughing. The other photo was the four of us with the cake before we cut it. I passed it around the room for everyone to see.

"Please tell me what other evidence you may require that my marriage to Noah is very much real. I could kiss him right now, but I'd like to keep things professional."

Noah snorted, and my mom shook her head.

"The next thing I'd like to discuss is this." I held out the brown envelope with the photos.

39

———

NOAH

My HEART SANK when Lior got the envelope out. I hadn't seen the photos since Lex had taken them away, and I didn't want to see them again.

"Inside this envelope are a bunch of photos that show Noah in compromising situations with other men," Lior said.

Most of the partners were shocked, but Getty looked almost smug.

Lior continued. "These contents were intended to humiliate my husband and create doubt and division between us. Someone wanted to embarrass my husband and me to weaken our relationship and attempt to remove me from this company. There are two reasons this person will not succeed."

Everyone hung on Lior's words. I looked at his mom, who smiled back.

"My marriage is solid. Noah and I love each other and intend to stay married for as long as he can put up with my ornery ass. False accusations and doctored photos aren't going to come between us. Yes, these photos have been proven to be fake. It's also not going to be easy to oust me from this company. For your convenience, I've arranged for copies of the relevant section of the company's bylaws to be handed out."

Lior's secretary handed out a thin folder to everyone. I took in their reactions as each partner opened their folder. Some looked relieved while others were confused. Getty would have smoke coming from his head if he was a cartoon character.

"As you can see from the highlighted area, the only person with any real power in this room is my mother."

I looked at Mathilda, who stood up. Lior put his hand on my leg under the table.

"As you might take from this information, gentleman, even if my son hadn't met the stipulation of my husband's will, he would still be the first in line to run this company. I assure you I have enough money to buy my husband's shares, and I don't need to tell you who I will pass them on to. Save yourselves the extra work and leave Lior to do what his father intended all along, especially as he met the stipulation of the will by getting married within the timeline, and as he's confirmed, he will more than meet your request to remain married for at least a year. Can I have a nod of agreement?"

The majority of the partners acknowledged Mathilda's request. Getty was predictably as stiff as a board.

"That's settled then," Mathilda said, sitting back down.

Lior stood. "Thank you all. I will continue to do my best to earn your trust and I hope that together we can take Van Stern Enterprises to new heights. Well, most of us. Mr. Getty, is there anything you'd like to say?"

Getty straightened his tie. "No. What would I have to say?"

"How about an apology and a confession?" Lior asked. "Gentleman, Mother, it has come to my attention that Mr. Anderson Getty hired a personal investigator to follow my husband because he didn't think our marriage was real.

When he didn't find any evidence of that, he did the next best thing, he faked it. The photos we received anonymously were paid for by Mr. Getty."

Getty stood. "He's lying. This is preposterous. I worked with Lior for over twenty years. I would never have done such a thing."

Pierce stood. "That's not exactly right, is it, Anderson?" He didn't have to say anything else because Anderson knew his scheming was up.

"I don't have to stand for these accusations. You'll be hearing from my attorney." Getty grabbed his folder and left the room.

Lior turned to the room. "I want to close this meeting. My secretary will be in touch with a date for us to meet to discuss the future of the company, which does not include Anderson Getty. I would like you to consider Mr. Pierce Dellcourt to take the future vacant position left by Anderson Getty."

The partners agreed to continue the meeting another time and, one by one, left the room, stopping to congratulate Lior and shake my hand. Some even apologized that we had to go through the ordeal Getty put us through.

Pierce stood rooted to his seat.

"You okay?" I asked.

He stared at me. "I have a confession to make. What I told you about Lior cheating was a lie."

"I know. Lior would never do that. But thank you for telling the truth." I left him and joined Lior because I didn't know how to process that a lot of my feelings of guilt about the situation had stemmed from the conversation with Pierce. But now he'd come through with some really vital information.

Pierce remained in his place and didn't say a word until everyone was gone.

"Lior, are you insane? Putting me up for partner?"

Lior looked at me. "I'm not insane, but I'm in love, and I've been told repeatedly by the wisest woman I know that having someone to love is more important than anything in life."

I hugged him tight. "Love you too, Lioreo."

"Are you sure you want me around?" Pierce asked.

"Who else is going to snitch to my mom when I miss lunch breaks?"

"This is true." Pierce stood and held his hand out to Lior. "Looking forward to working with you, boss."

Lior scrunched his face.

"I'm not calling you sir."

"You can call him Lior," I interjected.

Pierce laughed. "You're growing on me."

I leaned closer to Lior. "Meh, I could learn to tolerate you."

"God, you two are going to become best friends, aren't you?" Lior groaned.

I wasn't sure about that, but I was glad to be on okay terms with Pierce, especially if he was going to end up working with Lior.

Pierce left, taking Mathilda with him, which meant I was alone with my husband again.

"That took too long," Lior said.

"Getty's face almost exploded."

We stared into each other's eyes, smiling.

"What do we do now?" I asked.

Lior cradled my face in his hands, his thumbs caressing my cheeks. "I'd like to take my husband home and show him exactly how much I've missed him. Would that be okay with you?"

"Meh, I guess."

"I could turn my computer back on. There's a bunch of

reports with my name on them. It'll take me days to go through them all."

I grabbed his hand and dragged him out. "Come on, we have places to be, asses to fuck, and this time we're using the goddam bed. I didn't buy the best mattress in the store for nothing."

He laughed but followed me out.

I wasn't joking.

Living downtown was bad for grocery shopping, but it had its perks. My apartment was equidistant from my office and Lior's, which meant that in just three blocks, we were making out in the elevator as we rode up to my floor.

When we got out, Lior pushed me against my front door, kissing the back of my neck. His beard tickled my skin, making me shiver.

"I fucking missed you so much. Can't wait to be inside you."

I groaned. "Wait. I need to do something." I took my phone out and messaged my brothers to give them the signal that everything had worked out and I would be away from the office until Monday. With any luck, we'd stay in bed the rest of the weekend.

I turned the phone off and got the keys out to open the door.

As soon as we got inside, Lior lifted me onto his shoulder and took me to my bedroom.

"You're a caveman."

"Tell me to stop, and I'll stop."

"No way. I want you to pillage and plunder my cave like a Neanderthal."

He laughed. "You're nuts."

When he put me down, I went straight for his tie, being careful to not undo the knot completely. I threw it on the bed. "For later."

Lior held my hand up, kissing my ring finger. "You put it back on."

"It didn't stay off for long. Don't tell anyone, but I kinda love being married to you," I said, running my hands over the hair on his chest.

"It'll be our little secret." His eyes searched mine for something. "Noah…"

"Yeah?"

He sat on my bed, taking me with him. I straddled his legs and rested my arms on his shoulders.

His fingers brushed my sides softly.

"Before we get naked and my brain stops functioning, I need you to know I was coming for you regardless of what the partners decided."

"You were?" My voice was barely audible over the lump in my throat. This meant I was more important to him than anything else. No one had ever put me in that place.

"Before you strolled into my life with your confidence and swag, I'd given up on finding someone to share my life with, Noah. My passion was the museum and, newsflash, it's not the best place to meet people."

"I don't know. Charlie is kinda cute."

He put his hands on my ass and pulled me closer. "He's also straight and married with children and a grandchild on the way."

I sighed dramatically. "The best ones always are."

"I'd accepted my attraction to you as something I couldn't fight, but I didn't expect it to turn into this kind of love."

"I think I have some work to do until I believe you really love me. Crazy run-away-with-me mouth and all," I said.

"Your mouth might be one of the things I love the most about you."

I ran my fingers through the hair on the back of his head and pulled him in for a soft, wet kiss.

"I don't know what I have to offer to you, Noah, but I love you so fucking much."

"I can tell you. You married a stranger to keep your family business. I don't know about many things, least of all feelings. I spent so much time avoiding them that I had to be hit with the brutal force of my love for you to understand it for what it was. But there's one thing I do know, and that's family."

"I hate that I have to bring this up. It has never an issue between us, but one day it could be. Aren't you worried about my age? What happens when I'm seventy and you're still in the prime of your life? Or when I die?"

"I will love you until your dying breath."

"That's the problem, Noah. I know you will, and I'm not sure I want you to. It's not fair on you."

"Can we not talk about you dying? You are still very much alive."

I stroked his cock over his slacks, proving he was not just alive but ready to play.

"You were amazing in that meeting. I was so hard for you. If you'd banged your fist against the conference table, I would have come on the spot."

"Do you have a corporate sex kink?"

"Fuck yeah. Have you looked at you in a suit?"

"Enough talking, Noah Spencer."

I undid the top buttons on his shirt and impatiently pulled it over his head. He tried to do the same to me, but I held his hands behind his back. I was in charge now.

I worshipped his nipples with my tongue until they were little peaks of pleasure.

Noah moved against me, trying to get more of what felt good. I loved how unashamedly hedonistic he was.

With one arm around his waist, I flipped us so he lay on the bed. I covered his body with mine.

His legs went immediately around my waist as he tried to get some friction. I ignored it and proceeded to cherish his body the way I'd wanted since the night we met.

"You taste delicious, Noah."

"I know. I'm a fucking strawberry cocktail. Just eat the fruit already."

I licked his sternum and kissed all the small ridges of his abs, the sexy V hiding under his jeans.

He unlocked his legs to give me room to move. I undid

his jeans and pulled them down only enough to bury my face in his crotch.

"Lior," he panted.

"God, Noah, you're so intoxicating." I kissed the head of his cock through his underwear. "I want you so fucking much."

"You have me."

He pushed his jeans farther down his hips. I loved teasing him, but torture wasn't my thing, and I was right there with Noah. I needed this too much.

I pulled his clothes the rest of the way off until he was naked, splayed out for me to enjoy, to relish.

My clothes followed his into a pile on the floor.

"Look at you. I don't even know where to start."

He bit his lower lip and raised his legs, hooking his hands on the backs of his knees.

"Is that what you want, baby? You want me to eat you?"

"Like your last meal."

Before I indulged, I reached over to the bedside table to grab the lube.

I placed it by his side for easy reach, then dove face-first onto his tight pink hole.

I circled it with my tongue, tasting his unique Noah flavor. It certainly wasn't strawberries, but it was so much better. Noah was musk and pine and man. My favorite.

"Oh god, Lior. Feels so good." He released a shuddering breath and then a moan when I added suction at the same time my finger pressed against his hole.

Noah relaxed under my touch, eager to be stretched. I grabbed the lube and applied some to my finger.

As soon as it disappeared inside him, I moved my mouth to his balls. I sucked and licked, making sure not an inch of him was untouched.

His dick leaked a bead of precum onto his stomach, so I licked that too, and then I sucked his cock down to the root.

Noah's hands fisted my hair. I didn't think he even noticed me opening him up with more fingers.

"You're so ready, Noah. Turn over." I helped him place a pillow under his belly to raise his ass.

I covered my cock with lube and then pushed my way in slowly.

"Oh god. Fuuck," he cried.

"I love that you love being fucked so much, Noah."

"Only when it's your fat dick splitting me open. I want to feel every inch of you when I get up from this bed. Wreck me, Lior. Fucking wreck me."

My body sang when he talked like that. I loved that he didn't want gentle. He wanted to be commanded, to be led to paradise, and I was more than up for being his tour guide.

I pushed back and entered him again in one motion. I kept a slow and steady pace for as long as I could, enjoying the small punctuated moans out of his sweet mouth.

As I sped up, he hid his face in the pillow, muffling the sounds. My legs and arms burned from keeping this position, half on him and half raised.

I sat back on my heels, taking him with me.

"That's it, Noah, fuck yourself on my cock."

His skin was flushed red. He raised his head and glanced behind. Our eyes met, and his lips curled up in a smile.

"You feel so good, Lior. I will never get tired of this." In a surprising show of dominance, he flipped onto his back, aligned my cock with his hole, and with his heels, pulled me back inside.

"Agh," I cried as his tight hole swallowed me.

I fell forward on top of him. My mouth searched his in a claiming kiss. I was drowning in Noah and loved it.

"Tie my hands," he asked, holding my tie he'd discarded onto the bed earlier. I'd forgotten about it.

The way his big blue eyes stared at me with so much trust and love as he held his hands together filled the rest of my heart. There was no more empty space. Noah was all of it. He was everything.

I twisted the neck of the tie and put his hands through the holes, pulling tight, and then I wrapped the ends around my hand so the tie couldn't come undone.

His eyes rolled to the back of his head, and he sighed.

"My beautiful man. You're not afraid to push and tell me what you want, even when what you want is to give up control."

"I'll give you everything, Lior. You're the only one I can do that with. I trust you implicitly. You can pull the ties, spank me, fuck me into a goddam wall. I'll always want more." He gasped as I started moving inside him again. "I'll never have enough of you, Lior. Ever."

"Yes," I hissed. I increased my pace until the only noises in the room were broken gasps, skin slapping skin, and his headboard hitting the wall.

It was a fucking carnal symphony of love.

In one last attempt to draw out this pleasure, I silenced Noah's moans with my mouth, drinking in every beautiful note. There wasn't an atom between us. I wasn't even pulling out of him that much because I just wanted to live in this moment, forever inside my man. *My husband.*

Noah shook uncontrollably, a sign he was coming. I kept it all up, the thrusts, the kissing, the touching. My hand gripped the tie harder as my orgasm built inside me, and I let go, filling him the way he craved.

My sight went dark and stars filled my vision.

"Fuck, fuck, Noah," I rasped, trying to regain my breathing.

I let go of the tie, and he released himself. His hands caressed my face, my beard, my back.

"I don't want you to ever leave me," he said.

"I won't. That's a promise."

We stayed like that for a while until the need to go to the bathroom and clean up became too pressing.

"Have I ever told you married sex is the best?" he asked as he took a leak and then turned on the water in the shower.

I chuckled. "I'll have to agree with you, but I think it's you that makes it so good."

"I was never like this, you know?"

"Like what?"

"Submissive. Letting go of control. Women expected me to take charge. Don't get me wrong. I loved sex with women. I had fun with guys, but on the rare occasion I bottomed, I could never truly let go."

"Maybe you didn't trust them to take care of you."

"Maybe. I carried the hurt from my college relationship all these years. It wasn't healthy, and now I know that. When we met, there was something about you that spoke to me straight away."

I grabbed the soap and lathered his skin, cleaning him from head to toe. He melted under my touch. What was it about taking care of him in that way that was almost better than sex?

We returned to the bed, discussing if we wanted to order food in or force ourselves to go out. I knew if we didn't leave now, we'd be holed up until Monday.

The noise of the front door opening made me sit up while Noah just sighed as if he'd expected the intrusion.

"Cover up your junk, boys, because I will look, and my phone is ready. Have I told you this new phone has a super high resolution? It can catch the tiniest details."

Ellie stumbled into my room, followed by Lex, Emery, Adam, River, Jax, Tanner, and Meatball.

I pulled the covers up to our waists, but Noah didn't seem too worried about anyone seeing his junk.

"Is this a usual occurrence or just a rite of passage?" I asked.

"Rite of passage," Noah said, keeping his eyes on the crowd in front of us. "How dare you come into my castle and insult my goods?"

"Castle?" Ellie asked, raising a brow.

Noah pointed at me. "He's my dragon, I'm the princess, and unless six out of the eight of you want to be the rescue army, I suggest you respect my manhood and leave me to spend the weekend being ravished."

He crossed his arms over his chest. I'd swear if he was standing up, those hands would be on his hips.

"No one's joining us," I said. "Just to be clear."

"Not even Meatball? Look at his thighs."

I put my arms around Noah's waist and pulled him tighter against me. My hardening dick pressed against his back.

"Not even him."

"Ugh, worst husband ever."

I turned to the group. "How can we help you?"

"We're throwing a pre-bachelor party for Adam. And also for you because we didn't get to throw you one," Lex said.

Noah jumped off the bed, practically taking the bedsheets with him and almost exposing me.

"Noah!" I managed to get a hold of the extra blankets at the foot of the bed in time to cover myself.

The sound of a camera shutter echoed in the room. I looked at Ellie as she put her phone away.

"What? I like this picture." She pointed to the wall beside her. "I want to find one like this for my living room."

"Can we have some privacy to get dressed?" I asked since no one seemed bothered about standing in our bedroom while we were naked. "Unless you want to watch what you interrupted when you barged in. You all know Noah is a whore for attention, and I'd do anything for my dear husb —" They ran out of the bedroom, slamming the door shut.

Noah jumped back into bed. "Were you serious?"

"Fuck no. We're getting dressed."

He smiled wide, his eyes coming alive. "Lioreo, when I couldn't possibly love you more, you go and stoop to my level to tease my brothers."

I wrapped my hand over the back of his head and drew him in for a kiss.

"I told you I'd do anything for you, husband."

41

NOAH
TWO MONTHS LATER

I PICKED up my pace as I walked through the park to the basketball court.

Today was one of those days I wished I lived on the other side of the park because I was running late.

Lesson to myself. A quick orgasm in the shower with my husband was never just a quick orgasm.

Was I ever going to get tired of waking up to Lior? Of snuggling on his chest? Of playing with his beard as I fell asleep?

No way. He was the endgame for me.

With the basketball court in sight, I ran the rest of the way, but I slowed when I saw no one around.

I tried to think if West and Drew had canceled the game but couldn't remember anything. Shit, did I miss a notification from this morning? I'd run out of my apartment because I was late and hadn't thought to check it.

The gate was locked.

Ugh, I could have stayed in bed with Lior. I was going to murder the guys.

"Hey, Noah."

I turned around and saw West and Drew.

"Hey, guys. Where's everyone?"

"They're at a different location."

"Oh, new court? I kinda liked this one," I said, looking back at the old court. We'd had some fun times here, but I knew, eventually, we'd move to the hospital when the reno was all finished.

"Um…not quite," West said. He joined me by the fence. "I'm going to need you to go with it, okay?"

"Go with what?"

Before I could do anything, my head was covered with a dark cloth bag.

"What the fuck? What's going on?"

"We're just the messengers. You're the package," Drew said.

"What?" I tried to remove the bag from my head, but they held my hands and then tied them behind my back.

"Don't fight it. We have orders from…um…someone important."

I sighed. "If my brothers have anything to do with this, I'm going to break into their apartments and put bags of fleas inside their beds."

All I heard was laughter as they guided me away from our location.

There was nothing I could do but go along with it. After a short walk, they helped me into a car.

"Where are we going?"

"You'll see."

"Not likely with a fucking bag over my head. How am I supposed to sit with my hands like this?"

There was a silence.

"Um…if you promise not to take the bag off your head, we'll untie you."

"Fine. This is ruining my hair." When they released my

hands, I sat back and felt my way to lock the seatbelt into place.

I had no idea where they were taking me, but it took for freakin' ever.

"We're here," West said. "We're going to hand you over to someone else. They're helping you get dressed. Please don't ruin this."

That was unlikely because now I was curious about what was going on so I played along nicely.

They helped me out of the car and then asked me to wait. The air smelled familiar, like a park or somewhere with a lot of grass.

"Do you think if we abandon him here, we can split his half of Mom and Dad's inheritance?" Adam asked.

"Absolutely."

I heard a high-five.

"Assholes. What's going on?"

"Raise your hands," Lex said. He helped me out of my T-shirt, careful not to remove the bag. Then he put my arm through a sleeve and went around my back to the other arm, doing buttons up to my neck.

"I hope this is ironed, and it's one of my nice shirts," I moaned.

It took longer to get me fully dressed in what I had to guess was a suit than if they'd taken the bag off and allowed me to dress myself.

They finished with shoes, and then I was led away again.

The gravel under my feet turned to soft grass.

"I better not get bag hair when you take this shit off," I complained.

"We're here," Adam said.

"Where?"

Silence.

"Uh, hello?"

More silence.

"I'm going to take this off in five seconds," I threatened.

I started counting but stopped when someone touched my arms, and then the bag was gone.

I squinted as I got used to the light again, but I didn't need to see to know who was with me. His cologne always gave him away.

"Lioreo, what in the fresh hell is this?"

He cradled my face and kissed my forehead.

"Our families had an idea—"

"Say no more. Let's run to another country. I'm sure I can get us into Portugal with ancestry links or something," I said as I looked down at the clothes I'd been dressed in. Thankfully, it wasn't a clown outfit. My guess on the suit was correct. It was one of mine.

"As I was saying, your parents, brothers, and my mom wanted us to have a wedding with an actual reception since we didn't have a proper one in Vegas."

"Yeah, we did. That cake was the best cake I've ever had in my life. The only criticism I have is that I didn't get to eat it off your abs."

He leaned over and kissed me gently. "Today you can… later."

He turned us around until I faced the other way where all my family, Tanner, Jax, Ellie, Meatball, Lior's family, West, Drew, the kids from Star Finders, and even Pierce were all gathered in their finest clothes.

They parted like the Red Sea to show an aisle made of flower petals leading to the glass gazebo.

"Oh my god, I'm gonna cry." I leaned against his chest.

"You? Noah No Feelings Spencer? Cry?"

"Shush, it's Noah No Feelings Van Stern now."

Changing my name was a decision I hadn't taken lightly,

but it had felt so right for me. Yup, I was that person. Nope, I never thought I would be.

Adam and Lex agreed that at work, I'd still go by Spencer so we wouldn't have to change all our stationery, emails, business paperwork, and god knows whatever else my name was printed on.

Lior took my hand and led me to the aisle.

"This is crazy, but thank you, everyone, for being here," I said as we walked toward the gazebo.

I screeched when we got to the top and the same celebrant who married us in Vegas was right there, holding her cards.

"Oh my god, you're here!" I ran to give her a hug.

"Are we getting any butts this time?" she asked, smiling.

"I've graduated to—" Lior covered my mouth with his hand.

"Don't you even dare."

Everyone gathered around us. The perfect lighting of the gazebo bathed everyone in color.

I leaned over to the celebrant and whispered, "You did marry us for real the first time, right?"

"I did. We're doing a vow renewal and celebration." She turned to Lior. "Thank you for getting in touch. I have family out this way, so it was the perfect excuse to see them."

"I literally could not love you more, Lioreo."

"You say that every time."

It was true. Every day he came through the door of our place in the city or our place at the museum was a special day. He bought me flowers, special dinners, took me out dancing, and once a month, we spent a night at the hotel in the city where we relived the night we met.

He also walked around barefoot wearing nothing but gray sweatpants and never complained when I jumped him. He let me cuddle him when we watched TV, and better than anything, he let me be myself. He loved me for the crazy that I was and never asked me to change.

A tear slipped unchecked down my cheek.

"Hey, you're not supposed to cry until the vows," he said, cleaning my wet cheek.

"I only ever dreamed of having the same kind of marriage I grew up watching with my parents. I never believed I was good enough to deserve it. Every day with you is a gift, Lior."

The celebrant coughed. "You're not supposed to say the vows before we start."

"How about if I recite the ode I wrote to my husband's butt? I bet everyone would love to hear that."

The sound of laughter surrounded us.

"Let's leave the odes for the speeches." She turned to everyone. "We are gathered here today to join Noah Van Stern and Lior Van Stern as they renew the vows they promised each other on the day of their wedding…"

My gaze moved from Lior to our group of family and friends. Everyone was smiling. Okay, Victoria looked like she was about to puke, but nothing today would make it less than perfect, down to the fake kidnapping.

When the ceremony ended, everyone congratulated us, and then we had a buffet and celebration in the museum's gardens.

I learned later that Lior had closed the museum for the day to make sure our family could enjoy the celebration in private.

Pierce came over just before we were due to cut the cake.

"The ceremony was beautiful. I'm really happy for you two."

"We've come a long way, Pish. I'm having some squishy feelings toward you right now. You should probably go," I said.

He laughed and shook Lior's hand. "I think you're right. I heard it's a free bar. See you around."

I turned to Lior, wrapping my arms around his waist.

"Let's cut the cake and then throw everyone out. You promised I could eat cake off your abs, and now that's all I can think about."

He kissed my nose. "Don't be impatient, my sweet husband. We have our whole lives ahead of us."

I grinned. "Oh my god, how many orgasms do you think we can have until one of us dies? Do you think we should start keeping a record?"

He shook his head.

"You are something else, Noah."

"A good something else, right?"

He captured my lips with his. "The most perfect something else there has ever been."

42

LIOR

Noah slept soundly against my chest, but no matter how much I tried, I couldn't get back to sleep.

Jetlag was a bitch even after flying first class.

I sighed. The perks of getting older.

Not that I felt my age. Marrying someone seventeen years younger sure kept me on my toes.

I caressed his hair.

Life with Noah was a beautiful adventure.

He sucked in a deep breath and then stretched like a cat, settling back against me with a contented sigh.

"Morning," he said.

"Hey, beautiful."

"I'm beat. Whose idea was it to have a honeymoon on the other side of the world?"

I chuckled. "I believe that was yours."

"Well, I blame you for giving in to my whims."

"I'll remember that next time you want something."

He opened his eyes and looked at me. "It was a pretty good honeymoon."

"The best."

"We should have a honeymoon every year."

"Uh-huh."

He rested his chin on my chest. His big blue eyes stared at me with so much love. Noah No Feelings was the most open person I'd ever met. And he did have feelings. He felt everything.

"What time's the wedding?" he asked.

"After lunch. We can order room service breakfast and go down just before the ceremony."

"I should message my brothers to say we're here in case anyone needs anything."

"Okay, you do that. I'm going to grab a shower. Join me after?"

"Absolutely." He turned over to grab his phone.

I pulled clean underwear for both of us from our suitcase and went into the bathroom.

The warm water was heaven for my tired muscles. We'd arrived at the vineyard so late last night that we'd jumped straight into bed.

Traveling from our late honeymoon straight to Adam's wedding was probably not the best idea we'd ever had, but when Noah found out about a fundraising event for a charity that helped foster children in Melbourne, we extended our honeymoon to attend.

We were paying the price of that decision now. Thankfully, I'd also extended our stay at the vineyard for a few days after the wedding.

Adam and Victoria would leave for their honeymoon tomorrow, and then we'd get to hang out with the rest of the guys until we went back to work in a few days.

The shower door opened, and Noah stepped in.

"The family has been informed, and I've double-checked the locks on the room door. No one's interrupting us this time."

He stepped under the water spray and then reached for the soap.

"I'm going to wash you all nice and clean," he said like he didn't have an ulterior motive.

His hands kneaded my back muscles, then moved down to my ass and legs. I groaned as I relaxed under his touch. My dick hardened. I gave it a few strokes before Noah turned me around.

He was on his knees.

I thought he'd go straight for my cock, but he just kept washing my legs. Then he stood, his hands lathering more soap on my abs and chest.

"I am gagging to suck your cock to the back of my throat, but I need you in my ass more, so how about you fuck me until I come, and then you feed me your cum?"

I flipped him so he faced the tiles.

"What kind of husband would I be if I didn't grant you all your wishes?" I rasped against his ear.

He released a breath. "Fuck, Lior. I'm already so hard."

I searched the toiletries bag for the lube packet and then moved the water spray a little so it wouldn't hit Noah's back.

He widened his stance. His face was turned sideways.

I coated my cock with lube and applied some to his hole.

"I'm going to give you what you need." I pushed a finger inside him. His eyes fluttered closed and his mouth opened, releasing a short breath.

On the second finger, I leaned in to take his mouth. The kiss was awkward in that position, but it helped distract him from the intrusion. I knew he liked it rough sometimes, but there was something about him that I was always able to read when he was looking for that little bit of pain or when he wanted to be looked after in a different way.

I scissored my fingers in and out of him, avoiding his prostate until I added the third.

"Lior," he gasped.

"Look at your flushed skin, Noah. I love seeing you this needy."

He closed his eyes and bit his lower lip. My sign that he was ready.

I turned him around and lifted him off the ground. He wrapped his legs around my waist and held on until I aligned my cock with his hole.

He let his head fall back as I lowered him onto my length.

"You feel so fucking good. So tight."

"Ugh, fuck me, Lior. I need to come."

I pressed him against the wall to help with leverage and then started fucking him in earnest. Every thrust earned me a gasp from Noah. I loved the sound, which usually followed a moan.

The deeper I went, the shallower his breathing became. I knew he could be close any moment, so I just needed to hold on a little longer.

"Do you want to stroke your cock until you come?" I asked.

He shook his head.

I had both hands on his ass to keep him up, so with one hand, I eased a finger into his ass. That helped press my cock against his prostate with every thrust.

In less than a minute, Noah was shouting his orgasm.

I let him ride it out, which took supreme control because I was still rock-hard inside him.

When he was ready, I released him. He went straight down on his knees.

I lost my breath when he took my cock to the back of his throat and swallowed.

"Fuuck…"

He swirled his tongue around the head and sucked hard

as he took it all the way in again. His hands reached my balls, tugging them gently at first. When he groaned, his beautiful watery blue eyes staring up at me, lost in the act, and then tugged my balls harder, I came.

Noah closed his eyes as he swallowed every drop, his throat bobbing.

"Christ. That was too good," I gasped, trying to regain my wits.

I helped Noah to his feet and captured his mouth. "I fucking love you so much, Noah."

"I love you more, Lioreo."

We finished the shower, dried, and got dressed.

I was about to call down to order breakfast when there was a knock on the door.

We exchanged a complicit smile. Five minutes earlier, they would have had to knock the door down if they'd wanted to come in.

Noah opened the door, and Lex, Emery, Ellie, and River came in.

River looked frantic. The others looked confused, as if they'd been dragged here without knowing why.

"What's the matter?" Noah asked. "Don't tell me Adam did a runner."

"Worse," River said, pulling a small piece of paper from his pocket. "This was pushed under my door. Victoria is gone, and she's not coming back."

Noah gasped. Lex looked like he was going to be sick.

Ellie looked at River.

"Someone has to tell Adam."

Dear reader, thank you for coming along on Noah and Lior's journey.

Noah's personality just shines off the page in his story. No wonder Lior fell in love so fast and so deep. Do you think Lior will still find Noah as adorable and loving, when he comes home one day to what he thinks is a sexy surprise, but instead finds a different kind of adorable gift?

Sign up to my newsletter here (readerlinks.com/l/4008154) to read an exclusive bonus scene.

What's next for the Spencer brothers?

For the last two books we've seen Adam's tribulations with his wedding and his fiancée, who seems to have done a runner on her own wedding day. What do you think will happen when the only person Adam wants around to help him through it is his best man and best friend, River?

Get The Best Friend's Secret here: readerlinks.com/l/3610455.

Shhh I'll let you in on a little secret. Are you curious to find out why what happened in Vegas didn't stay in Vegas for Tanner and Jax? Check out their story, **The Convenient Groom**, readerlinks.com/l/4201711

BONUS SCENE
A COMING HOME SURPRISE

Lior

FOURTEEN DAYS, twelve hours, and seventeen minutes. That was how long I'd gone without seeing Noah.

I was so desperate to lay eyes on him, touch him, hear his hitched breathing as I kissed him that I was close to murdering the taxi driver.

Next time, I'd park at the airport.

Next time, I wouldn't be gone so long.

The trip to VSE's European headquarters had been a success, and taking my mom with me was the right decision. She was still getting used to being on her own, and since she'd always traveled with my dad, she had friends all over Europe.

While my mom had enjoyed seeing her friends and socializing for the first time since my dad passed away, I'd hated every minute of being away from Noah.

I never thought I'd be that guy, but here I was, jumping out of my skin, ready to see my husband. I was also trying to keep my mouth shut every time the taxi driver mentioned the puppy his wife had brought home that he hadn't wanted but had fallen in love with.

"Any plans for the weekend?" he asked.

Yeah, naked and preferably inside my husband.

"Nothing much," I said instead.

"Oh, here we are. You'll be home before I can say Golden Retriever," he said.

I smiled while gritting my teeth. The driveway to my house was in sight. Another five minutes, and I'd be running through that door and into Noah's arms.

He'd left a semi-cryptic message on my phone earlier about a surprise. Knowing him, he'd tied himself to the bed again.

My dick swelled at the thought. Once upon a time, my right hand had been more than enough to take the edge off, but now, nothing but Noah did it for me.

It had been a long two weeks.

I watched the taxi disappear down the driveway while I got my key out.

The house was surprisingly quiet, but the light from the bedroom was my guide into my husband's arms.

I dropped my suitcase by the door, removed my shoes, and by the time I got to the bedroom, I was shirtless and reaching for the button on my slacks.

"Noah?"

No answer.

I opened the door, but even though the light was on, the bedroom was Noahless.

The closet was also empty, although it looked like it had been visited by a tornado or a fashion-conscious bear.

The house wasn't huge so there was only one other place he could be. I stepped out of the room and into the guest room, which was now mostly Noah's dressing room.

I loved my man, but he was messy.

My slacks were left behind as I stepped into the guest room.

"Welcome back, husband."

I gasped. Noah was tied to the clothes rail in the closet with one of my ties around his wrists. He wore one of my work shirts and nothing else.

"Noah." I narrowed the gap between us, wrapped my arms around him, and slammed my mouth onto his.

I consumed him like a parched man drank water. He smelled like my shower soap, and his sounds…fuck, I'd missed him so much.

"You're never going away for that long again," he said as I nibbled his lips. My hands explored the curve of his ass, finding his pre-lubed hole.

"Agreed."

"Or I'll come with you."

"Probably not a good idea. We'd just end up staying in the hotel room, and these are actual work trips."

He lifted one leg, giving me better access to his hole. "I need you so fucking much, Lior. Please get inside me."

"Patience, baby."

"You were gone two weeks, twelve hours, and thirty-five minutes." His indignation was adorable.

I went down on my knees and sucked his cock into my mouth.

"Lior," he shouted.

Fuck, I'd missed his taste. It was a shame he'd already gotten himself ready for me because I'd have eaten his ass before fucking him.

I replaced my mouth with my hand. "Let me take the edge off, and then I'll fuck you slowly into the mattress."

He jerked in his ties and moaned loudly as I resumed my oral assault.

"Oh fuck, fuck!"

I sucked him into the back of my throat as my finger sought his prostate. In a few short seconds, Noah was coming, and I swallowed every single drop he fed me.

"Hmm…delicious." I stood and kissed him.

He was putty in my arms. Orgasm-drunk Noah was the sweetest.

Ignoring my erection had been easy while I was focused on Noah, but now, my dick demanded attention. If I so much as rubbed against him, I'd come.

I released the tie from around his wrists, admiring how he'd gotten himself into that position on his own.

As soon as his hands were loose, he wrapped his arms around me tight.

"I missed you so much," he said, kissing me again. "This is all kinds of sad and desperate, but I don't give a crap. I love you so much, Lior. The last two weeks have been hell."

I took him over to the bed and covered his body with mine.

"Tell me what you've been up to."

We'd had daily calls, so I already knew, but I wanted to hear his voice. I wanted to hear his breath catch while I sucked his nipples or licked his abs.

A whine sounded from somewhere in the house.

"What was that?"

"Huh?"

"That sound."

He pushed my head down onto his chest. "Keep licking. I like it."

I snorted but did as I was told. My Noah always got bossy when he wanted me inside him.

I pushed my underwear down past my thighs and pressed our dicks together.

The whining sound returned.

"There's something here."

"Don't stop," he demanded.

"I can't do this while it sounds like an animal is being tortured around here."

He huffed. "The only animal being tortured here is me. Stick that fat cock inside my ass now, or I'll demand a divorce."

I bit his earlobe. "What's going on, Noah Van Stern?"

"Nothing."

I stood and pulled my underwear back up.

"It's nothing. Let's have sex. More sex." He followed me out of the room, grabbing his boxer shorts on the way.

The whining sound was louder in the kitchen. I followed it to the laundry room.

When I opened the door, a small black dog ran out so fast he slid on the tile floor and almost bumped into the kitchen island.

"Surprise…" Noah said as the dog ran back to us, jumping around our legs.

I kneeled and was immediately attacked by a very excited wet tongue.

"This isn't the kind of action I was expecting tonight," I said, looking at my husband while trying to stop the slobbery kisses. "And who are you?" I asked the dog. Damn, those were cute black eyes.

Noah sat on the floor next to me. The dog immediately left me for him.

"This is Mango. Lex's gecko, Gordon, brought him home almost two weeks ago. They took him to the vet, and he's chipped and has all his vaccinations."

"So, he belongs to someone."

Noah's face flushed. In my oversized shirt, he looked

beautiful and mine. I was supposed to be getting lost inside him right now.

I sighed. "Noah?"

"He kinda does belong to someone."

"Let me guess, he belongs to us."

Noah beamed. "Yes."

The dog was cute. I'd give him that.

"He can't stay here on his own while we're at work, baby," I said, pulling him closer.

Noah leaned against me, rubbing the dog's ears.

"He's going to be with Charlie at the museum. Everyone loves him there. He even has his own bed and toys in the office. When we come home, we can get him so he spends the night with his daddies."

"You've thought of everything, haven't you?"

"Yup."

The dog yapped as if agreeing with Noah.

"What's your story, little dude?"

The dog yapped again.

"He escaped from the animal shelter. Lex found out from the vet when he took Mango to get checked. He felt bad leaving him there, so he took him home, but their cat didn't fall in love with Mango, so I brought him here."

I kissed the back of his neck. "Your big heart is one of the things I love the most about you, but please promise me we're not adopting every stray animal out there."

He turned to me. "Are you really happy to keep him?"

"Do I have a choice?"

"Of course. This is a big commitment."

I chuckled. "We got married when we barely knew each other. I think it's safe to say we're not afraid of big commitments."

"Best deal I've ever made."

We stayed on the kitchen floor until Mango fell asleep on Noah.

Moving him back to the laundry room was like handling a bomb ready to detonate, but we made it.

It was then that I saw the number of toys, pillows, and blankets Mango had at his disposal. He was a lucky puppy.

I dragged my husband to our room, removing the extra pieces of clothing and heading straight for the shower.

"You're going to have to learn to be quiet," I whispered into Noah's ear under the warm spray of the water.

He jumped up and wrapped his legs around me.

"Fill all my holes, and I'll be as quiet as a mouse."

"You say it as a promise, but it sounds like a challenge."

His big blue eyes were bright as they looked into mine. "Do it and find out."

I planned on it.

Maybe I wouldn't be spending the entire weekend naked and inside my husband after all, but it had taken a whole five seconds to fall in love with Mango. Only four more than it had taken me to fall in love with Noah.

Maybe I was that easy. Or maybe I was just lucky.

As I filled my husband and felt like I was coming home, I knew I was definitely both.

Dear reader, thank you for coming along on Noah and Lior's journey.

Noah's personality just shines off the page in his story. No wonder Lior fell in love so fast and so deep. Do you think Lior will still find Noah as adorable and loving, when he comes home one day to what he thinks is a sexy surprise, but instead finds a different kind of adorable gift?

What's next for the Spencer brothers?

For the last two books we've seen Adam's tribulations with his wedding and his fiancée, who seems to have done a runner on her own wedding day. What do you think will happen when the only person Adam wants around to help him through it is his best man and best friend, River?

www.ingramcontent.com/pod-product-compliance
Lightning Source LLC
Chambersburg PA
CBHW030528190726
48283CB00006B/1818